"So the opinion of the good folk of Golden Prairie hasn't changed?"

Linc's words were low, as if resigned to the inevitable.

Sally didn't answer.

"What do you think?"

His question, so direct, so void of emotion, jarred her from trying to maintain disinterest. She jerked her gaze to him and saw something in his eyes that said he wasn't as uncaring as he tried to portray.

She swallowed hard. "I think…" Her heart opened up and dumped out a tangle of emotions—things she couldn't identify and didn't want to own. They seemed to pull her in a hundred different directions. "I think Abe is right. You deserve a chance."

His expression faltered. He shifted on his feet, then nodded. "Does that mean we can be friends?"

She smiled softly. "It looks like we already are."

"Good to know." His words were brisk.

Had she disappointed him? Friends was good, wasn't it?

Strange, then, how it
As if she'd fallen short

Books by Linda Ford

Love Inspired Historical

The Road to Love
The Journey Home
The Path to Her Heart
Dakota Child
The Cowboy's Baby
Dakota Cowboy
Christmas Under Western Skies
  "A Cowboy's Christmas"
Dakota Father
Prairie Cowboy
Klondike Medicine Woman
*The Cowboy Tutor
*The Cowboy Father
*The Cowboy Comes Home

*Three Brides for Three Cowboys

LINDA FORD

shares her life with her rancher husband, a grown son, a live-in client she provides care for and a yappy parrot. She and her husband raised a family of fourteen children, ten adopted, providing her with plenty of opportunity to experience God's love and faithfulness. They've had their share of adventures, as well. Taking twelve kids in a motor home on a three-thousand-mile road trip would be high on the list. They live in Alberta, Canada, close enough to the Rockies to admire them every day. She enjoys writing stories that reveal God's wondrous love through the lives of her characters.

Linda enjoys hearing from readers. Contact her at linda@lindaford.org or check out her website, www.lindaford.org, where you can also catch her blog, which often carries glimpses of both her writing activities and family life.

LINDA FORD

The Cowboy Comes Home

™ LOVE INSPIRED BOOKS

ISBN-13: 978-0-373-82907-1

THE COWBOY COMES HOME

www.LoveInspiredBooks.com

Printed in U.S.A.

My God will supply all you need according to
his riches in glory by Christ Jesus.
—*Philippians* 4:19

For Sierra.

As my eldest granddaughter you hold a special place in my heart. It has been my joy to watch you grow and see you become a beautiful young woman. I hope we can become closer in the future. My prayer is that you will find true joy and meaning in life through opening your heart to God's love. I love you.

Chapter One

Golden Prairie, Alberta, Canada
Spring 1934

She needed eyes in six places at once to keep track of that child.

"Robbie!" An edge of annoyance worked itself into Sally Morgan's voice. Yes, she understood how a boy who was about to turn six might be upset by so many changes in his life. His mother had passed away just after Christmas. His maternal grandmother had stayed until spring and then Sally started coming during the day. But the child needed to realize life was easier if he didn't fight every person and every rule.

Sally found Carol playing with her doll in the patch of grass next to the big tree at the front of the lot, her plain brown hair as tidy as when she'd left for school. Even her clothes were still neat and clean. The girl was only eight but had adjusted much better than her brother. "Have you seen Robbie?"

Carol didn't even glance up from her play. Simply shook her head.

"Where can he be this time?" As soon as she'd realized he was missing she'd searched the house. She'd looked in the shed in the back of the lot where he often hid. Now she marched toward the barn. The children's father would be home shortly and expecting his meal. She'd left the food cooking on the stove. If she found Robbie soon she could hope to keep supper from burning.

She stepped into the cool, dark interior of the barn, now unused. Mr. Finley didn't own a horse. He drove a fine car instead. "Robbie!" she yelled, then cocked her head to listen. She heard nothing but the echo of her voice, the flap and coo of pigeons disturbed by her noisy presence and the scurry of mice heading for safety.

She left the barn and turned her gaze to the narrow alley separating the fine big yard on the edge of town from the farm on the other side. Would Robbie have ventured into forbidden territory? Most certainly he would if the notion struck.

Sparing a brief glance at the house where the meal needed attention, she headed for the gate, pausing only long enough to call to Carol, "You stay there while I find Robbie."

Her steps firm with determination and mounting frustration, she strode across the dusty track to the sagging wire fence. From where she stood she saw nothing but the board fence around the back of the barn. Sighing loudly, she stuck her foot on the wobbly wire to clamber awkwardly over the fence. She landed safely on the far side and hurried forward. Three steps later she skidded to a halt.

A man leaned against the fence. A man with an I-own-the-world stance, a cowboy hat pushed back to reveal a tangle of dark blond curls, and a wide grin wreathing his face. She spared him a quick study. Faded brown shirt, tied at the neck like a frontier man of years ago. Creased denim trousers. He dressed like he'd very recently come off a working ranch.

Sally's worry about Robbie collided with surprise at seeing a man in Mrs. Shaw's yard. A sight, she added, that made her feel a pinch in the back of her heart. It had to be the way she'd hurried about searching for Robbie that made her lungs struggle for air.

Robbie. She'd almost forgotten she was looking for him. Her gaze lingered on the man two more seconds. Then she forced herself forward another step, following the direction the man looked.

Her heart headed for runaway speed.

Robbie stood within reach of the hooves of a big horse.

She choked back a warning. If anything startled the animal he could trample Robbie, which would certainly reinforce some of the things the boy had been told, like don't go near a horse that doesn't know you. Stay out of people's yards unless invited—but she had no desire to see him learn in such a harsh fashion.

"That's it. No sudden moves."

She didn't need to turn to know the deep voice came from the man leaning against the fence. He sounded every bit as relaxed as he looked. Her gaze darted back to him. Yes. Still angled back as if he didn't have a worry in the world. He was a stranger to her. She knew nothing about him except what she saw, but it was enough to convince her it took a lot to upset his world.

She envied him his serenity.

"His name is Big Red. I just call him Red."

"Can I touch him?" Robbie's childish voice quivered with eagerness.

She shifted her attention back to him. Normally the boy didn't ask permission and if he did, he paid no mind if it was refused, but he stood stock still waiting for the man to answer.

"Sure. He's as tame as a house kitty. But speak to him first. Maybe tell him your name and say his, like you want to be friends."

Sally watched in complete fascination as Robbie obeyed.

"Hi, Big Red. My name is Robbie Finley. Can I be your friend?" Slowly, cautiously, perhaps a bit fearfully, the boy reached out and touched the horse's muzzle. The horse whinnied as if answering the boy.

Robbie laughed out loud.

The horse lifted his head, rolled back his lips and gave an unmistakable horse laugh.

Sally chuckled softly. It was all so calm. Sweet even. Not at all the way Robbie usually behaved.

"I suppose you've come for the boy?" The man peeled himself from the fence and headed in her direction.

Her amusement fled. Feeling exposed and guilty, she glanced about. She was trespassing, along with Robbie. But that didn't bother her as much as the foolish reaction of her heart and lungs, her thoughts and skin— she'd never known her skin to tingle so that it made her cheeks burn. It was how the man grinned that filled her with a need to run and hide.

"Allow me to introduce myself. Linc McCoy."

She nodded, unable to push a word to her brain let alone her mouth. The name had a familiar ring to it. Or was it only her stupid reaction making her think she'd heard it before?

"Are you Robbie's mother?"

Words jolted from her mouth. "Oh, no." A rush of them followed. "His mother is dead. I'm only the house-keeper. I take care of them. Every day. I make meals and—" Then a blank mind.

"Oh. I don't believe I've had the pleasure."

Pleasure? Yes, it was a word that fit this man. He seemed to embrace life with his smile, his relaxed stance. Even his dark eyes—brown as mink fur—said life was good. Fun. To be enjoyed. Ah. That would explain why Robbie had responded so well to him. Robbie didn't have much use for rules or anything interfering with his idea of fun. She tried to think how unnatural it was in a grown man but instead she smiled back, as bemused as Robbie was with the horse. Suddenly she realized he grinned because she hadn't given her name. When had she ever been so foolish? So slow thinking? "I'm Sally Morgan."

"Looks like we'll be neighbors."

Another burst of words shot from her mouth. "Oh, no. I don't live here. I only come in the daytime. I live out of town." She waved in vaguely the direction of the Morgan home. "Not very far from town. Just a nice walk. I come to take care of the house and the children."

How could she have forgotten her responsibility? "Come along, Robbie. Your father will be home shortly."

Robbie stuck out his lip in an all-too-familiar gesture.

Linc McCoy strode to the boy's side with a rolling gait. "Nice meeting you, Robbie. Red says so, too, don't you, Boy?"

The horse whinnied and nodded his head.

"See. He agrees."

Robbie giggled, but when he turned back to Sally his look overflowed with rebellion. He had the same coloring as his sister, brown hair, brown eyes. On Carol it was sweet. Not a word she would use to describe Robbie.

Mr. McCoy planted a hand on Robbie's shoulder and turned him toward Sally. "You run along now. Perhaps you can visit again."

"Only with permission," Sally warned.

"That's right. You have to ask before you come over. Wouldn't want to worry Miss Morgan, would you?" He shifted his warm, steady gaze to Sally, and her breath stuck halfway up her windpipe. "It is Miss, isn't it?"

She nodded. It was an innocent enough question. It was only her befuddled brain making her think it brimmed with interest. "Yes." If she didn't get back in a matter of minutes, not only would supper be ruined but she was bound to say something really and truly stupid.

Robbie didn't protest when she grabbed his hand and hustled him to the fence. He scampered over, but she hesitated. There was no graceful way to climb over and land on her feet.

Mr. McCoy followed her. "Allow me." He pushed the wire down with his foot and extended his hand to help her over.

What a predicament. Place her hand in his and most

certainly stumble over her tongue, or climb over on her own and most certainly stumble to the ground.

She chose dignity over wisdom, placed her fingers in his cool firm palm and wobbled her way over the swaying wire. "Thank you," she murmured, managing to make her thick tongue say the two syllables without tangling them.

Abe's car pulled into the narrow driveway.

Oh, no. She couldn't possibly make it back before he discovered her absence. "Run, Robbie." She grabbed his hand and fled for the back door.

They burst into the house. Sally choked on the burnt smell. Abe held a smoking pot in his tea-towel-protected hand.

"I'm sorry," Sally gasped and rushed to take the pot. The potatoes were ruined. She dumped the pot in the sink and quickly checked the rest of the meal. The green beans she'd shoved to the back of the stove looked a little limp but were edible. The meat simmered in now glutinous gravy, but it could be salvaged with the addition of hot water. "Everything will be ready in a minute or two. I'll call Carol." But when she turned to do so, Abe blocked her way.

"Where were you? I come home expecting supper and discover my daughter home alone, you and my son missing. Did you let him run away again?"

Her tongue seemed to stick to the roof of her mouth. She sucked saliva to moisten it. Why did he blame her when Robbie was so difficult?

"I need someone who can handle my home and children."

She nodded miserably. She had always considered

herself efficient until she started work here. And her future depended on proving it. Everyone knew Abe Finley was in need of a new wife and mother for his children. He was a man with a good home and a government job that offered stability. Too bad he couldn't smile with as much pleasure as Mr. McCoy did. She dismissed the thought before it had a chance to roost.

"It won't happen again." Not if she had to chain Robbie to the stove.

"I'm glad to hear that." He turned on his heel. "Call me when you have things properly organized."

She was organized. She did watch his children with due care. A thousand protests sprang to her mind but were quickly squelched as she turned back to the stove. Abe wasn't unkind. He simply liked things done properly, neatly. It wasn't too much to expect. Especially if she wanted him to offer marriage to make the arrangement permanent.

Too bad he couldn't enjoy life as much as Linc McCoy appeared to.

Sally slammed a pot lid on the cupboard with more force than necessary. Why was she thinking about a stranger when her future lay in this house? If she proved herself acceptable—and she vowed she would. And who was Linc McCoy to be hanging about Mrs. Shaw's place like he owned it?

She managed to present a passable meal, substituting slabs of bread for the potatoes. Her father had always said there was nothing quite as good as bread and gravy, but she could tell Abe didn't share the opinion. However, he ate without complaint and pushed from the table a little later, having eaten enough to satisfy most any appetite.

"You did fine despite your mistakes. Thank you."

"You're welcome." She met his gaze for a moment but as always felt awkward and darted her glance past him to the dirty dishes. "I'll wash up before I head home."

"I appreciate that."

Yet somehow she wondered if he did, or if he expected it. Immediately she scolded herself for her wicked thoughts. Why was she suddenly so keen to criticize him? She had no right. She was here to do a job. With the unspoken agreement that it could lead to more.

A window stood over the sink and as she washed dishes, she glanced out frequently. She faced the back of the yard, toward Mrs. Shaw's place. A gate near the barn swung back and Linc, astride Big Red, rode out. He sat on the horse like the two were one, his hat pulled low to shield his eyes from the slanting rays of the sun. Red raced down the alley between the two properties. Linc and Red flowed like fast-moving water down the fence line. At the corner, the horse reared.

Sally's heart clamored up her throat. He was going to be thrown.

But instead, he let out a loud whoop that reached her through the open window. Then he laughed and rode back.

He saw her staring at him and waved his hat, grinning so widely and freely it tugged at some remote part of her heart. Oh, to feel so free and full of enjoyment.

With another whoop, he guided the horse past the barn and out of sight.

She didn't know who he was, but he certainly seemed to think life was a lark. She forced her attention back to the stack of dirty dishes and hoped he would ride fast and far, out of her thoughts.

Linc galloped two miles down the road before he turned and allowed Red to keep a sedate pace on the way back to his grandparents' farm—now Grandmama's farm. Grandpa had died two years ago and ever since, Grandmama had been begging Linc to come back and help her.

He might never have come, except for the way things had worked out.

He settled back in the saddle and thought of the afternoon. Little Robbie had ventured into the corral, unaware Linc watched. The little boy wore nice clothes but an unhappy expression. He wondered what brought such a look to a child's face until Sally said the boy's mother had died. Linc understood how that felt. His own mother had died when he was but fifteen. Much older than Robbie, but still too young to be motherless. Mothers kept the family together, provided a moral compass. Without a mother…well, his family had certainly gone downhill. Not that he intended to dwell on it or try to find someone or something to pin the blame on.

His mood shifted and he grinned as he thought of Sally. He didn't remember her from before, so the Morgans must have moved in after they left when he was sixteen. Otherwise he would have certainly remembered her. Even then he liked a good-looking woman. And Sally was certainly that, with wavy brown hair falling to her shoulders, capturing the sun's rays like miser's gold in each wave. Eyes the color of olive-green water, like he'd seen in the mountains to the west. Eyes that widened in surprise at seeing him, narrowed with caution before taking his hand. He rubbed his hand against the warm denim on his leg. He had only meant to be helpful, but her cool flesh against his had felt like a hot iron, searing her brand on his palm. He pressed his fist to his chest, feeling marked inside as well and ignored the urge to thump himself on the forehead at such silly ideas. He dropped his hand back to his leg.

Obviously a proper young woman.

Even if she didn't know the McCoy reputation, she would soon enough hear it. Not that it mattered what people said. He'd tried to tell his pa and older brother so six years ago. Stay and prove the rumors false, he'd said. But he was only sixteen and they weren't about to listen to him.

Now he was back and determined to do what he'd wanted back then—prove the McCoys were not sticky-fingered scoundrels.

And of course, care for his injured father.

Time to get back to the task.

Despite the duties calling him, he took his time unsaddling Red, then spent a leisurely thirty minutes grooming him and tidying up the barn before he headed for the house. He paused inside the door and breathed in the homey scents of yeasty bread and cinnamon. No matter where he'd gone in the past six years, he'd missed this place.

Grandmama sat in her favorite spot—a rocking chair by the window—doing needlework. "I 'spect you're missing your freedom."

He understood what she didn't say. That she feared he would leave again as soon as Pa—

Memories of a pretty face flashed through his brain. Even if he had planned to leave, getting to know Miss Sally better was enough to make him reconsider. "I never wanted to go in the first place."

Grandmama glanced up then. "You should have stayed. You could stay now and run this place."

He wondered if anyone else would hope he'd remain. "I had to go with Pa and Harris." Though he couldn't exactly say why. Guess the same loyalty that brought him back with Pa. "How is he?"

"Haven't heard from him."

Which meant he was sleeping. The painkiller the doctor provided was doing its job. Once it wore off, Pa would start hollering and cussing. Poor Grandmama— having to listen to Pa in one of his rages. Yet when Linc showed up on the doorstep dragging his injured father, she had calmly opened the door and welcomed them. And she'd cried when Linc said Harris had died in the mining accident that injured Pa.

"He was my oldest grandson. Despite his rebellious ways I have never stopped loving him and praying for him." She'd hugged Linc long and hard. "Are you still walking in your faith?" she asked when her tears were spent.

He'd had his struggles, his ups and downs and times of doubt, but he was happy to be able to give her the answer she longed for. "I hold fast to my faith and God's love."

"I don't suppose Harris or your Pa ever made that choice?"

"Not Pa. I don't know about Harris. You know how he always tried so hard to please Pa." Even if Harris believed in God, he might well hide it from Pa so as to not incur his displeasure.

"Then this is why God sent you home. To allow Jonah another chance to change his ways. My Mary would want her husband to become a Christian."

Linc permitted himself a moment of aching emptiness at the mention of his mother's name, then pulled his thoughts back to the present. "I'll check on him." He strode to the bedroom off the front room where Grandmama had made up a bed for Pa. Pa murmured in his sleep. Doc said the drugs made him restless, but for the moment he seemed comfortable. The bruises on his face had faded to yellow and the swelling had subsided. His leg was bound and splinted. Doc changed the dressings on it every day. But it was the injuries to his chest that had done the most damage. Doc said he couldn't tell how badly Pa's internal organs had been damaged. His chances were slim, Doc had been honest enough to say. "About all we can do is keep him comfortable."

Which meant giving him pain medication.

Linc shook the bottle of medicine. It was almost empty. As were his pockets. It had taken a whack out of his savings to bury Harris and the rest to get himself, Red and his father home. He'd have to find himself some sort of work in order to keep the bottle full.

Satisfied his Pa didn't need anything for the moment, he returned to the kitchen and sat at the table, turning his chair to face Grandmama.

"I met a young lady today. Sally Morgan. Do you know her?"

Grandmama carefully put away the yarn and folded the piece of fabric she worked on before setting it on the little table beside her chair. "I know the Morgans. Mr. Morgan died a few years back. The two older girls have married recently. Louisa, the eldest, married a widower with a little girl. They adopted one of the orphan girls before they headed west where he has a ranch. Madge and her husband now own the Cotton farm. They're a hard-working young couple."

"Uh-huh." He wasn't so interested in the family as in Sally.

"Miss Sally is working for our neighbor, Abe Finley." He knew that, too.

"He's a widower with two young children."

"I met Robbie. He came to visit me and my horse."

"Young Robbie has been a bit of a…" She hesitated. "A concern since his mother died."

Linc smiled. "You couldn't come right out and say he's a defiant child?" He'd seen the way he'd glowered at Sally when she said he had to go home.

Grandmama sniffed. "I don't believe in speaking ill of others."

"Too bad others don't share your view." If they did, Linc and his father and brother wouldn't have felt they had to leave town six years ago. And maybe Harris would still be alive. He missed his brother. A blast of sorrow hit Linc and he looked out the window, waiting for it to pass.

He saw the corrals out the window and remembered he was asking about Sally. "So what do you know about Miss Sally?"

Grandmama gave him her best warning expression.

"Everyone expects she and Abe will decide to marry. So you stay away from her, you hear?"

"This understanding that everyone has, is it official?"

Grandmama's eyes narrowed. "There's been no announcement, if that's what you mean. But you listen to me, Lincoln McCoy—"

Uh-oh. When she used his full name, he knew she was deadly serious.

"Abe Finley is a fine match for Sally. Don't you go interfering with it."

And he wasn't suitable? Is that what she meant?

"You hear me?"

Linc sighed. He wouldn't argue with her. After all, she had given shelter to Pa and she didn't even like him much. Just as she'd welcomed the four of them when they returned eight years ago, when Ma was filled with cancer and dying. And perhaps she was right. He was a McCoy, after all, and even if he convinced everyone they hadn't stolen the things they'd been accused of, he would still be a McCoy—and who were they but wanderers? Pa never stayed long in one place. In fact, come to think of it, the two years they'd spent on this farm made the longest he could remember being in one place.

Grandmama nudged his leg. "You hear me?"

"I hear ya." What he heard was there was no formal agreement between Sally and Abe.

Chapter Two

Sally pulled a tray of cookies from the familiar oven of home and scooped them to a rack to cool. Ginger cookies perfectly rounded, nicely browned with a sprinkling of sugar. She was a good cook. Yet she experienced so many failures at the Finley place. She must be trying too hard. She sucked in spicy air and pushed her frustration to the bottom of her stomach. She needed to remember she was a child of God, and as such had His approval. "I'll take these over to the Johanssons as soon as they cool," she said to her mother. "I'm sorry to hear the mother is still not feeling well." Mrs. Johansson hadn't regained her strength after the birth of daughter number five. "The children will appreciate fresh cookies."

"How did your day go at the Finleys'?" Mother glanced up from sewing a button on a sweater.

Sally didn't want to trouble her mother with tales of her struggles with Robbie and news of a ruined meal. "There was a man at Mrs. Shaw's."

"Really? How do you know that?"

"I saw him out in the corrals. He showed Robbie his horse. Big Red, he's called."

Mother studied her with watchful eyes.

Fearing her expression would reveal more than she wanted, Sally shaped more cookies.

"So you met this man?"

Sally nodded. "When I went to bring Robbie back. His name is Linc McCoy. I thought I'd heard the name before but can't place it."

"The McCoys are back?" Mother sounded as if a murderer had escaped into their presence.

"I only saw the one. Are there more?"

Mother pushed to her feet and strode to the window. "I don't suppose you know the story. It was fresh when we first moved but died down shortly after."

Sally stared at her mother's back. "What did they do?"

Mother faced her and sighed. "Mrs. Ogilvy kept some expensive jewelry in her home."

Sally waited for more. Everyone knew Mrs. Ogilvy to be the richest lady in town. She lived in a big house at the opposite end of the street from where Mr. Finley lived. She lived alone except for a woman who came in to help care for the house. Mrs. Ogilvy had once ruled Golden Prairie society but had been ill for the past couple years. She was on the mend now and again dominating social activities. Why, at Christmas she'd instigated a town party for everyone, including hobos from their shelter down by the tracks. Sally had even heard Mrs. Ogilvy allowed some of them to live in the old coach house she no longer used. Sally liked the woman who used her worldly goods to help others.

Mother sighed and continued with her story. "Mrs. Ogilvy's jewels went missing. It was never proven, but all the evidence pointed toward the McCoys. They were known as the kind of people who—" Mother stopped. "I don't like to speak ill of others, but from what I understand they had sticky fingers."

"The McCoys?" This news didn't fit with the relaxed, smiling man she'd met. "How many were there?"

"A father and two sons—the younger several years younger than the older."

"What do they have to do with Mrs. Shaw?"

"Mrs. McCoy was Mrs. Shaw's daughter. Her only child. She came home to die of cancer." Mother shook her head sadly. "I can't imagine how she must feel to lose her daughter, then have her grandsons and son-in-law branded criminals."

"But you said they were never convicted."

"No, they weren't, but people believed it was only because of poor police work. They left town to avoid the censure of the community."

Sally pulled out another tray of baked cookies and put them to cool, then slipped a tray of unbaked ones into the oven, welcoming the chance to contemplate all her mother said.

"You say you met Linc McCoy? I'm not certain but I think he was the youngest son. From what I recall, about fifteen or sixteen when they left town."

"They might be innocent. You know what gossip is like."

Mother crossed to Sally's side. "Where there's smoke, there's fire. I don't want you feeling sorry for this man. It would not serve your purpose to get involved with him. Whether or not they've stolen the jewels, their name carries trouble."

Sally met her mother's eyes without flinching. She understood what Mother meant. People would likely feel the same way about the McCoys now as they had back then. She shifted her gaze. The lowering sun shone through the west window, highlighting the ever present dust in the air. Through the window, she studied the struggling garden. "I need to take water to the garden." She'd saved the dishwashing water. "I'll feed the chickens as soon as I finish the cookies."

Mother returned to her sewing, knowing they were in agreement. Sally would do nothing to besmirch her reputation or put her security at risk. She'd avoid Linc McCoy, which shouldn't be hard.

Mother paused. "I wonder what brought them back."

Sally wondered if all of them had returned. She'd seen only Linc—the man who seemed to think life was for enjoyment.

Well, so did she, only she liked to enjoy it on her terms. She recalled one of her memory verses. *A good name is rather to be chosen than great riches, and loving favour rather than silver and gold.*

She could well say, rather than Mrs. Ogilvy's jewels.

She wanted nothing more to do with Linc McCoy and the shady doings associated with his family.

Sally slipped into the Finley kitchen and began breakfast preparations. Overhead, she heard the family rising. They would soon descend—Carol ready for school, Abe dressed and groomed for his job and Robbie with his eyes silently challenging her.

She sighed. She and Robbie would become friends sooner or later. She just wished it would be sooner.

A short while later, the children descended, Abe's hand firmly on Robbie's stubborn shoulder. Carol was dressed for school, not a seam out of place. From the beginning she insisted she could manage her hair on her own and did a fine job. Robbie wore wrinkled overalls with threadbare knees. If she didn't miss her guess, his shirt was buttoned crookedly, but she would ignore it unless Abe insisted it be corrected. Abe was even neater than Carol, as if he'd pressed his suit while on his body so not a crease was out of place. Freshly shaven, smelling of bay rum with his dark brown hair brushed back. One thing about Abe: he knew how to make the most of his looks, and there was no denying he was a good-looking man and well respected—a good Christian, a devout churchgoer, a man of honor.

Sally recited his attributes as she dished up porridge and poured Abe a cup of coffee. She hated the stuff, preferring a pot of well-steeped tea, but had learned to make a brew to satisfy his requirements. She'd eaten with Mother before leaving home but sat with the family and drank tea as they ate.

Abe left as soon as he finished. He spared them all a hurried goodbye.

Sally found it easier to smile once he'd gone, even though she still found his rushed exits strange. Her father had hugged each of the girls and kissed Mother when he left the house. He always had a kind word for them. She'd told herself several times it wasn't fair to any man to compare him to Father, and yet she wished Abe would at least read a chapter from the Bible and pray with the children before he left for the day.

At first, she'd debated with herself as to whether she

should take on the responsibility. The deciding factor had been that she should begin as she expected to go on, and if she were to become a permanent part of this home, Bible reading and prayer were what she wanted.

But rather than read from the family Bible, she brought a series of Bible stories on cards with pictures on one side and text on the other that she'd collected in her Sunday school days. She chose the next in the stack to read.

Carol listened intently. Robbie fidgeted, wanting to leave but knowing Sally would insist he stay. They'd fought that battle the first day and Sally had won, knowing she must.

She made her prayer short, asking for the children and their father to be safe. In her heart, she prayed she could live up to expectations and not let foolish thoughts distract her. And why the thought shaped into a grinning man in a cowboy hat, she wouldn't let herself consider.

Carol departed a short time later then Sally turned to Robbie. "Play out back where I can see you."

She washed dishes and put together soup for dinner when both Abe and Carol would come home. Every few minutes she glanced out the window to check on Robbie. He'd dug a hole in the end of the garden and used the dirt to construct a barrier, no doubt hoping to build a place where he could hide from his troublesome world.

Sally grinned. After Father died she'd done the same, only she'd had the loft of the barn where she used loose hay to encircle a little patch where she took her books and an old school notebook, in which she wrote copious amounts of purple prose full of emotionally charged words like hopelessness, emptiness and loneliness. She had felt safe and secure in that little place.

Forbidden, her gaze sought the area across the alley. Quickly, telling herself she was only allowing her eyes a chance to look into the distance, she glanced to the corrals, past them to the bit of yard within her view. Maybe he had left again. No reason such a thought should make her sad. She snorted as several of the words she'd used in her loft hiding place resurrected.

The soup simmered on the stove. She mixed up baking powder biscuits to go with it.

Another glance out the window showed the Shaw yard still empty and Robbie struggling to build his dirt walls higher. The soil was so dry it sifted into a slack pile.

Remembering her own efforts to create a safe place, she ached for the little boy. Hoping he wouldn't be angry at her interruption, she hurried outside. "I can show you how to build higher walls if you like."

He didn't move for a full three seconds.

She knew he warred with a desire to dismiss her and frustration over dealing with the piles of dirt.

"How?" He made certain to sound as if he was doing her a favor.

"I saw some scraps of lumber in the shed. I think you could use them to provide support. Come. I'll show you."

He followed her to the shed and allowed her to fill his arms with bits of lumber.

Back in the garden, she drove the thinner pieces into the ground as uprights and showed him how to place the wider pieces against them and hold them in place with the dirt. As they worked, she told him about the place she'd made in the loft.

She heard a horse trot down the alley and kept her gaze averted to the count of five before she glanced up. Linc on Big Red rode toward the center of town.

He nodded at them, grinning. "Playing in the dirt, I see."

She tossed her hair out of her eyes. "We're building."

"What are you building?"

"I'm not sure. Robbie, what are we building?"

"A fort." He didn't pause from scooping dirt against the walls.

Linc looked from Robbie to Sally, paused a moment then returned to Robbie. "What sort of fort?"

"To keep out the bad guys."

For a moment Linc didn't move, didn't say anything and his grin seemed narrower. "Guess we all need a safe place." He touched the brim of his hat. "Perhaps I'll see you later."

Sally waited until he rode out of sight then pushed to her feet. "I have to check on dinner. Call me if you need any help."

Robbie kept shoveling dirt.

We all need a safe place. Exactly her sentiments. She paused outside the door and studied the house. A good solid house. A safe place? She glanced over her shoulder. Safer than a man on horseback who dropped in from who-knows-where and would likely drop back out as quickly and silently.

She hurried indoors and put the biscuits in the oven to bake.

The meal was ready when Abe stepped into the house. The table was set neatly. She'd put the soup in a pretty tureen in the middle of the table and arranged the biscuits on a nice platter. She'd even found a glass dish for the butter.

Robbie had come in without arguing. He'd dusted his clothes and washed his face and hands. Hardly any evidence remained of his morning spent playing in the dirt.

Sally was satisfied the meal looked as good as it smelled. Everything was done to perfection. As she'd taken care of the many details of creating this meal, she'd taken care of one other thing—sorting out her thoughts. She needed a safe place and this was it. Nothing could be allowed to take that away from her. Especially not a man on a horse.

They all took their places and without any warning, Abe bowed and said grace.

It still startled Sally the way he did it. Father had always said, "Let us pray." And waited for them all to fold their hands and bow their heads.

Abe did things differently. Nothing wrong with that.

He ate in silence for a few minutes, then, as he broke open another biscuit and drenched it in butter and jam, he said, "I hired a man to work on the barn. I want it converted to a proper garage. The yard could do with some cleaning up, too, so I gave him instructions to fix the fence out back, prune the apple trees and generally take care of the chores."

"I see." Abe was one of a handful of people who could afford to pay someone to do repair work for them.

"I don't have time to show him around so perhaps

you would do so. Give him access to the tools in the shed. Make him feel welcome. Perhaps offer him coffee in the middle of the afternoon. That sort of thing."

"Will he be taking meals with us?"

"I shouldn't think so. He lives close by."

She quickly did a mental inventory on the neighbors, wondering which one had been so favored by Abe.

"I think he's down on his luck. As a Christian man I feel it my duty to give him a helping hand."

That tidbit didn't help her. Most of the families in town were having trouble making ends meet.

He pushed back and reached for his hat. "He said he'd come over after lunch. It would please me if you helped him in any way you can."

Sally waited, expecting a name, but Abe headed for the door. "Wait. You didn't say who was coming."

"Oh, didn't I? Sorry. It's Linc McCoy. He's staying at his grandmother's just next door." He pointed toward the farm.

Sally's heart quivered. Linc was coming here to work? Abe expected her to help him? The man did strange things to her equilibrium. Things she didn't like or welcome.

Abe must have read her hesitation. "There have been cruel rumors about him in the past. This morning I saw Linc in the store asking after a job and overheard some not-so-kind-hearted women saying no one in town would hire the likes of him. Not a very Christian attitude in my opinion. I believe our church should do what it can to dispel such unkindness. As a deacon I intend to take the lead. I hope I have your support."

"Of course." Thankfully her voice didn't reveal her

confusion. "It's very noble of you to give this man a chance."

Her praise brought a pleased smile to Abe's lips.

Sally vowed she would do what she could to help Abe's cause.

Linc considered this job an answer to prayer—an opportunity to earn money to buy more medicine for Pa, but even more, the chance to prove a McCoy could be trusted. Grandmama seemed troubled by the job offer and warned Linc that Sally's association with him, even indirectly, could harm her reputation. He understood her warning and was prepared to stay as far away from Sally as the large yard allowed. But Abe had told him to go to the house for instructions on where to find tools.

He first toured the yard, noting all the things needing attention. Abe wanted the barn converted to a garage for his car. Linc went inside to study what it needed.

"What are you doing here?" Robbie asked from the dark interior.

"Looking."

"At what?"

"The barn."

"You never seen a barn before?"

"Oh, yeah. Lots of them. I could tell you all sorts of stories about barns."

"Nothing special about barns."

"Nope. Guess not. Seems a shame to take the stalls out though."

Robbie emerged from the shadows. "Why you going to do that?"

"So your father can park his car in here."

Robbie made a rumbling noise with his lips. "I'd sooner have a horse."

"Me, too, little guy."

They stood side by side in shared sorrow at the way horses were being replaced with automobiles and tractors.

Linc moved first. "I need to ask Miss Sally to show me the tools. Want to come along?"

"Yep."

Linc wasn't sure who needed the other the most. He, to keep his thoughts in order when he spoke to Sally, or Robbie, who seemed to crave attention, but together they marched to the back door. Robbie stood by his side as Linc knocked.

Sally opened the door. "Mr. Finley said to expect you. He said I should show you what needs doing."

Linc backed up two steps. Robbie followed suit, though not likely for the same reason. Linc did it to gain a safety zone. Even so, he felt her in every muscle. She smelled like home cooking and fresh laundry, the most appealing scent he'd ever experienced.

She slipped through the doorway. "I'll show you around."

I've already looked about. The words were in his brain but refused to budge. Instead he nodded, and he and Robbie fell in at her side.

She led him to the back corner of the yard. "Mr. Finley said the crab apple trees should be pruned."

Robbie climbed one of the trees and sat in a fork, pretending he had a spyglass as he looked out across the yard.

Linc and Sally stood under the scraggly trees that were shedding the last of their blossoms and trying to bud, finding it difficult because of the lack of moisture. He examined the three trees. "Lots of dead branches that need to come out."

She nodded. "I figure they must be tough as an old cowhide to survive the drought and wind and grasshoppers. Especially the grasshoppers. The little pests have gnawed most of the trees to death around here."

"Then I guess they deserve lots of care."

He turned from examining the branches. She stood under a flowering bough. Their gazes collided. Her eyes were wide and watchful. Wary even. No doubt she had heard about the McCoys by now. "You know I'm Beatrice Shaw's grandson?"

She nodded. "My mother told me."

"Did she tell you about the McCoys?"

Sally's gaze never faltered. "She said your mother had died and you have a father and older brother."

"My brother is dead, too. In a mining accident."

"I'm sorry." She brushed his arm with her cool fingers then jerked back, as if she was also aware of the tension between them.

"Pa was injured, too. That's why I'm here. To let him rest and recover." He clung to the hope Pa would get better.

"How is he?"

"Not good."

"Again, I'm sorry. If there is anything I can do to help...."

He stood stock-still, letting her concern filter through

him. Not many around here knew of the accident. No reason to hide the fact but no reason to tell it either. He didn't want or expect sympathy—just a fair chance to prove the McCoys were an okay bunch. Yet the way her eyes filled with regret and concern made him realize how much he wanted to share his sorrow.

He leaned against a tree. "I was working on a ranch when I got word about the accident. Harris—that's my brother—was killed outright. Pa was in terrible shape. I made arrangements to bury Harris." He told her details of the funeral. "It was ten days before Pa was able to travel. The doctor out there said to take him home so he could die in his own surroundings. Grandmama's place is the only home we've ever had so I brought him here."

She listened to his whole story without uttering a word, but murmuring comforting sounds.

He fell silent, feeling a hundred pounds lighter having told her. Suddenly he jerked upright. "Sorry. I didn't mean to tell you the story of my life."

She laughed softly. "I expect there's more to your life than that and I didn't mind. Helps me understand."

He didn't ask what it helped her understand, and she didn't explain. Perhaps they both knew the answer without speaking it—his tale helped her understand him, just as sharing it helped him understand how kind and sympathetic she was. He had never before felt so comfortable with another human. Sure, he had unburdened himself to the occasional horse—Red heard lots of his woes—but never before to another person, and most certainly not to a woman.

Grandmama warned him she was a genuinely gentle person. Now he understood what she meant.

Guilt flared through his blood, searing his nerve endings. He glanced over his shoulder as if Grandmama watched.

Chapter Three

"Abe said you would show me where the tools are."

Linc's words jerked Sally back to her responsibilities. "Of course." She didn't offer to show him the barn but marched toward the shed at the back of the yard. She paused as they reached the garden. Robbie followed at their heels and veered toward the hole he'd been digging this morning.

She watched him and spoke her thoughts. "I'd like to plant a garden."

"I'll dig the ground for you."

She thought of arguing. Would she look as if she couldn't manage? On the other hand, his help would certainly make the work go faster. Still undecided about how she should handle his offer, she opened the door and stepped aside as he entered. But two feet of distance did not protect her from acute awareness of the warmth of his body as he passed, nor the scent of leather and freshly cut hay. And something more she could not identify, nor did she intend to try. But whatever it was made her feel as if a weight pressed against her chest, making her lungs reluctant to work.

He took his time looking about, then emerged with a round-nosed shovel and a rake.

She had thought long and hard about planting a garden. Well, actually she'd only thought of it this morning and decided growing a garden would prove to Abe she was efficient and capable. Her plan had been to dig the soil on her own, but suddenly accepting Linc's offer to help seemed the wisest thing in the world. It would enable her to get the garden in sooner, which was good.

When he told her about his father and brother, she sensed a man who valued his family above people's opinions. She respected him for that.

He strode to the edge of the garden and began turning over the soil.

Robbie stood before the hole he'd dug. "You can't touch my fort." His expression dared anyone to do so. Sally knew he would fly into a rage if they did.

Linc leaned on the shovel, his expression serious, and pushed his hat back to reveal a white forehead. Brown dirt dusted the rest of his face, and a thin layer wrapped about his pant.

Sally smiled gently. The man could look as handsome in work-soiled clothes as in a polished and pressed suit.

He nodded toward Robbie. "I respect a man who defends his property."

Robbie's expression revealed confusion. "What's that mean?"

Linc scratched his hairline and seemed to consider his answer with due seriousness. "It means I think it's a good thing you want to protect what you've made."

"It is?" Robbie suddenly stood up straighter. "I sure

'nough plan to do that." He picked up a stick and brandished it like a weapon.

Linc held up a hand. "Now hang on a minute. Did I threaten your fort? Did I say I was going to mow it down? No. I listened to your words. No need to get physical when your words work."

Robbie dropped his weapon.

Linc returned to digging, his back muscles rippling beneath the fabric of his faded brown shirt.

Sally stared. The McCoys had a reputation for taking things. What no one had said, perhaps had not noticed, was this McCoy had a way of giving things. He'd given Robbie the assurance his words could convey his desires. He'd given Sally a feeling of safety.

Now why had she thought such a foolish thing?

She spun around and stared at the house, as if it provided the answer to her question. Just because Linc knew what to say to Robbie to defuse his anger did not mean he offered safety. Safety meant a house. Assurance of staying in one place. Steady employment. Enough to eat.

Her heart burned within her at a rush of other unnamed, unidentifiable things that safety and security meant. She grabbed the rake and smoothed the garden soil behind Linc.

He turned. "I can do that." His voice rang with amusement and so much more.

She stopped and considered him. Did he think she needed protecting?

No one had thought so since Father died, and a lump lodged in the back of her throat. She swallowed hard.

"Is there something wrong with the way I'm doing it?" Confusion made her words sharp.

He studied her, a grin slowly wreathing his face. "Can't say as I ever considered there might be a right or wrong way to rake." He leaned on the shovel and contemplated the idea. "I suppose if you had the tines upward. Or tried to use the handle—"

Her tension disappeared and she laughed. "You're teasing."

"Seems like a good idea if it makes you laugh. You should laugh more often, don't you think?" Without waiting for her to say anything, he turned back to digging.

She stared at his back. Didn't she laugh often enough? Or was he saying he liked hearing the sound of her amusement? Perhaps liked making her happy? As she bent to resume raking, she tried to think how she felt about the idea. No one else seemed to care if she laughed or enjoyed life. Abe certainly didn't. Seems all he cared about was if she kept his life orderly.

There she was again, comparing Abe to another. It didn't escape her troubled thoughts that this time it wasn't her father but a man hired to do chores.

She banged a clump of dirt with the rake, taking out her annoyance on the soil. She knew what she wanted and how to get it. And it wasn't by comparing poor, unsuspecting Abe to every man she knew or met.

Linc worked steadily up the length of the garden, turning over clumps of dry hard dirt. She followed, smoothing the soil for planting. Without rain she would have to baby the plants along with rationed bits of water, the same as she did at home.

Neither spoke as they worked. Crows flapped overhead, cawing. The wind sighed through the grass and moaned around the buildings. Robbie yelled some sort of challenge to an unseen intruder. Sally paused to watch the boy.

Linc had stopped, too, and grinned at Robbie's play. Then turned his smile toward Sally, capturing her in a shiny moment.

The amusement they shared made her eyes watery, and she turned away. The feeling was more than amusement but she refused to acknowledge it. She riveted her attention to Robbie.

He leaped out of his dirt fort and charged at the invisible foe, brandishing the same stick he had waved at Linc. He turned, saw them watching and lowered his weapon. Then determination filled his eyes and he marched toward Sally, his stick held like a sword. "You are my captive. I will take you to my fort. You will stay with me until someone rescues you." He shot Linc a narrow-eyed look.

Sally backed away, uncertain how to respond.

Linc straightened and grew serious. "Never fear, fair maiden. I will rescue you from your wild captor."

She giggled and allowed Robbie to shepherd her into his fort. The hole might be the right size for a five-year-old but barely accommodated her legs, so she stood awkwardly while Robbie guarded her from the solid ground of the garden. They were on eye level with each other, close enough that she saw the mixture of excitement and worry in his eyes. She understood how badly he wanted to play, yet couldn't believe any adult would play with him. When had she ever seen Abe play with the boy? Never. When did she play with him? Almost never. Sure, she read to him. Gave him crayons and coloring books. Even helped him do jigsaw puzzles, but she had never romped with him. Why not? Father had played with her and her sisters. She could remember games of tag and hide-and-seek. He'd even taught them to play ball and croquet.

Her thoughts stalled as Linc crouched low and worked his way cautiously to the edge of the garden. "Someone has captured my fair maiden," he murmured. "I must rescue her before she is harmed."

Robbie pressed a hand to his mouth to silence his excitement and wriggled with delight.

Linc pretended to search behind a clump of grass. "Where can they have taken her?" Keeping low, he ran to the shed and opened the door. "Maybe they will capture me, too. I should hide." He darted inside and pulled the door shut.

Silence followed his disappearance.

Robbie stood stock-still, seemed to consider his next move then yelled out in his fiercest voice. "Mister, I got your lady over here."

The door cracked open. Linc peeked out, and seemed surprised to see Robbie and Sally. "The fair maiden. I will come to her rescue." He emerged, brandishing a length of wood matching Robbie's. He planted one hand on his hip and danced forward in some kind of fancy step while waving his wooden sword. "I challenge you to a duel. Come out and face me like a man."

Sally chuckled softly, but her enjoyment ran much deeper than amusement. Linc made a mighty impressive swashbuckler.

Robbie, holding his sword high, stepped forward, meeting Linc at the edge of the garden. *Crack. Whack.* The swords crashed against each other.

Sally sat on the edge of the hole, grinning at the pair. One thing about Linc—he seemed to know how to have fun. He also knew how to talk to Robbie in such a way as to bring out the best in him. Guess she'd have to give him credit for being loyal to his family, as well. It couldn't have been easy to bring his father back to a place where he knew he'd face censure. But he'd returned so his father could recover…die…in comfort. Her eyes stung with unshed tears.

Linc fell to the ground, and Sally jolted to her feet. "Are you hurt?"

He pressed his hands to his chest. "Mortally wounded, fair maiden. Mortally wounded."

Instinct brought her out of the hole, but Robbie waved his sword and ordered her back. "You must stay until you are rescued."

She shook her head as she realized it was all play acting and sat down again on the edge of the dirt hole.

Linc groaned, rolled on his side and heaved a deep sigh. Then he was quiet. So quiet and still that Robbie tiptoed over. Linc waited until he bent over him to check if he was okay, then grabbed Robbie's sword and held it to the boy's chest. "You are my captive. Set the fair maiden free or prepare to die."

Robbie backed toward the dirt fort. He signaled Sally. "You have been rescued. Go and never bother me again."

Linc reached out and helped Sally from the hole in the ground. He pulled her to his side.

All pretend, she assured herself. Her silly feelings of being protected were not real.

Linc laid Robbie's wooden sword on the ground and edged away, keeping Sally pressed close behind him. "We will meet again, you scoundrel. Next time you won't be so lucky." He turned, grabbed Sally's hand and raced around the shed and out of sight to lean against the warm, rough wall. He laughed, long and hard.

Sally giggled, as delighted with his merriment as she was by his sense of play.

Finally he sobered enough to speak. "Harris and I used to play war games."

"Who was your fair maiden?"

"Usually some poor unsuspecting neighbor girl." He laughed again. "It got so the girls ran indoors when we approached."

She chuckled, enjoying the mental picture of girls running away screaming. Suddenly her amusement died. She doubted the girls ran from him still. Not that it mattered to her if they did or not.

Robbie tiptoed around the edge of the building. "What are you doing?"

"Is it safe to go back to digging the garden?" Linc asked.

Sally sprang into action. "I have to get to work. No more play." She hurried back to her raking. What had she been thinking? She had responsibilities.

Behind her Linc spoke to Robbie. "She didn't mean it. There will always be time to play."

Sally snorted. Showed what he knew. "Play is for children."

"Do you really mean that?" Linc picked up the shovel and resumed digging.

"I guess there is a time and place for play. And people who can take the time." She spoke the words firmly, as much to convince herself as him.

"I gather you don't count yourself one of them."

"Not when I have responsibilities."

He worked steadily. "There will always be responsibilities."

"True."

He reached the end of digging and stopped to wipe his brow on his shirt sleeve. "So you don't play? Grandmama says you have two sisters. Surely you played with them."

"I used to. When I was young and carefree." Why did she feel she had to defend herself? She expected him to ask why she wasn't any longer carefree, but instead he asked, "What games did you and your sisters play?"

"Dress up. Plays. Tea parties." She didn't want to mention the games she'd played with Father.

Linc placed the stake in one end of the garden and stretched a length of twine to the far end, marking a row for Sally. As he worked, he was acutely aware of her studying his question, though her fingers sorted through a small tin bucket full of seed packets.

She'd been a good sport joining in Robbie's game. The boy seemed almost afraid to play. Or rather, to engage adults in his play.

Linc tried to remember a time his father had played with him, but couldn't. Harris, five years older, had been the one who roughhoused with Linc, threw a ball endlessly while he learned how to connect with the bat, and involved him in long complicated games of cops and robbers.

"My father died almost five years ago," Sally finally said. "Just before the crash. Mother says it was a mercy. That it would have broken his heart to see how his family had to struggle."

Linc sat back on his heels and watched her. She had forgotten about the pail of seeds and stared into the past. Her eyes darkened to a deep pine color. A splotch of dirt on her cheek made him want to reach out and brush it away, but he didn't want to distract her. He guessed she would stop talking if he did, and he longed to hear who she was, who she had been.

A shudder raced across her shoulders. "I can't believe how things have changed."

He didn't know if she meant from her father's passing or the depression that followed the stock market crash. Likely both. "It's been tough." It was both a question and a statement. So many unemployed men, many of them in relief camps in the north. The idea behind the camps was to give the unemployed single men a place to live, food to eat and meaningful work to do. Linc thought the reason was more likely a way to get the desperate-looking men out of the way so people weren't reminded of the suffering of others. He had seen women with pinched faces, aching from hunger and something far deeper—a pain exceeding all else—as they helplessly listened to their children cry for food. The drought and grasshopper plague took what little was left after the stockmarket crash. Things were bad all over, but he wanted to know the specifics of how her life had changed. He wanted to know how she'd survived.

"The whole world—my whole world—went from safe to shattered in a matter of days."

"Losing a parent can do that to you."

She blinked, and her gaze returned to the present. Her eyes, holding a mixture of sorrow and sympathy, connected with his. "I guess you understand."

Something in the way she said it, as if finding for the first time someone who truly understood her feelings, made him ache to touch her in a physical way, to offer comfort. And keep her safe. Only the distance between them stopped him from opening his arms. "Your sisters would, too."

She averted her gaze, but not before he caught a glimpse of regret. "Of course they do, but they coped in their own way. Madge, she's a year older than me, did her best to take Father's place. She guided Mother in making decisions about the farm, and because of her efforts our house is safe and secure." She brought her gaze back to his and smiled, as if to prove everything was well in her world. "Louisa is two years older and spent so much of her time sick and forced to rest that she lived in her books. Father's death hit her hard." This time she seemed to expect the shudder and stiffened to contain it to a mere shiver. She brightened.

He discovered he'd been holding his breath and released it with a whoosh.

"I didn't mean to get all sentimental. I mentioned my father because you asked about games. He taught us to play softball."

"Ball, hmm." He pushed his hat far back on his head

and stared away into the distance, imagining a father and three little girls laughing and giggling. "Did you like the game? Were you good at it?" His question seemed to surprise her.

"I tried really hard because I wanted to please my father, but I preferred a game of tag. Father knew a hundred different ways to play the game—frozen tag, stone tag, shadow tag—" She giggled nervously. "I guess that's more information than you expected."

It wasn't. In fact, he wanted more details. "Why did you like tag better than ball?"

She shuffled through the seeds and waited a moment to answer. "Because—" Her voice had grown soft, almost a whisper. "It's just for fun. No one can be disappointed because you couldn't hit the ball." She again turned to the bucket of seeds. "Now I must get this garden planted. And I've kept you from your work long enough."

Her words hung in his ears. She seemed to care so much what her father thought. But then, didn't everyone? His father made it clear he thought Linc didn't measure up to Harris. Although he didn't want to be the sort of man his brother had been—rowdy and hard living, caring little for laws or who got hurt in his schemes—Linc did wish his father viewed him as more than a mother's boy. Too soft for real life. Of course, his father's version of real life hadn't exactly worked out well for either him or Harris.

But Sally was right. Work called. He'd promised a day's work for a day's pay, and he intended to provide it. He went into the shed, found a ladder and saw and carried them out. Sally bent over a row, dropping seeds into a little trench. He paused, thoughts buzzing in his head like flies disturbed from a sunny windowsill. Noisy but nameless. His heart strained with wanting to say something to her that would—what? He could offer nothing. She came from a good family, and he? He was a McCoy.

Until today it hadn't mattered so much.

He hurried across to the struggling crab apple trees. Every step emphasized the truth. He was here to take care of his injured father. She had aspirations to marry Abe Finley.

But as he tackled his job, he stole glances at her. She worked steadily, seeming unmindful of the searing sun and the endless wind whipping dirt into her face as she bent over the soil. At that moment the wind caught the branch he had cut off and practically tore him from his perch on the ladder. He struggled to keep his balance, and had to drop the branch. It lodged in the heart of the tree. He jerked to free it, and managed to kick the ladder out from under him. He clung to a solid branch with his feet dangling. The branch cracked ominously, and he stopped trying to pull himself upward.

How inglorious. Hanging like a kitten gone too far out on a limb. "Sally. Could you give me a hand?"

He couldn't turn to see her, but he knew the second she realized his predicament.

She gasped. "Oh, my word. Hang on. I'm on my way."

"Hang on?" he sputtered. "I fully intend to."

She giggled a little as she trotted across the yard. The ladder was heavy and awkward and she struggled to place it in a spot that would enable him to use it. "Try that."

He swung his feet, found the rungs and eased his weight to them. His body angled awkwardly between his hands and his feet. The limb cracked as he shifted. "Step back in case this breaks."

"Hurry up and get down."

He had to let go of the relative safety of the branch and fling himself toward the ladder. He sucked in air, tensed his muscle and made his move. The ladder shuddered but stayed in place. He looked down. Sally steadied it. His heart clawed up his throat. If the branch had broken...if he'd fallen... "I told you to step back." He sounded angry.

She blinked and looked confused, as if trying to decide if she should obey, then her eyes cleared. "I will once your feet are on the ground."

He caught two rungs on the ladder on his descent. His feet barely touched the ground before he swung around to face her and planted his hands on her shoulders. He wanted to shake her hard but resisted and gave her only a little twitch. "You could have been hurt if that branch gave way or if I fell. Next time listen to me when I tell you to get out of the way."

Suddenly, as if obeying his words, she retreated a step, leaving him to let his hands fall to his side.

"If you had fallen and hurt yourself, how would I explain to Abe—Mr. Finley? He gave me instructions to see you had what you needed and offer you coffee. You do drink coffee, don't you?" Her eyes alternated between worry and interest in his reply.

"Yes, I like coffee just fine." His anger fled, replaced by something he had no name for. The dark churning feeling in the pit of his stomach made coffee sound bitter.

Her only concern was pleasing Abe, meeting his expectations.

"Fine." She turned toward the house, called over her shoulder. "I'll holler when coffee is ready."

"Fine. I'll get this tree done."

Her steps slowed to a crawl and she slowly turned. "Make sure the ladder is secure before you go back up."

"I don't aim to break any limbs, except the damaged ones on the tree." He didn't even try to keep the tightness from his voice. After all, how could he care for his father and earn enough money for pain medication if he broke an arm or leg?

No sir. He had his priorities straight.

Chapter Four

Sally ground the coffee beans with a great deal of vigor. She had helped him and ended up getting scolded. She should have let the man fall on his head. Might teach him a lesson.

The coffee grinding forgotten, she stared at the far wall of the kitchen. He might have killed himself. Or done serious physical harm. The stupid man. Did he think himself invincible? She shivered as her mind filled with a vision of his battered body beneath the tree.

She sprang to the window to make sure he wasn't sprawled motionless on the ground. Her breath thundered from her lungs as she saw him astraddle a branch.

She sucked in air, finding her ribs strangely stiff, then turned back to the task of making coffee. She didn't want him hurt on her watch. Abe would surely think she'd neglected her duties if he was. There was no other reason. But her lungs stiffened again as she thought of looking up in anticipation as he called her name and how her heart jolted when she saw him dangling in midair. The remnant of a panicked feeling lingered behind her breastbone, and she forced it away with determined deep breaths.

She poured the ground coffee into the pot and set it to boil. Carol would soon return from school, and Sally always prepared a snack for the child. Carol was way too thin and barely ate enough to keep a mouse alive. Sally ached for the child, understanding that she mourned her mother's death. Much as Sally had done for her father.

Linc would have to wait for coffee until Carol got home. She ignored the reason for her decision—there was safety in having both children to hide behind.

How ridiculous. He was only here to do odd jobs for Abe. And she was here to establish how well she could cope. Having focused her goal clearly in her mind, she gave herself a good study. Her skirt carried a liberal amount of dust from working in the garden, and her shoes needed cleaning. Moving toward the plate glass mirror over the couch in the front room, she saw blotches of dust on her face, her unruly curls frosted with the ever invasive brown soil filling the air. "Sally, you look like a homeless tramp. Go clean up," she said.

A few minutes later, shoes cleaned, skirts dusted, face washed and hair brushed until it gleamed, she paused again in front of the mirror and smiled at herself. Now she'd pass inspection. And just in time, as Carol slipped through the back door. Only because Sally knew enough to listen for her did she even notice her entrance. "Hi, Carol. How was your day?"

"Okay." She sank into her customary chair at the kitchen table and let her head droop.

"Anything special happen?"

"No." The word seemed to require a great deal of effort.

Sally studied the child a moment longer, wishing she could offer comfort, but Carol would shrink back if Sally tried to hug her. What she needed was her mother, but her mother was gone. Sally touched the top of Carol's head. "We have company for snack time."

Carol perked up. "Who?"

"Why don't I let you see for yourself?" Sally went to the door and called. "Coffee's ready. Come and get it."

Linc dropped to the ground and gave her a wave to acknowledge he'd heard.

Robbie straightened, glanced toward Linc and when he saw the man wave, he turned to Sally and did the same. When Linc dusted off his pants, so did Robbie. Only in Robbie's case, the result was a brownish cloud.

Sally watched another moment, smiling as Robbie imitated everything Linc did. She wondered if Linc noticed.

The distance prevented her from seeing his eyes, but he flashed a grin at her that made her gasp and duck back inside. She pressed her hand to her chest and instructed her heart to beat calmly. She did not understand this out-of-control reaction. She, Sally Morgan, twenty years of age, was a cautious young woman who did not do foolish things. Nor was she about to change because someone had a wide smile that made her think of wildflowers and open spaces.

Having set her mind back on a corrected course, she put out a coffee cup for Linc, poured milk for the children and placed a selection of cookies on a plate.

Linc and Robbie came through the door together.

"I got a real good fort built," Robbie said. "I think I'll put a fence around it."

"Good fort needs a good fence." Linc sounded as if it was the most important thing he could discuss.

"You seen any forts?" Robbie asked.

"Only in museums. I'm grateful we don't need them to protect us anymore." He glanced about. "Is there a place I can wash up?"

Sally indicated the sink in the back room that served as pantry and laundry room.

Robbie followed Linc and washed his hands without being told. If only the boy could be so cooperative all the time. She poured coffee into the cup she'd set out for Linc and waited for the pair to return.

Robbie scampered to his chair and downed his glass of milk in loud gulps. "Can I have more?"

"Whoa. Slow down," Linc said. "You wouldn't want to drown yourself, now would you?"

Robbie giggled and planted himself more squarely in his chair, apparently intending to wait patiently.

"And who is this pretty young gal?" Linc indicated Carol.

His words jarred Sally into action. "This is Carol Finley." She told the girl who Linc was, saying he visited his grandmother across the alley, leaving out all the vicious rumors.

"Pleased to meet you." Linc reached for Carol's hand and bent over slightly as he shook it.

Carol flushed a dull red, pulled her hand to her lap and ducked her head.

Guess he had the same disconcerting effect on both young and grown girls. The thought comforted Sally, but she experienced a twinge of sympathy for Carol's confusion.

Linc shifted his attention to the table, nodded toward the cup of steaming coffee. "For me?"

Sally jerked herself out of her thoughts. "Yes. And please, sit down and help yourself to cookies."

He sat and tasted his coffee. "Yum. Hard to beat fresh coffee."

Sally refilled Robbie's glass and passed the plate.

Carol lifted her face as she took a cookie. Her eyes darted toward Linc and she ducked away again.

Smitten, Sally thought. *And as embarrassed about her reaction, as I am about mine.*

"Did you bake these?" Linc lifted a ginger cookie to indicate what he meant.

"Yes." Sally prayed her cheeks wouldn't darken in echo of Carol's reaction. She was, after all, a grown, self-controlled woman. "My father's favorite cookie."

"They're good." He sighed. "Not at all like the hard tack and beans a cowboy gets used to eating."

Robbie nearly squirmed right off his chair. "You a real cowboy?"

Linc held out his arm. "Feel."

Robbie pressed his hand to Linc's forearm.

"I feel real to you?"

Robbie giggled.

Carol watched the pair. "He didn't mean real in that way. He meant do you live out on the hills, camping with cows and herding them?"

Sally almost dropped her cookie. It was the most she'd heard Carol speak at one time since she'd started caring for them a month ago. She tore her attention from

Carol back to Linc, as curious over his answer as either of the children.

Linc leaned back, a faraway look in his eyes. "I spent many nights sleeping on the ground with a herd of cows bawling in my ear. Lots of fun but hard work, too. And like I said, often the food wasn't that great."

He might not appreciate the food, but there was no mistaking how much he liked his sort of life. A shudder crossed Sally's shoulders. She could imagine nothing appealing about such an unsettled existence.

"You cook your own food?" Robbie asked, his eyes and mouth as round as the top of his glass.

"Depends on whether I was alone or with a crew. If I was alone, I didn't have much choice. Either cook or starve to death. But when we had a roundup the ranch provided a cook wagon. That was great." He sighed and patted his stomach. "Some of those old cooks worked magic with flour and water and fresh beef."

Carol had slid forward on her chair, mesmerized by the way Linc talked. "Did you sing to the cows?" She lowered her gaze a brief moment. "I heard that cowboys sing to calm them. Our teacher taught us 'The Old Chisholm Trail.' She said the cowboys like to sing that song."

"Come a ti-yi-yi-yippy-yippy-ah." Linc half sang, half spoke the words.

Carol's eyes glistened. "That's it."

Linc chuckled. "We had one old cowboy by the name of Skinner. He always brought along his fiddle and played it after supper, just as the moon cast a glow on the trees, making them look like pale white soldiers. I tell you, there's nothing more mournful than a fiddle playing "Oh Bury Me Not on the Lone Prairie." He shivered but his face belied his words. He looked as if it was the best part of life.

Sally didn't take her eyes off his glowing face. Without looking, she knew both children were equally as mesmerized. She blinked and forced her attention to other things. Her responsibilities. "Children, finish up. Do your chores and then you can play until suppertime."

They downed their cookies and milk and raced away—Robbie to take away the pail of coal ashes Sally had scraped out of the stove earlier in the day. He often made a big deal of the chore, when all he had to do was carry the pail to the ash heap at the far corner of the yard and bring the empty pail back. This time he didn't utter one word of complaint. Carol's chore was to sweep the front step and sidewalk. She grabbed the broom and hurried outside.

Linc drained his coffee and pushed back from the table. "I thank you." He grabbed his hat off the back of the chair and headed for the door where he paused. "You coming out again?"

Why did her heart pick up pace at his innocent question? She half convinced herself he spoke out of politeness, not out of any real desire for her to join him. With the portion of her brain that remained sensible, she brought out the right words. "I can't. I have to make supper and…" At a loss to think what else she needed to do, she let her words trail off.

"Of course." He pushed his hat to his head and stepped outside. "Thanks again." He strode away, his long legs quickly creating distance.

She stared after him as he returned to the crab apple

trees and gathered the branches he'd removed. His arms full, he headed for the garbage barrel by the ash pile and broke the branches to stuff them into the barrel. What did she hear? She lifted the window sash and listened.

"Oh, do you remember sweet Betsy from Pike?"

He was singing.

She listened in fascination. He didn't have a particularly fine singing voice. In fact, it was gravelly, as if he sang past a mouthful of marbles, and he missed a few of the notes. But what he lacked in talent, he more than made up for in enjoyment. The notes fairly danced through the air and frolicked into her heart, where they skipped and whirled until they were well embedded.

The front door slammed. Carol skidded into the kitchen and stored the broom. She headed for the back door. "He's singing." She left again so fast, Sally didn't even have time to close the window and pretend she hadn't been listening as eagerly as young Carol.

Carol trotted to the garden to stand by Robbie. Shoulder to shoulder they watched and listened to Linc, who continued to break branches, oblivious to his adoring audience.

Sally studied the two children. Both were under his spell. She slammed the window shut. They were children, prone to hero worship. She, on the other hand, was a grown woman who knew better than to chase after… after what? She didn't even know what she thought she'd been chasing. Certainly not stability or sensibility. She turned and studied the kitchen. Very modern, with an electric refrigerator Abe had shipped all the way from Toronto. A gas range stood in the corner to be used in hot weather. He'd shown her how to light the pilot and how to set the controls on the oven, but Sally had never used a gas stove and wondered if she would ever be comfortable doing so. She preferred to use the coal cookstove.

Abe was very proud of the modern fixtures, especially the stove. "It's a Canadian invention," he said with enough pride that Sally thought he would like to take credit for the innovation.

She shifted her gaze, itemizing the benefits of the house. Two stories. Four bedrooms and an indoor bathroom upstairs. All the bedrooms had generous closets.

Downstairs, besides the kitchen and back room, there was a formal dining room, complete with a china cabinet holding a fancy twelve-place dishware collection. Sally thought the plain white dishes with gold trim rather unnoteworthy. Her choice of pattern would have been something with a little color in the form of a flower. There were so many lovely rose patterns.

"I like to entertain here," Abe had said, indicating the formal dining room and the array of dishes. "Dinner parties for my business associates." He eyed the dark wood paneled room with windows covered by heavy forest-green drapes shutting out most of the light. Obviously it was his favorite room in the house.

Sally had nodded, her smile wooden. She could cook a meal for twelve with no problem. But a dinner party? Business associates? It sounded stiff and dull.

She gave herself a little shake. Of course she could do a dinner party. No need to be nervous because she didn't know Abe's business associates and had never given a formal dinner. How hard could it be? Cooking was cooking.

And if she didn't get to her meal preparations this minute, she would be hard-pressed to have supper ready when Abe came through the door.

She hurried to the back room and found potatoes. As she peeled them, she enjoyed a view of the backyard. Robbie played in his fort. Carol sat cross-legged nearby, scratching in the dirt. She paused often to glance up, a dreamy look on her face. Sally didn't need to follow the direction of her gaze to know the reason. Linc had returned to pruning the crab apple trees. From what she could see, he removed a great number of branches. The trees looked downright sparse. *I hope he knows what he's doing.* Abe would be very upset if Linc killed the trees.

Linc stepped back and surveyed the damage, then hoisted the ladder to his shoulder and went to the little shed. After stowing the ladder, he headed for the house. His gaze flicked to the window and he smiled.

Sally developed a sudden interest in the task of peeling potatoes and hoped he didn't think she'd been staring.

He knocked.

She dried her hands on a towel, smoothed her apron and walked slowly to the door just to prove she had other things holding her attention. "Yes?"

"I'm headed home to check on my pa. Tell Abe I'm done with the trees and will start working on the barn tomorrow, unless he prefers I do something else."

"I'll let him know." Abe no doubt would have specific ideas of what he wanted done and in what order.

"I'm off then." He took a step toward the back gate.

"I hope your pa is okay. Say hello to your grandmother for me."

He touched the brim of his hat. "I'll do that." His mouth pulled to one side. He seemed to consider saying something more, then nodded without voicing his thought. "See you tomorrow." And he swung away, passing the garden. He echoed a goodbye to the children before he vaulted over the fence, not bothering with the gate.

Sally stared after him until he disappeared from view behind the board fence. Even then she continued to stare. What was it about this man that pulled at her so hard? Like a promise. Of what? The man was a cowboy. By his own confession, he slept on the cold, hard ground, often with nothing but cows for company. It should have turned him into a recluse or at least a man with poor social skills. Linc might not fit into everyone's idea of a refined gentleman, yet there was something about him. Something she couldn't put her finger on, but she also couldn't deny its existence, even though she wanted to.

"Is he coming back tomorrow?"

Sally's gaze lingered one more heartbeat, her mind indulged in one more puzzled thought, then she turned to Carol who stood before her, her face a mixture of hope and fear. "Your father has hired him to do yard work. I should think he'll have enough to keep him busy for a week or two. Perhaps even a month." She utterly failed to keep a note of joy out of her words.

"Good." Carol marched past her, into the house and up the stairs. The words of a song trailed after her. "Oh, do you remember sweet Betsy from Pike?"

An echo sounded from the garden in a low, monotone singsongy voice.

Sally stared. Robbie was singing? Come to think of it, he'd been pleasantly occupied all day building his fort. She watched, her eyes narrowed in concentration. In her experience, Robbie being content was foreign. The few times it happened had led to a major explosion. Maybe he'd wait until she left to shift into defiance. Except…how would Abe deal with it? He had little patience with Robbie acting out. "Losing his mother will not be tolerated as an excuse," Abe insisted. Yes, she understood Robbie must find a better way to express his displeasure but—

Lord, these children are hurt and frightened by their loss. Help me help them. Help them find joy in life and be able to believe they can again be safe.

She thought of how she'd found the feeling of safety after her father died, through helping her mother and sisters keep things organized and in control, doing what she thought her father would approve of. How could she help these children find the same sense of safety?

"Robbie, come wash up for supper."

He jerked as if she'd struck him, and his chin jutted out. "Leave me alone."

"Your father will soon be here, and he expects you washed and ready to sit down."

Robbie gave her his fiercest glower.

"Robbie, I think your mother would want you to do your best to please your father."

His scowl deepened. "She won't know what I do."

"Maybe not. But you will. You know what would please her. You can honor her by doing it."

He turned his back to her and continued moving a pile of dirt. It seemed he did his best to make sure most of it fell on him.

"Robbie, please come to the house." She kept her tone firm and soft.

"You ain't my mother."

"I know that." She didn't expect she could replace their mother if she married Abe—when she married Abe, she corrected. "No one can replace your mother." She let the words sink in.

"I betcha Linc didn't wash his hands when he camped out with cows."

"I have no idea if he did or didn't, but I noticed how well he cleaned up before coffee." She'd noticed far too well, taking in how his face shone from the scrubbing and how his hair, bleached almost blond on the ends but darker where it had been hidden from the sun, had been plastered back in an attempt to tame the curls. How they slowly returned to their own wayward tangle.

She'd had to refrain from checking her hair to see if her curls were doing likewise. "He cleaned up really well." Her words had a difficult time squeezing past the tightness in her throat.

Robbie studied her reply for a moment, then bolted to his feet to race across the yard. He didn't slow down as he passed her, nor did he glance toward her. His whole attitude clearly said he would wash up because a man like Linc, a man he admired, had done so. He would not do it to please Sally. No siree.

She sighed and followed him inside. Would she and Robbie ever have anything but an uneasy truce? She didn't have time to think about that at the moment with dessert to finish, potatoes to mash and the meat to check. She took dishes from the top shelf—the best everyday dishes—found a red checkered tablecloth and set the table as nicely as she could. Too bad she didn't have flowers to put in a vase in the middle of the table.

This meal would be flawless. Abe would see that she could run his home as well as any woman.

Robbie came from the back room, water dripping from his ears. He'd combed his hair back.

"You look very spiffy."

He jerked to a halt and gave her a look fit to fry her skin. "I do not."

Instantly she realized she'd offended him. Actually, it was pretty hard to miss. She knew exactly what she'd done wrong. She'd made him sound like a sissy. "You're right. You look like a frontier man. Maybe even a cowboy. Ready to get out and ride."

He held her gaze a moment then tipped his chin in barely there acknowledgment before he crossed to the table with a faintly familiar swagger.

She didn't have to think hard to know where she'd seen it before. Robbie had done his best to imitate Linc's rolling gait.

No, she definitely wasn't the only one in this house to be affected by his presence. She stiffened her spine and held her chin high. Only she wasn't a child. She was an adult who knew exactly what she wanted. A stable life, a nice home. No way she'd ever consider camping out on the prairie to be something romantic.

The strains of "Oh, bury me not on the lone prairie," echoed through her head. She meant every word of the song.

Chapter Five

Linc crossed toward his grandmother's house, singing that silly song he couldn't get out of his head. Several times he'd discovered he sang it aloud and stopped instantly. He ought to have more consideration for his surroundings. It wasn't like he was with a bunch of cows or even some cynical, fun-making cowboys who would josh him good-naturedly, or otherwise, depending on their personal objectives in life.

Once he heard Robbie singing along in a voice lacking both strength and musical ability. Not that Linc thought he had the latter. Lots of people had felt free to point that out to him. He countered with the same words every time. "Mostly I sing because I'm happy. Sorry if it has the opposite effect on you." Mostly he continued to sing, unless it seemed likely to start a fight.

But when he heard Robbie, he figured now was not the time to have second thoughts about raising his voice in song. Seems the boy had little enough to be happy about in this life. Sure he had lots of good things—a warm home, a father with a steady job and the hope of gaining Sally for a stepmother. Momentarily the thought made the song die on his lips. He sure hoped that Robbie, Carol and their father would appreciate Sally the way she deserved. But that thought aside, Robbie didn't realize how good he had it because right now likely all he considered was what he'd lost. His mother. Linc knew how sorrow could make all other thought impossible.

He'd mostly gotten over his own loss, though there were times when missing his mother seemed like having a pile of hay lodged in his stomach. It just wouldn't go away. Now he had the fresh pain of losing Harris. And the dreadful specter of his father's possible death.

But the day had been pleasant. Seeing Sally's smile, playing with Robbie, watching Carol light up when he sang a cowboy song. As he hit the back step of Grandmama's house, his happiness dissolved into reality. He flung the door open. "How is Pa?"

"Same, my boy. I gave him more medicine an hour ago. He's been resting since then." She turned from arranging slices of yeasty-smelling bread on a platter. "I heard you singing as you crossed the yard." Her smile was gentle. Not at all reproving.

But Linc felt as if he stood before ten pointing fingers. How callous to be happy with his brother buried in the mountains and his father likely dying a slow, painful death. Yet for a few hours this afternoon he'd shoved the knowledge to the back of his brain and enjoyed himself. Yes, he'd had fun.

He didn't realize he smiled so openly until his grandmother straightened. "What have you been up to, Lincoln McCoy?"

He sobered so quickly his lips almost knotted.

"Grandmama, I was working all afternoon." Playing with Robbie and Sally most surely qualified as work. He was amusing the boss's son, after all. "Did you know the Finleys have a tiny grove of crab apple trees? I pruned them. Hopefully they will become stronger and more productive now. And I turned over the garden soil."

Grandmama sniffed. "Those trees have been there longer than the Finleys." She studied him a full thirty seconds. "First time I ever saw someone so pleased about a little yard work."

His sigh was long and purposely exaggerated. "Would you feel better if I dragged through the door, my chin bobbing on the floor and moaned and groaned about how hard life is?"

Her sigh was equally long and exaggerated. "Of course not."

He started to smile, but she held up a warning hand.

"But I'd feel a lot better if you told me Sally Morgan was away for the afternoon."

He narrowed his eyes, vowing he would not let her guess how glad he was that she wasn't gone. "Now why would that make any difference to you?"

She matched his narrowed eyes. Not for the first time in his life he realized how alike they were in their gestures, and often in their speech. "Because I fear it means a lot to you."

He wanted to protest. Say it didn't make a speck of difference. Assure her he never once looked at Sally. Never even noticed her. But he couldn't lie. If he tried, she would know immediately. The trouble with two people having the same mannerisms was she would see his attempt at lying as clearly as if she had lied. Instead he shifted directions. "Didn't you say she was unofficially promised to Abe Finley? Practically engaged to be married." He hoped his silent emphasis on *unofficially* and *practically* didn't come across in his words.

"I said it. Did you hear?"

"I must have, since I repeated it to you."

Grandmama took three steps toward him, stopped with her very sturdy shoes toe-to-toe with his dusty cowboy boots. "I mean, did you hear it here?" She tapped his forehead. "Or is it stuck somewhere between there?" She touched his right ear. "And here?" She flicked his left ear.

"Ow." He jerked away and grabbed at his ear, pretending a great injury. "Why'd you do that?"

"You don't need to think you're too big for me to handle, young man. If you don't behave yourself I'll hear, and if I hear, I'll deal with you."

"Ho, ho." He bounced away a few feet. "You might find it hard to put me over your knee and smack my bottom."

"Your size doesn't intimidate me."

He stalked right up to her and leaned over to meet her eyes. Never once did she falter. Not that he expected her to, any more than he expected she would consider trying to carry out some form of corporal punishment. "I'm a big boy now. Maybe you should be afraid of me." To prove his point, he wrapped his arms around her waist and lifted her off the floor.

She squealed. "Put me down, you naughty boy."

He spun around the room, accompanied by her choked laughter. "Not until you tell me what a good boy I am."

"Never."

He swung around the room again.

"Put me down. I'm getting dizzy."

"Am I the best boy in the world?"

"You're the best grandson this old woman will ever have."

"Good enough for me." He set her down and steadied her as she regained her balance. "Hey, wait a minute. I'm your only grandson."

She chuckled and gave him a fond look, liberally laced with teasing. "Now do you want supper first or you want to check on your father first?"

He laughed. "Still good enough for me." He glanced toward the bedroom. "I'll check on Pa first."

"Good idea. Call me if you need anything."

He headed for the doorway and paused before he stepped into the room. It always shocked him to see Pa like this—all busted up, his color almost as bad as Harris's had been.

He scrubbed his hands over his eyes and pushed away his morbid thoughts. To neutralize them, he allowed one mental picture of Sally. He had many to choose from— her laughing as they escaped Robbie's kidnapping, her concern when he faked a mortal injury, her anger when he almost fell from the tree, her shyness over coffee, the way she watched him out the kitchen window, all the time pretending she wasn't.

He chose the way she shied away from him at the table. If he needed any further proof she was aware of him, that was it.

He smiled, let the thought smooth his tension. Yes, he understood she and Abe were meant to be, but he promised himself he would deal with reality after he was through caring for his father. He stepped into the room. "Pa?"

His father stirred, managed to drag one eyelid open. "Linc. Where am I?"

Doc had warned Linc that Pa's mind would become more and more confused. "We're in Golden Prairie, at Grandmama's house."

"Harris is dead, isn't he?"

"Yeah, Pa. We buried him back at Coal Camp."

"He had a nice putting away?"

"Best possible. All the miners came out. They even shut the mine down for the funeral. There were lots of flowers. Harris's friend, Sam, sang 'Amazing Grace.' It was very nice." He would never hear the song again without choking up with sorrow.

"Good." Pa groaned again. "I'm in terrible pain." His words were tight.

Linc poured out a spoonful of the medicine and held it to his pa's lips, then pulled a wooden chair close to the bed and sat by his father, talking softly, his voice providing comfort until the medicine took effect.

He wet the facecloth in the basin of water and wiped his face gently. "Pa, I wish I could make you feel better."

"Me, too." His father's voice cracked.

"You want a drink?"

"You got anything stronger than water?"

Linc's lopsided grin quivered. "Coffee?"

Pa snorted. At least, he attempted to. "Ain't what I meant."

"You know Grandmama would sooner swallow tacks than have the devil's drink in her house."

"I sort of recall." Pa's voice faded. Talking consumed all the energy he could muster.

Linc held a cup of water to his lips and supported his head as he drank.

Pa fell back, exhausted. He would sleep until the medicine wore off, then Linc would be there to give him more.

But oh, it hurt to see his powerful, stubborn Pa like this.

Again, he found solace in picturing Sally. This time he chose the mental picture of her planting the garden. How she straightened and met his gaze across the yard. Even that far away, he enjoyed the way her eyes watched him. He couldn't see the color across the distance, but he didn't need to. He supposed officially they were hazel, which seemed a flat word when describing her eyes. Golden brown with flecks of green. He'd been fascinated to watch the color shift from almost green to gold when she turned toward the light. It had been all he could do not to stare.

His mind smoothed as he let his thoughts drift along the pleasant trail. Pa moaned and Linc sighed. Try as he might, he could not ignore his father's plight. He wished there was some way to help him. All he could do was pray. Not only for God to ease his pain, but also for his father to realize eternity waited—and he needed to choose where to spend it.

He touched his father's arm. "I'll be back later." He returned to the kitchen where Grandmama waited to serve supper.

She sighed. "I wish I could spare you this. Spare both of you."

His face must have revealed his pain. He made no attempt to disguise it. "I wish it, too." He rubbed his eyes, suddenly so weary he could think of nothing he'd rather do than sleep for the next three days.

"Sit and eat."

Food held no appeal, but his grandmother had spent the afternoon cooking. The least he could do was show some appreciation. He waited for her to sit across from him and reached for her hands before he bowed and said grace.

Soon enough he discovered he could eat heartily, even though he ached inside. His energy returned with eating. He dried dishes for Grandmama then returned to the bedroom. Already Pa was growing restless as the pain medication wore off. He reckoned it was safe to give another dose and waited for the medicine to ease Pa's discomfort.

Pa began to breathe easier as the medicine did its work.

Linc rose, planning to slip away and let his father rest.

"Don't go," Pa gasped.

Linc sat back, his legs rubbery. Was this the last breath his father would draw?

"It gets mighty lonely in here." Pa's voice was reedy.

"I'll stay with you until you fall asleep."

Pa opened his eyes long enough to give Linc a grateful look.

Glad he could do something that earned Pa's approval, Linc eased himself into a more comfortable position.

"I miss your ma," Pa whispered.

"Me, too."

"She used to read to me."

"I remember." Pa could write his name, decipher enough to buy something in the store, but not much else. "Do you want me to read to you?"

Pa's eyes flew open, filled with a combination of pain and hope. "It might give me something else to set my thoughts on."

Linc gained his feet.

"Not the Bible."

"Okay, Pa." He didn't bother to keep the disappointment from his voice. In the front room stood a huge cupboard, the lower shelves crammed with books. He searched the titles. *Pilgrim's Progress*. Perfect. He pulled it out, returned to the bedroom and began reading. "'As I walked through the wilderness of this world, I lighted on a certain place where was a den, and laid me down in that place to sleep; and as I slept, I dreamed a dream.'"

Pa made no protest, though the message was almost as clear and pointed as any scripture. Indeed, he lay quietly, breathing slowly.

Linc paused, wondering if he'd fallen asleep.

"Continue," Pa said.

Linc read for an hour until his voice was hoarse. Quietly he closed the book, waiting to see if Pa would protest.

His father cracked one eye open. "More tomorrow?"

"Of course."

He remained until he was certain Pa slept, then tiptoed away, his insides knotted in dreadful anticipation of the fact that his father wasn't getting better.

Only one thing eased his mind—remembering Sally. According to what she said, she only stayed long enough to serve supper to the family. She'd be gone by now. Too bad. He might have slipped over to speak to her. The walls of the house seemed to press in on him. "Grandmama." She sat at the kitchen table doing some fancy handiwork. "I'm going for a ride."

"I expect you need to get away for a bit."

He paused at the outside door. "Where did you say the Morgans live?"

Grandmama dropped her handiwork and gave Linc a look fit to bleach his skin pure white. "I didn't say. And best you stay away."

Linc grew still. He barely breathed. "Even my own grandmother thinks I'm not fit to associate with decent people," he muttered.

Grandmama had the grace to look uncomfortable. "I didn't mean it like that. It's just—" She shook her head, unable to finish what she started to say.

"Just what? She shouldn't associate with the likes of me? Shouldn't even be seen in my company?" He spun on his heel. "I'll try and keep it in mind." He strode toward the barn as if chased by an angry posse and quickly saddled Big Red. He rode from town at a moderate pace, but once he reached the open road, he urged Red into a full-blown gallop.

He rode until the wind cleared his brain, then turned and rode back at a more leisurely pace. Rather than go directly back home, he rode up and down familiar streets. He'd been back in Golden Prairie for days, but his movements had been restricted to his grandmother's place, the Finley place and a few businesses in the heart of town as he looked for work. Now he was curious. How much had the place changed in the years he'd been away?

He passed the redbrick two-story school. The same dusty yard. The same worn playground equipment— a slide, a pole swing and two teeter-totters. The same flagpole directly in front of the main doors with parallel sidewalks where girls lined up on one, boys on the other to march inside. His time in this building had been mostly pleasant.

With a flick of the reins, he moved on. Houses on either side of the street had faded, their yards threadbare. Everywhere he saw evidence of the drought. He recalled the names of people who had lived in the houses. The Stewarts—a middle-age childless couple. The pair sat on matching rockers on the veranda, watching him with all the interest of a small town resident seeing a stranger in the midst of their lives.

Next to them, the Rowans lived with a houseful of young ones who would be mostly grown by now. Charity Rowan had been in his grade. She'd always been friendly. Wonder what became of her? He paused before the house and considered going to the door to ask after her and the other children.

Mr. Stewart rocked to his feet and moved to the top step. "Hey, there."

Linc turned toward the man. Although the greeting wasn't unusual, the tone of the voice was far from friendly, and Linc's shoulders tensed. "Hello, Mr. Stewart. How are you?" Far as he knew there was no reason for rancor between him and this man.

"You're that McCoy boy, aren't you?"

"I'm Lincoln McCoy." He didn't normally give his full name, but somehow he wanted the man to know he bore a noble name, though he doubted Mr. Stewart or anyone would think Abraham Lincoln in the same thought as Lincoln McCoy.

"Heard you lot were back in town."

Linc half expected the man to spit. His wife sat behind him, her arms crossed firmly over her thin chest.

"Came to see my grandmother. Help her out a bit."

"Likely help yourself to anything else you can get your hands on. No one has forgotten how Mrs. Ogilvy's jewels disappeared. Maybe they couldn't find evidence, but none of us have ever believed you innocent."

Linc tried to think how to answer. He had nothing to hide. No shame to disguise. He hoped coming back would prove his innocence to the townsfolk. But only if they gave him a chance.

His hopes had risen when Abe offered him a job. Linc was more than grateful after he'd spent the morning going from business to business and being flatly turned down. He knew it had more to do with his name than the depressed economic atmosphere. If he'd had any doubt, the clucking of tongues by a group of gossipy women in the store where he'd gone to ask for a job made it clear. That's when Abe had stepped in, taken in the situation and said he needed a man for yard chores. Abe had given him a chance to prove himself.

Not that Linc was foolish enough to believe Abe was anything more than an exception to what most people thought, but he owed the man for offering him a job. He directed his attention back to Mr. Stewart. "I have my eyes on nothing that isn't my own." Guilt stung him.

Could he honestly say those words in regard to Sally? But that wasn't what Mr. Stewart meant, any more than Linc did.

Knowing his interest in Sally ran against his gratitude to Abe sent a twist of guilt through Linc's thoughts.

Mr. Stewart made a noise ripe with disbelief.

Stung by the man's unwillingness to accept the facts, Linc didn't bother to moderate his words. "Seems to me a man who refuses to abide by what a court of law decided—namely, that the McCoys are innocent—is as guilty of dishonoring the law as a man who steals."

Mr. Stewart gave Linc a hard look. "You might have fooled the law, but you didn't fool me."

Linc kept his words low but let each one carry a weight of protest. "Sounds to me like you've appointed yourself judge and jury." He wondered if the man had heard of Harris's death and their father's injuries. But it was unlikely such knowledge would influence the man's attitude. He seemed pretty set on seeing the McCoys as undesirables.

"Just consider yourself warned. We'll be watching you. Don't think you can pull a repeat performance." Mr. Stewart returned to his rocker, crossed his arms and glared, he and his wife a matched set of disapproval.

Linc studied them a full thirty seconds. His insides protested. He ached for a way to prove his family's innocence. The McCoys were restless, sometimes aimless. His brother and father had chased after adventure and the next big chance. None of those things made them bad people. The theft of Mrs. Ogilvy's jewels had been conveniently laid on the McCoys. Likely someone passing through had seen an easy mark and lifted them.

But no one ever considered that. Not with the McCoys handy.

But the harsh look on Mr. Stewart's face and the equally forbidding one his wife wore informed Linc there was no point in further argument with this pair. He prayed they didn't represent the attitude of the majority of Golden Prairie residents.

All he wanted was a chance to prove the McCoys were good people.

He reined away and headed straight for his grandmother's home. At least she had never accused him. A suspicion burned the edges of his brain. Did she suspect Linc's father and simply not say so to spare Linc's feelings? Did she have doubts about Linc? Hadn't she said he should stay away from Sally? As if in her heart she didn't believe he was good enough to be in the same circle of friends as a Morgan girl?

He allowed Red to slow his pace.

Did anyone in this town believe a McCoy was capable of being a decent person? Did his own grandmother?

How long before Sally heard everyone's opinion of him? How long before she looked at him with the same guardedness or outright suspicion?

Not that it mattered. She intended to marry Abe Finley. He wondered if the two of them had discussed it already, or if it was merely an unspoken understanding.

Never mind. He was in town to ease his pa's dying hours and perhaps help his grandmother. He wouldn't let the opinion of a few…or many…drive him away.

He rode into the yard, took Red to the barn and brushed him down before he headed for the house. His palms were sweaty, and he scrubbed them on the side of his trousers. One thing he intended to get straight right here and now—what did Grandmama think?

The door crashed open.

Grandmama looked up, startled by his noisy entrance. "Linc, is something wrong?"

He jerked out a chair and dropped into it. "I saw Mr. Stewart." He tried to tame his thoughts lest they burst out in unfair accusations. "He made it clear I am under suspicion as a McCoy and not welcome in this perfect little town."

Grandmama's short laugh was mirthless. "The town is far from perfect, and I'm sure Mr. Stewart doesn't speak for everyone. At least, I've never heard that anyone voted him official spokesman."

Linc gave her a direct, demanding look. "Does he speak for you?"

His grandmother looked shocked. "You have always been welcome here."

"Do you think the McCoys stole those jewels?" He deliberately aligned himself with his father and brother.

She shook her head. "I don't want to think so, but after your mother died.... Well, your father was pretty upset and didn't much care what he did."

"So you think he might have taken them?"

She considered his question for the briefest moment. "I prefer to believe a person is innocent until proven guilty. And in this case, there was no evidence against your father. That's good enough for me. It should be good enough for you and for all those people out there, too."

Satisfied, he nodded and went to check on his pa.

He appreciated his grandmother's attitude, but it wasn't shared by everyone.

He wondered what opinion Sally held.

Or perhaps he didn't want to know.

Chapter Six

Sally watched from the window for Linc's appearance the next morning. Abe left instructions for her to tell Linc to paint the front fence before he started converting the barn into a garage.

Abe had left for work early. Carol had already departed for school.

It had been a good morning. Robbie came to the breakfast table on the first call, dressed neatly and ready for the day.

She and Abe looked at one another in surprise. As they studied each other, she saw in his expression something she'd never seen before—approval. But even more. Something that made her want to fidget.

Sally lowered her eyes first. She wished she could take credit for Robbie's compliant behavior, but knew it was Linc's doing. The boy was eager to see him again.

She tried to make herself believe she didn't share the anticipation.

"Nice to see you here on time," Abe said to Robbie.

"I got work to do," Robbie said with utmost sincerity.

Again Sally sent Abe a look of surprise and amusement.

Abe shifted away first this time to study his son.

"Really? What are you doing?" He sounded every bit as doubtful as surprised.

"Building a fort."

"Ah. Of course. Well, eat up and do your chores first."

Sally had smiled at Robbie's eager obedience as he ran to obey and then dashed outside. She looked out the window. Robbie had found a bunch of twigs and began to construct a fence around his hole. She realized with a start these twigs were from Linc's pruning yesterday. He must have broken them to the right length for Robbie to use. Her heart felt bathed in warm honey to think he would do this little extra for the boy.

Robbie looked up and waved to someone she couldn't see, then bounded to his feet and raced toward the barn.

Yesterday Linc came to the door upon his arrival. Today it seemed he didn't intend to, which meant she would have to leave the security of the house in order to relay Abe's instructions.

She removed her apron and draped it over the back of the chair. Then she changed her mind and again tied it around her waist. This was not a social call. He was here to work, and she had her own chores to take care of.

Ignoring the mirror in the back room, she went directly out the door. Robbie had disappeared, hopefully into the barn. The big doors stood open and a murmur of voices came from inside.

She paused at the gaping doorway and stared into the gloomy interior. "Hello?"

"We're over here." Linc's voice came from a distant corner.

She hesitated, not wanting to join him in the shadows. Afraid of revealing too much of her confusion in the low light. "I need to talk to you."

Muffled footsteps brought Linc to the bright patch of sunshine, Robbie at his side. "What can I do for you?"

A thousand things flooded her mind. Fun things. Picnics in the sun. Walks at dusk. Star watching—she jerked her thoughts into submission. "Abe said to ask you to paint the front fence first. He says there is paint in the last stall of the barn."

"Sure. Not a problem." His eyes flashed with humor, as if he'd read her wayward thoughts.

She lowered her gaze to Robbie. "Don't get in Mr. McCoy's way."

Robbie stuck out his bottom lip. He hung between wanting to impress Linc with his good behavior and wanting to inform Sally what he thought of her order. Normally he would have exploded into a rage, but after a moment of struggle, he crossed his arms over his chest. "I ain't bothering Linc, am I?" He appealed to the man at his side.

Linc ruffled the boy's hair. "I have no complaints."

Sally considered her options. Forcing Robbie to leave Linc alone would surely precipitate a scene, and she didn't feel up to dealing with one of his tantrums. "What about your fort? I saw you building a fence."

"Yup." But no indication the boy meant to move.

Deciding it was up to Linc to tell the boy to leave if he didn't want him hanging about, she retreated into the sunlight and turned toward the house. "I'll be back to check on you."

"Okay," Linc and Robbie said in unison.

She stopped and slowly turned. "I meant Robbie."

Linc grinned unrepentantly. "You're welcome to check on me, too."

Their gazes locked and went deep. Her heart stirred with a feeling unfamiliar, unsettling and equally unwelcome. "I'm sure you don't need it." She fled for safety behind the kitchen door.

She would avoid returning to the pair, but she worried Robbie would get into trouble. She could imagine him doing a number of things she would regret. But they moved outside to start painting the fence, which allowed her to glance out the side window in the back room to see them. Of course, she couldn't help it if doing various chores made it impossible to avoid the room and just as impossible to avoid the window. So she told herself, even as guilt heated her cheeks. She had no business admiring the way a man's muscles rippled as he applied long smooth strokes of paint.

Enough. She spun from the window and did not return for fifteen determined minutes. She glanced out and saw Linc still at work, but she saw nothing of Robbie.

The boy could be anywhere. She rushed from the house and looked around. No Robbie. She called his name.

Linc straightened. "He's in the barn."

She lengthened her stride as she hurried for the building. "Robbie?"

"What?" he answered from the corner.

She edged closer and saw he'd found some cans and lengths of leather and was constructing something. If she had to guess, she'd say the cans were horses, and he'd hitched them to a piece of wood that might be meant to be a plow or some sort of equipment. The boy was a farmer at heart. Too bad his father was a town man. Too bad Abe didn't see the value of hard physical work.

Sally's mind wandered, forbidden, to Linc and the way he made work look easy, even seemed to enjoy it.

Her thoughts were particularly wayward this morning. She made up her mind to do something about it. "I have to go to the store. Clean up and come with me."

Robbie threw himself to the ground and kicked his heels. "Don't want to. You can't make me." His voice was tight.

Sally already knew defiance was his middle name. Nothing short of a lightning bolt would force the boy to change his mind. She stuck her hand in her pocket and pulled out two pennies. "I have a hankering for one of those candy sticks. I thought you might want one, too. I guess if you don't want to come, I'll buy myself two." She paused a beat. "Unless…" She waited.

He stopped kicking but lay still a minute, making sure she understood he didn't give in easy. "Guess I'll go," he muttered, as if he did her a great favor.

"Fine. Cinnamon is my favorite flavor. What's yours?" She reached for his grubby hand. Today she would not insist he wash up. Hopefully they would not encounter his father, who would surely disapprove of taking his son out in such a dusty state.

"I like 'em all, but maybe I'll get a licorice one." He took her hand and accompanied her peacefully.

They went out the gate and had to pass Linc on their way to the store. He stopped painting and watched them approach.

"I'm going to the store," she said quite needlessly, as if it mattered to him.

"Have fun." He waited for them to pass.

She continued onward, vowing not to look back, but as they turned the corner she glanced his direction. He still watched. Knowing he'd seen her looking, she jerked her attention to the sidewalk in front of them.

A few blocks later, she and Robbie entered Sharp's store. A gaggle of women turned as they stepped inside.

Sally's heart stalled. Why did they all stare at her? She handed Robbie a penny. "Go buy a candy stick for yourself."

He needed no second asking.

Sally turned to Mr. Sharp. "Can I get some canned peaches?" She planned to make peach cobbler for supper. "Two dozen eggs and…" She felt the women crowd close as she completed her order.

How long could she ignore them? She bent over an ad for Dodd's Kidney Pills tacked to the countertop and pretended a great deal of interest in the product.

Her pointed disinterest didn't deter the women one bit. Not that she really expected it would.

"I hear the McCoys are back in town." The words were accented by a loud sniff.

"Maybe they think Mrs. Ogilvy has more valuables to steal."

Sally straightened but kept her back to the women,

not wanting them to get any satisfaction out of her reaction. No doubt the protests flooding from her mind would be evident in her expression, but how dare they accuse Linc of such despicable motivations when he'd come because of his dying father?

"Don't suppose they'll do the noble thing and confess."

Several jeers greeted the remark.

Sally turned to face them. She knew each of the women. Mrs. Brennan was a known gossip, as were her three grown daughters standing at her side. Miss Carter, a bitter spinster who liked to imagine the worst of everyone. But seeing Bessy Johnson and Granny Smith with them surprised Sally. She faced that pair. "I would think you'd give a man the benefit of doubt." She spread her glance across the others. "And how cruel to think of such things when Harris McCoy is barely cold in his grave, and Mr. McCoy is not likely to recover from his injuries."

The women stared at her.

"Why Sally Morgan," Bessy Johnson protested. "Are you defending the likes of the McCoys? Surely you haven't fallen under their spell somehow."

As one, the group shook their heads and made tsking noises.

Sally's cheeks burned. She shouldn't have spoken out so harshly. So rashly. "I'm sorry. I know nothing about what happened before we came." All she knew was what she had seen and felt the past few days.

"I suppose that explains a lot." Miss Carter patted her arm, as if to say only Sally's innocence allowed her to speak out on behalf of the McCoys. "You didn't see the three of them always eyeing up things and ducking down abandoned alleys when a decent person came along."

"Maybe they understood the decent people of Golden Prairie meant to shun them and didn't plan to give them a chance."

As a group, the women sighed.

"You are far too innocent and trusting for your own good," Mrs. Brennan said. "But I warn you, Sally Morgan, watch yourself around that young McCoy."

Granny Smith leaned closer, favoring Sally with more than a hint of peppermint. "I hear Abe has hired the younger boy to do odd jobs. Is that true?"

Sally nodded mutely.

"How odd." Granny Smith turned to the others. "Doesn't it seem strange to you?"

They murmured agreement.

She returned her snapping gaze to Sally. "Why would he do such a thing?"

Relief eased the tension in Sally's lungs. She could answer this truthfully and freely. "He told me the man was innocent and deserved to be treated fairly. Said it was his duty as a leader in the church to show a good example."

The women drew back, practically creating a vacuum around Sally.

Mrs. Brennan was the first to recover. "He thinks he's being fair? Sounds like he's judging the rest of us. Well, I declare." She drew in a long-suffering gasp. "He'll live to regret his decision." She pinned Sally with her unflinching gaze. "I hope you are wise enough to give that young man a wide berth."

Sally tried to keep her expression blank, revealing none of her guilt and wariness, though she wondered if she succeeded when Mrs. Brennan's eyes narrowed.

"You must be careful around such men. They have a way of turning a person's thoughts into turmoil so what you always knew to be right and good suddenly doesn't seem enough." She turned her attention to her three gaping daughters. "Never let a man—any man— divert you from the straight and narrow path."

"Yes, Mama," they murmured in unison, then flashed looks ripe with accusation at Sally.

Is that what they thought? All of them? Sally went round the circle, looking at each woman and the variety of expressions. Some harsh and accusing, like the Brennans. Others leaned more toward resignation, as if feeling sorry for Sally. For something they had already decided she'd done. Miss Carter alone managed to reveal a touch of compassion.

Their silent accusations were unfounded. Their compassion unnecessary. She knew right from wrong. Even more, she knew what she wanted from life, and that was a home and security such as she'd known when Father was alive. Which Abe could give her. She drew herself up as tall as she could. Her voice rang with pride. "You judge me to be a silly young woman. I should think you would know better. You all know me well enough to know I always do what is right."

Mr. Sharp handed her the basket of things she'd ordered. She took it and faced the women again.

"I not only do what is right, as you all know, I do what is wise. Come along, Robbie." Her head high, she marched from the store, thankful that Robbie followed without making a fuss.

The women waited until the screen door slapped shut, then they all began to speak at once.

Sally couldn't make out what they said, but she heard the surprise in the collective chatter.

"What did they mean?" Robbie asked.

She'd hoped he hadn't heard or hadn't listened. "About what?"

"They said bad things about Linc, didn't they? He's not a bad man. He's a nice man."

"They were talking about a different time." But not about different people. She would do well to keep it in mind.

But who was Linc? She tended to side with Robbie. He seemed like a good, kind man. He'd returned to make sure his father was comfortable in his final days, even though he likely knew the kind of reception he would receive.

Or was she being naive? Choosing to see only what she wanted to see?

They were almost back. Linc continued to paint the fence. As they drew near, he stood and wiped his hands on a rag. "I'll take that." He grabbed the basket and carried it to the kitchen table.

"They were talking about you," Robbie said.

Linc shot Sally a look ripe with regret. "Looks like a great candy stick."

Sally realized she'd forgotten to buy herself one.

"Yup." Robbie sucked on it. "Why did they say bad things?"

"Did they?"

Robbie took the candy from his mouth. "I couldn't understand what they said, but they did this." He puckered his mouth and looked cross. "I know what that means."

Linc chuckled. "I guess you probably do. But seeing as I didn't do anything naughty, you must have heard them wrong."

Robbie studied him a moment longer then, seemingly satisfied, wandered out to the fort under construction.

Sally watched him cross the yard, all the time aware of Linc studying her.

"So the opinion of the good folk of Golden Prairie hasn't changed?" His words were low, as if resigned to the inevitable.

She didn't answer. Didn't pull her gaze from watching out the window.

"What do you think?"

His question, so direct, so void of emotion, jarred her from trying to maintain disinterest. She jerked her gaze to him and saw something in his eyes that said he wasn't as uncaring as he tried to portray.

She swallowed hard. "I think…" Her heart opened up and dumped out a tangle of emotions—things she couldn't identify and didn't want to own. One thought followed another before she could see the first clearly. Others came on the tail of each until they seemed to pull her in a hundred different directions. She lifted her words from that tangle and focused on the only solid thing she could grasp at the moment—Abe. She knew who he was, what he stood for and who and what he would be into the future. "I think Abe is right. You deserve a chance."

His expression faltered. He shifted on his feet. For a moment she thought he meant to walk away. Then he nodded. "Does that mean we can be friends?"

She smiled softly. "It looks like we already are."

"Good to know." His words were brisk and he left the house without a backward look, his shoulders squared as if defying the world.

Had she disappointed him? She watched until he disappeared from sight. Friends was good, wasn't it? She could offer nothing more. Likely he didn't want more, either. It was enough.

Strange how it felt totally unsatisfactory. As if she'd fallen short of gaining a prize.

Now she was getting downright fanciful, and she had no patience with such sentimental nonsense. She turned her attention to the groceries and put them away, leaving out the can of peaches to use for dessert.

All she needed to do in order to soothe her thoughts was keep her mind on her work, and she turned her attention to lunch, preparing pretty sandwiches and arranging cookies on a special plate.

Lunch came and went. Carol returned to school. Abe thanked her for a well-done job and left for work. Robbie went out to join Linc.

Sally looked around the empty house. It practically echoed with her thoughts…which she tried to avoid. Friendship was all she could offer.

The dishes needed washing. The floor needed scrubbing. The windows could do with a polishing. She immersed herself in a flurry of activity, yet the afternoon trudged by on slow-moving legs.

She glanced at the clock. Still an hour before Carol

would be home from school. Enough time to bake fresh cookies for the afternoon break. Linc had liked the ginger cookies. What would he think of snickerdoodles? Perhaps she could soothe her own disappointment by showing Linc—and ultimately herself—how nice friendship could be.

Carol slipped in almost unnoticed.

"As soon as you're changed, would you go tell Linc and Robbie that tea is ready?"

"Okay." Carol clattered up the stairs.

Chuckling at her uncharacteristic eagerness, Sally stared after her.

Carol raced back down and out the door.

The coffee boiled, and Sally grabbed it before it sputtered over on the stove. She would not admit an eagerness matching Carol's. It was only an after-school snack.

But when she heard him approaching, the children chattering at his side, she had to admit this was no ordinary snack time. She didn't mean just the way the children acted. Her heart did unusual things, too. As if controlled by a spirited puppet master who laughed and sang with joy.

He stepped into the room. She felt his presence, from the soles of her feet to the roots of her hair. And although she tried to ignore him, her gaze was drawn unerringly to his face. His eyes were dark and guarded. She gave a tentative smile. "I hope you like snickerdoodles."

His lips curled slowly, and as they did the ice in her veins she'd been unaware of melted. When his eyes flashed warmth, she started to breathe normally.

They could surely enjoy friendship.

"I love snickerdoodles. And fresh coffee. And—" He didn't finish, and she wouldn't allow herself to fill in the blank he'd left. "I'll wash up."

As he ducked into the back room with Robbie at his heels, Sally smiled in satisfaction. They were friends, and it felt good.

As they sat around the table eating warm cookies, she felt at peace. Abe would expect her to treat Linc well.

"How was school today, little Miss Carol?" he asked.

Sally expected the usual murmured one-word answer, but Carol put her cookie down and glanced at Sally and then Linc.

"The big girls told me a bad story."

Linc shot Sally a look full of regret. She realized with a start he expected it to be about him. She prayed it wouldn't be. Didn't the man deserve to be treated fairly and without prejudice? Was Abe the only one willing to do so? It proved what a good man Abe was. "Do you want to tell us about it?" Linc's voice was soft, inviting.

Carol studied her half eaten cookie. "They said you were a bad man. That you stole from Mrs. Ogilvy." Her bottom lip quivered.

Linc allowed Sally a glimpse of his sorrow and regret then turned his attention to Carol. He caught her chin and pulled her face toward him. "Carol, I assure you I am not a bad man. But you must choose what to believe. Everyone must." He let his glance rest on Robbie a moment, and then on Sally.

She felt his silent pleading. Oh, if only she could tell him all she felt—that he was good and noble and very brave to return to a town ready to judge him so harshly. But fearing speaking from her heart would unleash things she didn't understand and knowing they would interfere with her plans, she hoped her smile said enough. Then she turned to Carol. "Honey, do you think your father would hire Linc to work here if he thought he was a bad man?"

Carol shook her head.

"So who do you think is right? Your father or some girls at school?"

"Father, of course. He is always right."

"There you go."

Carol let out a hefty sigh. "I knew it anyway."

Sally shifted her gaze to Linc and looked deep into his eyes. "So did I."

Linc's grin threatened to split his face. "Ladies, I can't thank you enough for your confidence in me."

Sally had smiled at him long enough, but she couldn't pull her gaze away. The air between them shimmered with something far beyond friendship, but she couldn't—wouldn't—name it.

Robbie pushed his chair back. "Time to go back to work."

The moment ended, and Sally scrambled to her feet and hurriedly started to gather up the dishes.

Linc rose more slowly, as if aware of her confused feelings. "You're right, Robbie. Let's go paint the fence."

Carol trailed after them.

It wasn't until the door closed behind them that Sally sank into a chair and buried her head in her hands. What was there about Linc that left her so fractured inside? Unable to remember who she was and what she wanted?

Or perhaps Linc wasn't to blame.

She could hold no one else accountable for her behavior, and she stuffed all her errant, confused thoughts behind a solid door.

She knew exactly who she was and what she wanted. Not for even a moment would she forget. At least not again.

Her mind full of determination, she turned her attention to the task of cleaning up the snack and preparing the evening meal.

Chapter Seven

Linc finished painting the fence, cleaned the paint supplies, scrubbed his hands and turned toward his grandmother's.

Friends, Sally said. Her eyes flashing with golden light as she said the word and smiled at him. A friend in this town was good news. But it felt like so much more than friends. The way her gaze captured his, probing, yearning. The way she defended him. She said she believed he was a good man. It seemed as if Heaven opened and showered her words down on him. A blessing beyond imagination.

He paused at the back fence of the Finley yard and waved at Robbie. "See you later."

Robbie glanced up. "You'll be back tomorrow, won't you?"

Linc nodded. "Got that barn to fix up. You want to help?"

Robbie grinned. "Can I?"

"Ask your father tonight, and if he agrees, I'd be glad of your help." The boy needed to feel useful. And Linc needed to believe he had something to offer besides—

Friendship?

He could no longer deny himself a glance toward the house. Yes, she stood at the window, watching. When she saw him looking at her, she tipped her head down as if whatever she did was vastly more interesting than him.

And why should he care? Friends didn't look for signs of interest, did they?

He almost convinced himself he wasn't the least bit disappointed when she looked up again and gave a little wave.

Maybe it didn't signify anything, but his heart felt years lighter as he sketched back a salute. He sang as he crossed to the other yard and marched up the steps into the house.

As always, when he crossed the threshold, the reason for being at Grandmama's hit him like being bucked off a horse, face-first into the dirt. His happiness at Sally's wave warred with the pain of his father's lingering death. Seemed neither of the emotions was about to win or lose. He simply had to contend with the inner turmoil. "How's Pa?"

Grandmama stirred a pot. The air filled with the delicious smell of butterscotch pudding. "I checked on him a few minutes ago and he appeared to be sound asleep, but see for yourself."

Linc paused as he passed the stove and took a deep breath. "Sure smells good." He hugged his grandmother around the waist. "You always did make the best puddings."

She smiled at him. "I guess I figure you only deserve the best."

He grinned. "Maybe don't deserve it, but sure do enjoy it."

"You're a good boy." She patted his cheek. "Don't ever forget it."

"I'll try not to." His grandmother's approval did a lot toward making him believe his worth, but didn't hold a candle to Sally's friendship. Though the word *friend* somehow grated across his thoughts, leaving them tender.

Friendship was good, he firmly informed his brain. But was it enough?

Grandmama studied him. Afraid she would read his mind—knowing if she did, she would point out yet again how Abe Finley could offer Sally all the things she needed and deserved, things he, Linc McCoy, could not—he stepped back.

Grandmama had one of those looks that said she read him like a book. Then she sighed. "Go see your father. I'm afraid supper will be a while yet. Some of the ladies got together to piece a quilt, and I just got home."

Grateful she refrained from saying all the things she thought, Linc nodded and went to the bedroom. So Grandmama had been out all afternoon. He didn't like to think of Pa being alone, but really, there was little anyone could do apart from giving him a little water if he'd take it and handing out the pain medication.

Pa lay spread eagle under the covers, his breathing catching every so often, which indicated the level of his pain, the doctor said. "Pa," he called softly. But Pa didn't stir, and Linc didn't try to disturb him. Let him sleep while he could. He studied the man a few minutes as pain and regret raced through him like raging flood waters. *Oh, Pa, I hate to see you laid so low.* Even more, he despised the way Pa had been treated in this town. At least his present circumstances spared him from hearing the comments of the townsfolk.

He returned to the kitchen where his grandmother labored over a pile of vegetables. "I think I'll go for a ride."

"Fine. Fine. Don't worry about rushing back. Everything will keep."

He went outside and threw a bridle over Big Red's neck. "I need to get some fresh air. How about you?"

Big Red was far more interested in a bit of green grass he'd discovered in the far corner of the yard.

"It'll be here when we get back," Linc assured him as he led the animal to the barn and saddled him. "A little exercise will do you good." He patted the horse's side. "Wouldn't want you to get fat and lazy."

He headed out of town, purposely in the same direction as last time, for no particular reason other than to avoid going the opposite way which, unless he chose an indirect route, would lead him past Mrs. Ogilvy's house. He was innocent. His father and brother were innocent, yet he felt branded. The idea of riding past her house made his skin tighten.

He rode into plenty of open space this way. In the distance he saw the boxlike orphanage atop a hill, as if whoever built it wanted it to always be visible. Perhaps so the people of the surrounding area wouldn't forget those in need of help and kindness. Letting his pain edge his thoughts, he wondered how often the orphans received those things. If the way Pa was treated indicated anything, likely not often.

Ahead of him on the trail he saw a woman walking. Sally.

He'd know the way she walked—quickly and purposefully—anywhere. Just as he'd recognize the way her curls bounced with every step, catching sunshine in each curve of hair.

His frustration and anger dissolved.

She turned as she heard his approach and waited at the side of the road for him to pass.

He reined in and jumped to the ground. "You're on your way home?"

"All done for the day."

"I'd think Abe would give you a ride." If he was Abe, he'd never allow her to walk home unescorted.

"He's offered many times, but the children are happy at home. I don't like to drag them out for no reason. Besides, I love the quiet."

He drew to a halt. Did he detect a hint of regret in her voice? "Would you prefer to be alone?"

She stopped walking, too, and her eyes widened in shock. "Oh, no. I didn't mean that."

"Good." The smile curving her mouth crowded into the corners of his heart. She plainly didn't mind his company. "Then I'll walk you home."

They fell into step, Red plodding along after them. At first neither of them spoke, then they both tried to say something at the same time.

Linc chuckled. "You go ahead."

"I was only going to ask where you've been the past six years and what you've done. What were you going to say?"

"That maybe the drought will end this year. Maybe

this will be the year prices recover." It was but a drop of all the things running through his thoughts to be said. He wanted to know so much. All about her. How she managed. What she did, liked, wanted.

She looked about. "If it doesn't, how will some of these people continue?"

Her question brought him back from his flight of errant thoughts. "It's tough to hang on."

"All that keeps many of them going, me included, is knowing whatever happens won't separate us from God's love."

"I believe in God's love and care, but love doesn't fill a child's stomach."

She slowed and looked toward the orphanage. "My sister, Madge, would argue. She says God will provide our needs." She gave a soft chuckle. "And He does." She told him how her sister prayed for a way to save their home and how she'd been offered a job that unexpectedly provided just the right answer. "In a way none of us could have predicted."

"So you are well taken care of now?" If she lacked anything, he'd do his best to supply it. Never mind that his limited resources barely allowed him to buy Pa's pain medicine.

"We live frugally, as everyone does, but we never go hungry."

His insides shifted from worry to a bubbling sensation of relief. "It sounds like this sister of yours is a real fighter."

Sally laughed out loud, drawing a smile to Linc's mouth. He liked her laugh. "She has a faith that moves mountains." Sally sobered. "I wish I had that kind of faith."

Their steps lagged so much that Big Red nudged Linc between the shoulders. Linc pushed him away. He was in no hurry. "What kind of faith do you have?"

She looked startled. Then seemed to consider her answer. "I've never tried to name it, but I guess I have a needy faith."

How intriguing. What did she need? Again, if he could in any way supply what she lacked, he'd do anything he could to do it. "Can you explain?"

"I need things from God, like security, safety, the assurance my needs will be met." She shrugged. "I don't expect you understand what I mean."

"Do you mean your faith believes God will provide all that He's promised? Or you'll believe it when you see it?"

"Ouch." She stopped and faced him. "That sounds like doubt, not faith. But maybe you're right. I want things to be in place." She considered him a moment, her gaze delving deep into his soul, seeking answers, perhaps wondering if he condemned her for her sort of faith.

"I didn't mean to sound critical." He'd only wanted her to realize God was bigger than her needs. He wanted her to feel secure in His love and care. He let her search his thoughts, hoping she would find something to make her feel safe.

How foolish. Wasn't it God she needed to depend on? But, he silently argued, it would be nice to help God in this matter.

"What kind of faith do you have?"

His grin felt lopsided. "I've never thought of it, either." He contemplated his answer. "I guess I have a surviving faith."

They moseyed onward.

"Explain what you mean."

"Okay." Again he sifted through his thoughts to bring some sense to them. "I've survived. My faith has survived through tough times and doubts."

"What sort of doubts?"

She was peeling back the layers of what he truly believed and how he'd arrived at that point. He'd never considered his journey too deeply, but now found he wanted to—and more, he wanted to share it with Sally. Wanted her to glimpse the workings of his inner being. "My mother tried to teach me about God, but I guess it didn't ring true. I knew she'd run off with my father, who had a terrible reputation. When I think of it now I realize how it must have hurt my grandmother."

She touched his elbow. "But she opened her home to them when they asked."

Her fingers on his arm carried a thousand unspoken messages. Likely they were only in his head, and she didn't have any idea of where his thoughts went—along a trail of a deep, intense…well, he'd settle for calling it friendship, seeing it was all that was available to him. "And she's done it again. Despite whatever she thinks of my father, she welcomed us without reservation. Her charitable attitude impressed me from the start. I wondered how she could be so kind even when she didn't approve. She offered unconditional love, so I could believe it when she said God loved me unconditionally. I chose to become a Christian because of Grandmama."

"What a wonderful heritage she's given you."

He agreed completely. "Tell me how you became a Christian."

Her gentle smile widened her lips and filled her eyes. And settled into his heart like a homing pigeon returned from a long journey. "My father led all of us to the Lord. I knelt at his knees when I was eight and prayed the sinner's prayer. I don't remember the words, but I know what I meant and felt. It was a special time."

"Your father was a special man."

"He was indeed, and I miss him." A break came in her speech, and then she continued. "I think of him so much, but most of all at bedtime. He made each of us promise to read a chapter from the Bible every night before we go to bed. I've missed very few evenings. I've found such strength and comfort in my daily reading."

Her words created a hunger in his heart.

"Do you read the Bible daily?"

"I haven't made it a habit, but maybe I need to."

"Now were you going to tell me what you've done, where you've been since you left here?"

"Nothing very exciting, I'm afraid. I went with Pa and Harris for the first few years, but they never stayed long in one place. They hunted gold in the mountains, worked on the railroad, drove freight for a few months, then they started working in the coal mines in the Crowsnest Pass. For some reason they seemed to enjoy that. I hated it. I didn't even make it through a full shift before I staggered out to the light and vowed I'd never go into the pit again."

She sent him a look so full of sympathy he had to stop and draw in air to clear his thoughts.

"I don't suppose you've ever seen the Frank Slide?" She shook her head.

"Boulders the size of houses came crashing down on the town. Seventy-six people were buried alive." Words poured from him, words stored up for so many years, things he'd never been able to openly say to his father and brother. "The rocks became their grave markers. The Indians called the mountain the mountain that walks. They knew it was unstable, but no one listened because there was a rich vein of coal beneath the mountain, and coal is worth a lot of money. It isn't worth a man's life, or the life of his wife and children though." He slowed his words and then went on. "I decided I preferred sky and grass to coal, and from then on I worked on a ranch."

"And then you lost your brother in a mine accident. How terrible."

"At least he didn't suffer."

"Unlike your pa. I'm sorry. How is he?"

"Not getting any stronger." He told how he had started reading *Pilgrim's Progress* to him. "I pray it will speak to my father and he will become a Christian before he dies."

"I will pray for it, as well."

He took her hand and squeezed it. "Thank you." So this is what it felt like to have a good friend? Except he wanted more. He wanted to be free to wrap his arms around her and hold her close, finding comfort in that. He ached to offer her what she needed.

Security and safety.

"This is where I turn off." They had come to a long

driveway. He saw a solid two-story house and a small but adequate barn.

"I'll walk you the rest of the way."

She stepped back, shock filling her wide eyes, darkening them to deepest green. "I couldn't let you do that."

He didn't need a blaring announcement to understand she didn't want him to. "Of course not." His voice cracked with disappointment. Up until this moment, he thought they were enjoying each other's company. Being friends. Isn't that what she wanted?

She shook her head and her gaze darted away to his left, to his right, always avoiding meeting his eyes. "Mother wouldn't understand."

Her words struck him so hard he stepped backward and bumped into patient Red.

Red. Escape.

Exactly what he needed. He flipped the reins over the horse's head and swung into the saddle. "I understand." He nudged Red and trotted toward town.

He understood all right. Way too well. He could be her friend, but not in public. Being seen with a McCoy—even by her mother—threatened the very things she needed—the things he allowed himself to briefly think he could offer. Safety and security.

The sky had darkened. He glanced upward. The sun still shone as brightly. It had simply lost its warmth. He was a McCoy. Not for the first time, he thought of changing his name to Smith or Jones or even Black. Yes, Black would suit just fine. But he didn't want to be someone else. He wanted to be seen as a good man with the name McCoy. Was that too much to ask? Seems it was.

Well, he had gotten along without friends most of his

life. That was nothing new. But all his excuse-making and reason-seeking did not ease the darkness in his soul.

He valued Sally's friendship. Obviously more than she valued his.

He reached the yard and took Red to the barn and cared for him.

As he stepped into the kitchen, the aroma of stew and pudding greeted him, as did his grandmother's smile, and he pushed his disappointment to the background.

Supper was good. He ate a good-size portion and hoped his grandmother wouldn't notice a certain lack of enthusiasm. Afterward, he dried the dishes for her then went to Pa's bedside.

"Where you been, boy?" His father sounded lonesome, not demanding.

"I went for a ride. You remember, I work at Mr. Finley's during the day."

"What'd you do today?"

"I painted the front fence. Mr. Finley likes things to look nice." Abe cared what people thought. He'd hired Linc because Abe did what was right and noble—out of duty. He stood for safety. Security. Just what Sally wanted. Thought she needed. But it sounded false, shallow and rigid at the same time.

"This man live alone?"

Linc told him of the two motherless children. "They have a housekeeper now who will likely become their stepmother." Saying the words out loud felt like bringing up bitter acid.

"She nice to them?"

He could gladly say she was. "She'll make a fine mother to them." But the idea of her living according to Abe's expectation of duty twisted his insides. She needed to know life was to enjoy. God's world was to enjoy, His salvation was to enjoy.

But if he took a good look at himself, did he really believe that? If he did, he wouldn't let gossip and spitefulness, nor even rejection from a friend rob him of enjoying all God had given. *Lord, help me see beyond these hurts to Your everlasting love.* He let peace fill him. "Would you like me to read to you again?"

He read another hour to his father, then slipped away and went to his room.

Sally read the scriptures every night because of a promise to her father. She asked if he read the Bible. He had never made a practice of it before, but now he found his copy of the Good Book and opened it at the beginning of the New Testament and began to read. As he did, all but a remnant of his bitterness disappeared. Somehow reading in his room and knowing Sally read in hers made him feel close to her and restored the feeling of companionship.

Perhaps it was all he could expect. Could it be enough? It had to be.

Chapter Eight

Next morning at the Finley house, Sally glanced around the table. Carol waited for her father to say grace. Robbie had a hand on either side of his bowl, and eyed the steaming porridge hungrily. Sally slowly brought her gaze to Abe. As usual, he wore his dark blond hair slicked back. His black suit was immaculate. He was a good, decent man; handsome in a gentle way.

He bowed his head and prayed, catching her off guard. By the time she bowed her head, he was done.

"Robbie will be six in two weeks' time," Abe said after he'd tasted his coffee and enjoyed a few spoonfuls of his porridge.

Robbie didn't stop eating, but he slid a look at his father—a rather hopeful look, Sally thought.

"Their mother thought the children should have a special party when they turned six and were grown up enough to start school. Do you suppose you could plan something?"

"What do you have in mind?" *What did your wife do? Can I do, as well?*

"Whatever you think Robbie would enjoy. Within reason."

She nodded, hoping he would give a clue as to what he meant by "within reason." But he didn't offer any details.

"I've prepared a list of guests." He pulled a piece of paper from his pocket and passed it to Sally.

She glanced over it. Six little boys from either business or church connections. Four little girls from Carol's class. At least he'd thought to include Carol in the celebration.

"Can you manage that?"

"I'm certain I can." She had no idea what he wanted, but she'd make sure it exceeded any expectations. She'd prove to everyone she was worthy of this job…even more, the role of Abe's wife.

Carol and Robbie watched her guardedly, perhaps afraid to get their hopes up for fear of being disappointed. Right then and there Sally decided she wanted to bring them pleasure, even more than she wanted to please Abe. Hopefully she could do both.

Abe finished and pushed back from the table. "And get rid of that pile of junk at the end of the garden before the party."

An instant pall covered the table. Robbie dropped his spoon and bunched his hands into fists. Sally stared at Abe. How could he order the destruction of Robbie's fort? Didn't he realize how important it was to the boy? Perhaps he didn't. After all, he only saw the boy in the evening. How was he to know Robbie spent most of his waking time playing there? She must explain its importance.

She rose. "I'll be right back," she said to the children and followed Abe through the dining room to the front door, where he prepared to leave for the day.

"Abe, may I speak to you a moment?"

"Of course. I hope you feel free to talk to me whenever you want."

She paused. Was he inviting her to share confidences? But this wasn't the time. Not that she could think of anything she wanted to tell him, apart from this one thing. "About Robbie's fort—"

He raised his eyebrows. "His fort?"

"Yes. That pile of junk in the garden. It's his fort. He spends a great deal of time playing there. It seems to give him a lot of pleasure. Would you reconsider having it destroyed?"

He looked at her so intently she wanted to squirm. "Do you think it's important?"

"I do."

"You feel I should leave it be?"

"It's important to Robbie."

"Very well. If you think it's best, I'll bow to your wishes." He headed back to the kitchen, Sally at his heels.

"Robbie, Sally says that—" he made a vague wave toward the fort visible from the window "—your fort is important to you. Is that right?"

Robbie nodded, his lips set in an angry frown.

"If it's important to you, then it may stay." Abe waited.

At first, Sally wasn't sure what he expected. Then it seemed plain. "Robbie," she whispered. "Thank your father."

Robbie looked ready to explode, unable to shed his anger so quickly. But he managed a muttered, "Thank you."

Satisfied, Abe left.

Sally and the children didn't move, even after they heard the front door close. Time was slipping away, and she read the children their Bible story then sent Carol off to school.

She turned her attention to cleaning up the meal as Robbie headed out to his fort. Smiling her satisfaction that she had succeeded in saving it for him, she watched out the window as he got a spade from the shed.

He carried it to the tangle of dirt and twigs that kept him happily amused for so many days. Perhaps he meant to make the walls higher but—

She gasped.

He banged away on the walls, destroying them inch by inch.

Sally threw aside the cloth and rushed outside. "Robbie, what on earth are you doing?" She grabbed the shovel. "You don't have to destroy it."

"He only let me keep it 'cause you said something. Give me the shovel." He lunged for it, but she jerked away.

"Does it matter why he let you keep it? After all your hard work you deserve to enjoy it."

But all Robbie seemed to care about was getting his hands on the shovel, and it took all Sally's concentrated dodging away to keep it from him.

"Hey, hey. What's going on?" Linc vaulted the fence and swept Robbie into his arms. "What are you trying to do?"

Breathless, Sally leaned on the handle of the shovel.

Linc lowered Robbie to the ground, but kept a firm grip on him. He squatted to eye level. "Care to tell me what this is all about?"

"It isn't a pile of junk."

Linc gave Sally a look of confusion.

"His father called his fort junk. Said it had to go." She turned to the boy struggling to escape Linc's hold. "He didn't know. Once I told him how important it was to you, he understood. He said you could keep it. Remember?"

Linc turned back to the boy. "I don't see why you were fighting with Sally. Seems she spoke up for you. Don't you think that calls for a little gratitude?"

The fight slowly drained from Robbie, and he sank to the ground. Linc released him, but stood ready to intervene if the boy exploded again. Robbie hung his head.

Linc glanced toward Sally, his eyes asking for an explanation, but she was at a loss as to what to do or say and indicated it with a shrug. Linc stared into the distance for two beats then sat down beside Robbie. "I guess you were pretty upset when you thought you were going to lose your fort. After all, a man likes to hang on to the things he's worked hard for. I understand that. But a man also has to learn to aim his anger and frustration in the right direction so he doesn't hurt the ones who care about him. Or destroy the things he wants to protect. Do you understand?"

Robbie gave no indication one way or the other, except to scuff his heels in the dirt.

Sally waited, not knowing what to expect and realizing how inept she was at dealing with the crises in Robbie's life—of which there seemed to be many.

"Sometimes I don't know who I'm mad at," Robbie said.

Linc sat beside Robbie. "That happens to me, too." He sounded as morose as the boy, and Sally almost smiled at the disconsolate pair sitting side by side in the dirt. They both wore such similar expressions. Except it wasn't a laughing matter. No one's pain was amusing, no matter how big or small. Being the youngest, she'd often wondered if anyone cared about her concerns. After all, it was old news to her older sisters and likely her parents. Everything that happened to her had previously been experienced and dealt with. Once her father had asked what bothered her. It was something small—so small she couldn't even remember what it had been. But she still remembered his words.

She spoke them aloud now, hoping they would encourage Robbie and Linc as much as they had her. "My father once told me anger only fuels pain. It misdirects our energies."

Two pairs of eyes turned to her, waiting for more, perhaps hoping she had an answer to how to deal with frustrating anger and disappointment. "He said the best way to deal with anger was to do something positive like help someone, make something, go somewhere. I guess that's why I like to help people. It makes me feel like life isn't out of control. I suppose that's why Linc rides his horse. It's a way to direct his feelings into action."

Robbie sighed. "I can't do anything."

She studied his fort. "Maybe you can."

Linc got to his feet and stood beside her, also studying the fort. "I think you could."

Robbie sprang to his feet. "What? What can I do?"

"Well, if your father thinks this looks like junk, maybe you need to make it look better. Finish the fence. Tidy up the dirt around it." Sally could see how doing so would improve the view from the window.

"There was a bit of paint left in the can. I could thin it, and you could paint these boards." Linc tilted his head from side to side. "How would it be if I showed you how to build a gate for your fence? Then it would look really great."

Robbie grabbed a twig and drove it into the ground next to the others forming the fence. "I'm going to finish the fence first."

Linc smiled at Sally and gave a subtle thumbs up. She grinned back. They had averted a crisis with the boy and given him a way to sidetrack his anger. Maybe it would help him in the future.

Her smile faltered when she remembered how she'd hurt Linc yesterday, when she refused to let him accompany her to the house. She hadn't meant to, but how would she explain to Mother, who feared any friendship between Sally and Linc would ruin her chances of marriage to Abe? Mother would never understand the friendship Sally had with Linc. In her room last night, she had worked it all through. She and Linc were forced to spend time together as coworkers. She admired his way with the children and the way he cared about his family. But she knew where her duty lay. She'd fought the word duty. What kind of relationship was based on duty? There was more to it than that. There was—

she'd plumbed her heart for what she felt toward Abe...
Safety, security—the very things she'd told Linc she
needed. Yet she appreciated Linc's company. She felt
comfortable opening her heart to him and talking about
her faith, her family, her fears.

They turned and headed for their own tasks—he to
the barn and she to the house. They reached the place
where their paths must diverge.

"You're good with him," Sally said, wanting to express how much she appreciated him, even though she
wouldn't let him walk her to the door.

"So are you."

They nodded mutual respect.

Linc adjusted his hat and seemed to want to say
more. She hoped he didn't want to discuss last night. It
took him a moment to form his words. "I wish I could
say it was because I'm all grown up and speak from
wisdom, but honestly, I feel like Robbie and I are on
equal footing. I look at my pa and want to be mad at
someone, but I don't know who it would be. It's a helpless, frustrated feeling."

"I think it's something we all struggle with. Remember how I have a needy faith? That's part of it. Standing back and knowing I'm helpless is a terrible feeling.
I need security. You asked if I trusted God or needed to
see before I believed."

"I wasn't questioning your faith."

"Well, I honestly don't know which it is. I know God
is my rock and salvation. I know He holds my future,
and that's a comfort. But I'm not sure I believe it's
enough. I watch families move away with all their pos-

sessions piled in the back of a truck. They have nothing left. How do they go on?"

"There is always hope."

"Hope is a pretty little balloon that won't last until morning."

He chuckled. "I guess if it's full of hot air, that would be true. What if it's full of something permanent, like God's promises? It wouldn't collapse or blow away then."

She stared into the blue distance as a bubble of something looking clearly like hope but feeling more solid landed in her soul. A verse her father had her memorize many years ago came to mind. "'Blessed is the man that trusteth in the Lord, whose hope the Lord is. For he shall be as a tree planted by the waters.'"

"Exactly. It's not a balloon, but a solid tree."

"I like that. It feels secure."

"I better get to work." He touched the brim of his hat.

"Me, too." It wasn't until she was back in the house that she recalled Abe's request for a birthday party for Robbie. What would a six-year-old boy want? She had only sisters, and they had loved dress up and tea parties. Robbie would obviously not like such things.

As she finished the breakfast dishes and tidied the house, she tried to come up with a plan. She wanted this party to be remarkable. She wanted to prove to Abe that she could manage anything he and his family required. But by midmorning she was no closer to a solution.

She watched out the window as Linc showed Robbie how to hang a gate. A smile tipped her lips and cheered her heart. Linc had once been a little boy. He would know what boys liked for a party. She waited until he headed back to the barn, leaving Robbie with some thinned paint and a brush, then went to talk to him.

She paused in the doorway and waited for her eyes to adjust to the gloomy interior. The squeal of spikes being pulled from old wood indicated his location. "Linc?"

"I'm over here."

She could see him now. "You used to be a little boy."

His grin gently mocked her. "I think that's pretty obvious."

"I guess I didn't need to point it out. I only meant to say I have never been nor known any little boys really well, and now Abe wants me to plan a special birthday party for Robbie, and I have no idea what he'd like."

Linc's arm fell to his side, the hammer dangling at his knee. "You're asking me for help?"

He needn't act so surprised. "Advice, at least. What would he like?"

Linc leaned against the stall and grinned. "I know exactly what he'd like." He glanced around like a coconspirator, leaned close and whispered, "A pony to ride."

"Oh, perfect! But I don't know anyone with ponies. Most people can't afford to feed pets like that."

His grin deepened, making her thoughts feel as if they had boarded balloons and were trying to soar or escape or—she punctured the balloons. She could not allow such nonsense.

"I know someone. Leave the pony to me." He must have seen the lingering doubt in her eyes. "Okay?"

Would Abe consider it suitable, safe for his son? "I better check with Abe first and get his permission." She turned her steps toward the house, then stopped. "I hope he agrees. Robbie would be thrilled."

Later, after supper was over and the kitchen cleaned she would normally hurry away, but Sally needed to talk to Abe. Alone. He'd said he hoped she would talk to him whenever she wanted, but she struggled to find the words to make this simple request. What was wrong with her that she turned into a tongue-tied child at the thought? Shouldn't she be able to speak her thoughts and wishes to him freely? After all, if they were to marry, she couldn't continue to feel so immature around him, but something about Abe made her anxious and uncertain of herself. She sucked in a deep breath. She must overcome this shyness.

He sat in his chair reading some documents. He preferred the children play quietly after their meal, so Robbie moved a little car across the floor and Carol colored a picture.

All she had to do was ask him to come to the kitchen. Or even go outside and walk around the yard. Instead, she wiped the table again and rehearsed her words.

"You're still here?" He stood in the doorway. "I thought you'd be gone."

Why should he think so? She always said goodbye before she left, and she hadn't done so. But his presence in the room gave her an opportunity to voice her question. "I wanted to speak to you before I leave."

"Go ahead." He filled a glass of water.

She lowered her voice. "I thought of having a Western-themed party for Robbie's birthday."

"Sounds fine."

"I'd like to have a live pony for the children to ride."

The glass of water, halfway to his mouth, stalled and he slowly lowered it. "Do you have a pony?"

She shook her head.

"Are you familiar with how to control one?"

"No, but Mr. McCoy offered to bring a pony and he knows about horses." She waited as Abe studied her, silently exploring her expression.

"Linc McCoy?"

She nodded.

He turned away as if he needed time to consider his answer. Then slowly faced her again. "I wanted to give McCoy a chance. I just didn't think it would involve my children."

A hundred defenses sprang to her mind. Wisely, she held them back, except for one. "It isn't like he'd be alone with the children." Though what difference that made, she couldn't say. Linc posed no threat to anyone, least of all a dozen children. But her answer seemed to satisfy Abe.

"Very well, but I want the pony to be under adult control at all times." He drained his glass and set it down. "I would not want any harm to come to my children—any of the children."

"I assure you they will all be safe." She washed his glass and returned it to the cupboard. "I'm leaving now." She called a goodbye to the children.

Would Linc ride down the road again? She could hardly wait to tell him Abe had given permission to proceed with the party. But she reached the turnoff to her house without seeing him. She paused and looked down the road, hoping to spot an approaching rider.

The road was as empty as the rain barrel at the side of the house.

It didn't matter. She'd see him tomorrow. But try as

she did, she couldn't deny how her heart practically burst with a need to talk to him, tell about her day, discuss ideas for the party.

Angry at herself for such foolishness, she stuffed the idea into a corner in the far reaches of her mind and resolutely turned her steps toward home.

Linc glanced out the window. From where he sat at his pa's bedside, he saw only the bright blue sky. He'd hoped to take Red out for a run. The horse needed to stretch his legs. Linc barely acknowledged the fact that if he was out there at this moment, he would likely overtake Sally on her way home. But Pa was restless today and Linc couldn't, in good conscience, leave him.

"What did you do today, boy?"

He told how he'd begun removing the stalls at one end of the barn in order to make room for Mr. Finley's car. "I told you about the children. Well, seems Robbie is about to turn six and his father says it calls for a birthday party. Sally didn't know what a boy would like, so I suggested a pony for the kids to ride."

"Sally? That the name of the woman who is going to be the new stepmother?"

Abe had a big solid house, a good job. He could provide security. Everything Sally wanted and needed. A needy faith, she'd said, and her words made him understand so much more. Sally wasn't one to take risks. Still, hearing his own father talk as if Sally was already Abe's wife made his throat spasm. Aware his pa watched him, he tried for a grin and missed. "Yeah, that's her." His voice betrayed him, sounding regretful rather than the nonchalant tone he aimed for.

"Uh-huh. Tell me about her."

"She seems like a good woman." It wasn't enough for Pa, so Linc provided details of Sally's family.

"Sounds like a good family," Pa said.

"I expect they are." Which about said it all. The Morgans were a good family, and the McCoys would never achieve a similar status. Good thing Sally planned to marry Abe. Now there was a good, upstanding man. After all, he'd even considered it his duty to give Linc a chance.

Not that Linc wasn't grateful. He glanced at the medicine bottle he could now refill. Yes, he was very grateful.

Though at the moment, he felt like Robbie. He wanted to find a shovel and whack something.

"You're a good boy, Linc," his father murmured. "Don't let anyone make you think differently."

Linc nodded. He could hardly point out that others thought differently, mostly thanks to the way Pa had acted after Ma died. But as he thought of Sally marrying Abe simply for security, he thought he understood a little better why Pa had gone a little crazy. Not that Linc would do so, but he couldn't abide the notion that Sally would settle for anything less than love and happiness simply for the sake of feeling safe.

It was almost dark before Pa settled and Linc felt free to ride Red away from town. He always took the same direction. Only now it wasn't simply to avoid passing Mrs. Ogilvy's house. Now it was because it took him the direction of the Morgan house. He rode to the turnoff, slowed enough to give the place a good study and was rewarded by the sight of Sally leaving a small fenced area he assumed was a garden spot. He watched until she stepped into the house, then he reined around and returned home.

He only wanted to assure himself she was safe and sound at home. He was only slightly disappointed to miss a visit with her. Or so he tried to convince himself, without much success.

The next morning, Sally hurried from the house before he made it halfway across the yard to the barn. "Abe says we can have a pony. He thought it was a fine idea. Isn't that great?" Her eyes sparkled like a precious gemstone. "He only says someone has to lead the pony at all times." She sobered a fraction. "Can you really get a pony?"

If only her pleasure was because they would be working together, not because Abe approved the party plans. "I know a man who'll lend me one. And I can certainly be in charge of it during the party, if that's acceptable." Perhaps Sally, or Abe, would object to a McCoy associating with the fine children of the Golden Prairie residents.

"Knowing you were in charge would give me utmost confidence." She clasped her hands and looked excited. "I know Robbie is going to be so happy." She paused. "Do you think we should keep it a secret?"

We? She put the two of them in the same thought? He tried not to let the idea fill him with sweet pleasure but failed miserably. Yes, it was only for Robbie's party. It was only so Sally could please Abe, but nevertheless, the words rang with all sorts of possibilities.

She looked puzzled as she tried to decide what was

best. "What would please Robbie more? To know ahead of time or have the pony as a surprise?"

Back to the subject at hand. "I think it would be hard for him to wait patiently. Why not keep it a secret?"

"Right." She tipped her head and her smile deepened, sending bright green shards through her irises. "There's so much to think about when raising children."

"It's likely easier if you've known them from birth."

Her smile faded slowly. "I wonder if I'll make a good stepmother."

He wanted to tell her to forget about being a stepmother, think about being—

He wouldn't allow himself to finish the thought, even though he knew he meant to say, *Think about being my wife. The mother of my children.* He knew he could never give her the solid acceptance Abe could. But again the troubling thought of last night surfaced—was security enough for a good marriage? But the worry lines creasing her forehead made him want to give her assurance. "You sincerely care about the children. I think that's important."

She nodded. "I hope so."

Linc noticed she hadn't said she loved them. Did she love Abe? He tried to convince himself he hoped she did because he didn't want to think of her in a loveless marriage. Would she choose such an arrangement simply to get the things she needed? Or thought she needed? He pushed away all disobedient, wayward feelings.

Yet errant thoughts flitted about like wild birds. She honored and valued a good name. He could not offer that, though given time, perhaps the McCoy name would stand for something besides suspicion.

He shifted his gaze to the big house. He thought of Abe's position in town and forced himself to acknowledge he had nothing to offer her. He had to remember it.

In the meantime he would help her make Robbie's birthday party a roaring success. If it enabled her to achieve her goal of becoming Abe's wife, he must console himself with the knowledge it was what Sally wanted. And he wanted what was best for her.

If only he could convince himself Abe Finley was better than a McCoy. Others would have no difficulty telling Sally it was so, but Linc believed he was equal to Abe in matters of honor and trust.

Did his friendship give him the right to ask Sally what she thought?

Chapter Nine

She was going to do this in a spectacular fashion. Sally spent hours creating invitations for each child in the shape of a cowboy hat. Besides date and time, the invitation instructed the children to wear clothing suitable for a cowboy party. Mothers of little girls in frilly dresses wouldn't want their darlings riding a pony. Nor would they want their little boys to get horse hair all over their Sunday best pants.

The day of the party arrived. Guests weren't due until after lunch, but she wondered if Robbie would last until then.

"What's the surprise?" he asked for the umpteenth time.

Sally smiled patiently, enjoying his excitement. "If I told you, it wouldn't be a surprise and I'd ruin it for you."

"I don't mind."

It was Saturday, so Abe was home. He spoke to his son. "Robbie, you have to wait. Is your room clean?" He didn't need to ask Carol. She kept hers spotless, as if afraid to have anything out of place. Sally understood it for what it was—an attempt to be in command of her life. Like Sally, she'd learned the value of being in charge of those things she could manage. Life had too many things she had no control over.

Robbie wolfed down his lunch and bolted from the table. "Is it time to start?" Robbie stared at the big grandfather clock in the front room. "Is the clock running okay?"

"See for yourself." The huge pendulum swung back and forth with patient regularity.

He sighed and moved to stare out the window. "Maybe I better get ready in case someone comes early."

Abe looked at Sally and shrugged as if to say he was fine with the idea.

"You might be right. Run up and change." She had helped him create a real Western outfit, complete with a cowboy hat Linc had located, a vest on which she'd sewn fringes and trousers with a fringe down each leg.

He was halfway up the stairs before she finished speaking. Carol followed at a sedate pace. Sally had added a fringe to a dark skirt she found in Carol's closet and decorated a matching vest for her. Linc had donated a cowboy hat that was once his mother's.

The children returned a few a minutes later. They looked great. Abe had not seen the outfits, and blinked at first glance.

Sally's throat clamped tight. Had she made a mistake in letting the kids dress up? Was he expecting Sunday outfits? "It's a Western-themed party," she murmured, although he knew.

"Of course." He shifted his gaze to the children, allowing Sally to draw in a steadying breath. "You look like…" His pause was noticeably long. "Little cowboys."

A knock signaled their first guest. With relief, she took in the cowboy outfit the boy wore. One by one the children arrived, and all were dressed appropriately for the day's activities.

With Linc's help, Sally had set up Western-themed games—a sawhorse with a saddle for the kids to play on, another sawhorse with a piece of wood to resemble a cow's head and a lariat so the kids could practice roping it. She'd drawn the heads of several animals—a sheep, a cow, a horse, a dog—on a sheet of wood, and Linc had cut holes where the mouths were, so it became a beanbag throw game.

With Linc's help she soon had all the children involved in the games. After a bit, when things seemed under control, Linc slipped away. They'd worked it out that he would bring the pony from the front of the yard so the kids wouldn't see it until it was right there.

Sally grinned. Things were going extremely well.

Mrs. Anthony, mother of one of the little boys, must have thought the same. "This is a lovely party, Abe." She sounded genuinely pleased. "Sally has done a good job."

Only a few feet away, Sally heard every word, though she wondered if the woman was aware of the fact.

Mrs. Anthony continued. "It appears the McCoy man has helped her."

Sally stole a look at Abe for his reaction.

Abe glanced around the yard. "He's made the place fairly gleam."

"You did right giving him a chance to prove himself."

Mrs. Anthony nodded approval as she followed Abe's gaze to the newly painted fence and the other improvements, courtesy of Linc.

Plump Mrs. Tipple sidled close to the pair. She darted a glance toward Sally and leaned in close. "You allow that man a lot of free rein in your yard. Aren't you the least bit concerned?"

Abe drew himself rigid in righteous indignation, although Mrs. Tipple seemed oblivious to it.

"He has done nothing to give me cause for concern. In fact, he is partially responsible for the games and the surprise yet to come."

Mrs. Tipple tried to appear regretful. "I admire your charity, Abe, but a con man is known to be charming. You must be cautious. After all, you have two young children and need I point out…an impressionable young woman?"

Abe shot Sally a startled look, which she pretended not to see as she developed a sudden interest in the way one of the children held the lariat. Would the unkind comments cause Abe to reconsider hiring Linc? The panic catching at her stomach made it difficult to straighten from her task. Her concern was only on Linc's behalf. He'd told her he needed the money he earned here to pay for his father's pain medication.

Abe shifted his gaze away, but Sally didn't relax. She couldn't, not knowing Linc's fate.

"I appreciate your concern." Abe spoke slowly. "But I'm sure you feel as I do. That a man should be judged fairly. No evidence. No crime. God warns us, 'Judge not, that ye be not judged. For with what judgment ye judge, ye shall be judged.' I'm sure none of us wishes to be condemned without evidence."

Sally's breath whooshed out. Abe was truly a good and righteous man.

Mrs. Anthony and the others murmured agreement, and Mrs. Tipple wisely withdrew, though Sally guessed from her expression she hadn't changed her mind.

At that moment, Robbie screamed. "A pony! You brought a pony! Can I ride it?"

Everyone's attention turned toward Linc as he marched across the yard leading a black and white pony. The children raced toward him. The adults drew in a collective gasp of surprise.

Abe grinned satisfaction at Sally. She flashed him a shy smile then turned her attention to Linc and the children. "Everyone line up and you can take turns riding. Mr. McCoy will lead him around for you. The birthday boy can go first."

Robbie needed no nudging. If only he would obey every suggestion so eagerly.

The other games instantly forgotten, the children lined up and waited for their turn. As soon as Linc lifted one off the pony's back, that child hurried back to the end of the line for another ride.

The sun dropped toward the west and still the children wanted to ride the pony, but Sally had sandwiches and cake to serve. The mothers had begun to grow restless. They had family obligations at home, and being a Saturday, baths to supervise and Sunday clothes to put out.

Sally clapped her hands. "Children, the pony is getting tired. He needs to rest. Why don't you come indoors for sandwiches and cake?"

They would have refused, but Linc held up his hands to signal the end of riding the animal. "Our pony needs something to eat and drink, and so do you. Run along now."

Amid a flurry of disgruntled murmurs, Linc led the pony out the back gate into the McCoy yard. Reluctantly, the children trooped inside, washed up and gathered around the table. But hunger had its place, and they wolfed down sandwiches and cake.

Sally passed Robbie his gifts. He received an assortment of crayons, coloring books, storybooks and balls. Sally had chosen two metal trucks for him. Abe presented him with a Meccano set. Robbie looked at the perforated metal strips and nuts and bolts as if the toy was broken.

"It's a building set," Abe explained. "I'll show you how to use it later."

"Thanks. Thanks everyone," Robbie said. "This is the best birthday ever."

The children cheered their agreement. Sally knew a moment of sweet victory.

Shortly afterward the guests departed amid a flurry of more "thank yous." As soon as the door closed behind the last one, Robbie headed for the back door.

"Where are you going?" Abe asked.

"To help Linc with the pony."

"He's gone home. I think you better stay here."

Robbie skidded to a halt. "Aw." He seemed about ready to defy his father.

Sally leaned over and spoke softly. "The pony needs his rest."

Robbie nodded, not eager to accept the inevitable.

"Come, Robbie," Abe said. "I'll show you how to use the Meccano set."

Robbie's expression said he didn't expect to have any fun, but he and Abe were soon creating something.

Sally cleaned up the kitchen. "I'm headed for home now," she said when the last dishes were put away.

Abe glanced up. "Thank you for the party."

Robbie bounced to his feet and ran to her. He threw his arms about her and hugged hard. "Thank you for the best party ever."

Her eyes glassed over with moisture as she hugged him back. "I'm glad you had fun." She couldn't look at Abe, embarrassed by her emotions, and simply called goodbye to them all, then slipped out the back door.

Instead of heading directly home, she went out the gate toward the McCoy place. Linc had made this all possible, and she meant to thank him.

She followed the sound of his singing into the barn where he watched the pair of horses. The pony had been brushed until his coat gleamed. Big Red allowed the smaller animal to share the hay in the manger.

Linc turned at her approach. "Party over?" He lounged against the corner of the pen, completely at ease.

She envied his ability to relax even when life was rather messy for him. It made her feel she lacked something. But she couldn't think what it could be and dismissed the thought. "Everyone is gone home, and the debris is cleaned up." She stopped at his side. Close enough to feel the heat from his body, but not touching. She knew something in her connected to him in a way she had never before experienced. The intensity of the unnamed, unacknowledged emotion frightened her. It must be denied. So she kept a space between them while allowing herself to stand close enough to feel him with every twitching nerve. "It was a great party. Thank you for making it possible."

"It was fun." He uncrossed his leg and planted both feet firmly on the floor. "Are you headed home now?"

"Yes. It's been a long day."

"I'll walk you home."

It wasn't a question, so Sally didn't answer. If she were honest with herself, she would admit she welcomed his company. Only, she excused herself, because she wanted to discuss the party. Share her sense of success.

He unwound himself from the post and they headed into the bright sun of the late afternoon.

She told him about Robbie's expression of appreciation.

"You're pleased with how it turned out?"

"Yes." Abe seemed pleased, too, but she didn't say so.

Their feet created little brown clouds of dust as they walked along the dry road. There had been only a hint of rain this spring. The hopeful farmers put their carefully hoarded bit of grain in the ground, but nothing had come up. Nothing would until rain came.

"The children certainly enjoyed the pony," Linc said after a few minutes of pleasant quiet. "They seemed to have fun with the games, too."

"It was a great day all around." She lifted her head. The orphanage windows flashed the reflection of the slanting rays of the sun. She slowed her steps. Linc realized she had fallen behind and stopped, turned, his expression concerned.

"What's wrong?"

"It's not wrong. It's right." She stared at the orphanage. "That was a great party. According to Robbie and his friends, the best ever. Seems a shame not to share it with some other children."

He followed the direction of her gaze. "You mean—"

"Yes. The children at the orphanage. Wouldn't that be a great surprise for them?"

Linc chuckled softly, a sound like a gentle breeze through trees. It brought her gaze to him. His eyes were warm as the sunshine, silently admiring her. She felt heat steal up her neck and pool in her cheeks at the way he looked at her, but she couldn't pull her gaze away.

"I think they would enjoy it immensely. Who do we get permission from to do this?"

He'd fallen in with her suggestion without one word of dissent, assuming they would do it together. It was like having someone read her heart. Her insides warmed to match her cheeks. "I'll ask the matron, but she won't object. She'll be pleased as can be that the children will have this opportunity."

Linc stood at her side, shoulder to shoulder as they looked toward the orphanage. She felt his eagerness match her own. "How many children are there?"

"Twelve."

"There's a lot more room out there, so I'll borrow

more ponies and we'll make games the same as Robbie's party."

"I'll make a big cake."

"I wish I could buy them each a gift."

Sally's pleasure at the generous idea filled her heart. "I don't think they will mind not having gifts."

"But—"

How her heart grew at his concern for these children. "Maybe we could think of something simple. Something we could make." She tried to think of something, but was distracted by the studious consideration on his face.

"Something small so they could each have one." He crossed his arms and studied the problem. Suddenly he brightened and faced her. "I could make little cars and trucks for the boys."

"I could make dolls for the girls."

His expression brightened with another idea. "Could you make tiny dolls?"

"I guess so. Why?"

"If Abe will let me use the leftover scraps of lumber in the shed, I could build a dollhouse."

She beamed at him. "Perfect. Just perfect."

They moved on, brimming with ways to make the party even better than Robbie's. Her turnoff was only a few yards away. She didn't want this time to end, nor did she want her enjoyment ruined by Mother's comments. "Will you attend church tomorrow?"

"I'll be there with my grandmother if Pa is resting so we can leave."

She stopped. This was where they must part ways. If only it didn't have to be. She stifled the thought before it could take root in her brain. But her thoughts proved to be stubborn today. When she was with Linc, something inside her broke free. There were many things she wanted to tell him, hopes and dreams to share.

Linc looked down at her, his eyes full of hope and promise and— "I better get back to town and take care of Pa." He touched the brim of his hat in a goodbye salute.

Regret. She saw it as clearly as she felt it, an echo of her own heart. Despite her resolve to keep her thoughts reined in, her insides suddenly flooded with secret joy that he didn't want this to end any more than she did.

"I'll see you tomorrow, if all goes well." He stepped back but didn't turn toward town.

She realized he waited for her to take the first step that would send them on different journeys. She inched backward. "See you tomorrow."

He nodded. "Tomorrow."

A promise pouring joy into her heart.

She spun around, lest he see the evidence in her face. Only once did she glance back. He sketched a salute as he headed toward town.

Tomorrow seemed a long way off.

She didn't realize how much her expression gave away until she stepped into the house. Mother stood in the kitchen doorway, her eyes steady and observant.

"That man walked you home again."

"Yes." Guilt clawed into her heart, ruthlessly destroying her happiness.

"Does Abe know how much time you spend with that man?"

"'That man' has a name. Linc McCoy. And we were

doing nothing to give Abe concern. In fact, we were discussing—"

Mother cut her off. "You better take a good look at what you are doing. Are you willing to risk Abe's displeasure for the company of this man?"

She wouldn't even speak his name. As if it was soiled. Sally knew better. Linc was a good man. Ready to help orphans. Willing to take care of his injured father. Concerned about his grandmother. But Mother saw none of the facts, nor would she welcome the words from Sally's mouth. "It was perfectly innocent."

Mother studied her solemnly, but Sally refused to squirm under her examination. They had done nothing wrong. Forbidden thoughts and wishes didn't count unless they were acted upon, and Sally didn't intend they should be.

Mother finally relented. "Very well. Just be a little more circumspect."

Sally went to the table and picked up a sock to darn. "I don't know what you mean." And she didn't. She and Linc had done nothing wrong. And what they did was in the open for everyone to see. And judge.

How would Abe judge them if he'd walked behind them?

Her cheeks stung with heat, and she bent her head so Mother wouldn't see. If he could read her thoughts he would have cause to wonder if she would make a suitable wife, but it wasn't like she hadn't done her best to control her thoughts. In the future she must do a better job.

"Robbie said it was the best birthday party ever. All the children seemed to have fun. Abe said I did a good job. He was pleased." He'd defended Linc against sly accusations.

The tension across her shoulders eased. Abe would understand and approve of Sally offering Linc friendship and acceptance. "Abe believes we shouldn't judge people without evidence. He almost scolded Mrs. Tipple for saying things that cast suspicion on Linc's reputation."

Mother joined her at the table and took up another stocking to darn. "Abe is a good man."

"Yes, he is."

"I hope you won't forget it."

"Mother." She puffed out her cheeks. "I don't intend to forget it." But Linc was a good man, too. She felt connected to him more than Abe. But then, what did she expect? She and Linc had worked together on a project that gave them both pleasure. Once she and Abe married and they spent more time together, things between them would change. They'd find things they were both keen about, like the children. She would not allow the thought demanding to know what else they had in common.

Abe was a good man with a solid reputation. He could give her what she needed. The safety and security she'd lost when her father died. She recognized a flaw in her reasoning, but would not examine what it was or what it meant.

Linc strode back to town. He found a small stone and kicked it ahead of him for several steps until it rolled into the ditch.

He'd almost asked her if he might accompany her to church. But he'd bitten back the request. She couldn't sit with him. She was more than half promised to Abe. They could only share the common goal of giving the orphanage children a special day. A smile curved his lips and eased through his insides. They had to build games, make toys. He would cut out the trucks and cars and small wooden dolls to fit in a dollhouse. She'd paint them and dress the dolls. Of necessity, they must work together to coordinate this party.

The idea settled into his thoughts like sweet tea.

The next morning Pa took his pain medication and slept. He seemed more comfortable these past few days. Linc wanted to believe it meant he was healing inside and would recover, even though the doctor offered no such hope.

He and his grandmother went to church together. Grandmama sat fifth row back on the right side, just as she had when he'd accompanied her six years ago. He sat beside her and glanced around.

Heads turned his way. Some people nodded a greeting. Just as many jerked away or gave him a hard warning stare as if to say, "We're watching you. You don't need to think you'll get away with anything this time." Grandmama, as aware as he of the murmur of disapproval rippling through the crowd, took his hand and squeezed it.

"God sees the heart," she murmured.

It should be enough. It had to be. But he felt like he'd been branded on the forehead with the giant letter *G*, for guilty. Though he'd done nothing. Nor had his father and brother. Seems not everyone was ready to believe his innocence.

Abe came in with Carol and Robbie, scrubbed and in

their best. They sat two rows from the front on the left, allowing Linc a good view of them. Abe looked neither to the right nor the left. He faced ahead and his children did likewise, though Robbie squirmed until Abe quieted him with a hand on his shoulder.

Abe had given Linc a job despite the rumbles of disapproval from the sainted men and women of the church. Linc owed him for the welcome he'd offered. He was a good man. The sort who could give Sally the things she needed. Things unavailable to a man who carried an undeserved but unrelenting bad reputation.

He shifted his gaze to the cross carved into the front of the pulpit. God accepted him. God knew his heart. But a part of him longed for more. Acceptance. Not by those squirming in the pews around him. But acceptance that made him able to think of marriage, a home and a family.

He'd never find it here with the cloud hanging over his family name. Things were different to the west in the ranching country. As soon as his pa was well, he'd return to that area. This time he'd find a place of his own, and a sweet woman to court.

The idea didn't ease his mind. In fact, it sat cold and lonely in his thoughts.

Sally wasn't in the church. He didn't have to turn around to know. The most obvious clue was that she didn't sit at Abe's side. But even without that information, he knew because of the emptiness he felt.

Suddenly the emptiness flooded with light. He smiled and glanced over his shoulder. She came down the aisle behind him and sat with an older woman, one row back and across from where he sat with Grandmama. He could almost reach out and touch her. He settled for a smile and nod of greeting.

The older woman's look was less than welcoming. It must be Sally's mother. Perhaps his glance had been more revealing than he meant. He quickly faced forward again. He gaze fell on Abe. Linc sat up straighter. Why hadn't Sally and Abe sat together? His spine softened.

They probably didn't think it appropriate until they made a formal announcement.

But if he'd been in Abe's shoes, he would have no regard for what people might say or think or how they would judge. He would sit proudly by her side, cherishing each moment of her company.

He wouldn't care about others. The truth of what that meant ached through him. More proof of how Abe was the perfect man for Sally.

And Linc McCoy didn't belong in the same league.

Thankfully the pastor rose and opened the service before Linc felt sorrier for himself.

The text for the sermon was Jeremiah chapter thirty-two, verse seventeen. The pastor read it in a strong deep voice. "'Ah, Lord God! Behold thou hast made the Heaven and the earth by thy great power and stretched out arm, and there is nothing too hard for thee.'" The scripture verse and the pastor's wise words were exactly what Linc needed for the day. For the week. Perhaps for many weeks and months and years. Whatever he must do, God would provide the strength he needed.

When the service ended, he took his time exiting the pew. Perhaps by delaying, he could avoid Sally and especially her mother's demanding look. He offered his arm to his grandmother and guided her down the aisle.

Sally and her mother were gone, but his chest refused to relax and allow him to breathe easy.

Many people greeted Grandmama. Some included him. Others avoided them. Linc clamped his teeth tight at how obvious they were. Grandmama would be hurt by their behavior. He wanted to rush her home, pack his pa across a horse and ride away rather than see his grandmother treated so poorly. But of course, escape wasn't possible. Not as long as Pa was mending. Or dying. He hated to admit the latter.

They stepped into the sunshine. The pastor waited at the door to shake their hands. At least he didn't shun them.

Linc's intention was to leave as fast as he could. Get back to his grandmother's home and his pa—his only reason for being here.

But Sally stood in the yard, surrounded by a knot of people. They all watched him. Were they waiting for him? He hesitated. Were they about to run him out of town?

Well, they could try, but he didn't intend to go anywhere until he was good and ready.

He descended the steps, Grandmama at his side.

Sally waited for them to draw near then called him. "Linc, come and meet my sister and her husband. And Mother." She introduced them. "Mother, Judd and Madge." One by one they greeted him. "I spoke to Matron about our idea of a party. She loves it."

"It's a wonderful gesture on your part," Judd said. "I understand you want to make some little toys. I have extra lumber you can use, and my barn is available if you need a place to work."

Linc allowed himself the briefest glance at Sally. Her eyes glowed with eagerness. Was it because her family supported their idea? Or was she anticipating time together, as was he? Aware of Mrs. Morgan's watchful eye, he kept his expression as bland as he could. "That sounds like a great idea. When can I have a look?"

"No time like the present," Judd said.

"Why don't you join us for lunch?" Madge added.

Linc tried to fathom if they meant Sally, too. Did they mean to encourage his wayward thoughts? "I have to take care of my pa, but perhaps later this afternoon if that's convenient?"

"That would be great. We'll see you later then." Judd and Madge moved on.

That left him and Grandmama alone with Sally and Mrs. Morgan.

Thankfully, Grandmama took Mrs. Morgan's arm. "Shall we visit the cemetery?" Grandpa was buried there. 'Peared Mr. Morgan was, as well.

Mrs. Morgan's glance at her daughter was unmistakably warning.

Linc waited until the two older women moved away before he spoke. "Does your mother disapprove of me?"

Pink stained Sally's cheeks, and she shifted so he couldn't see her expression. "She worries."

About what? But he couldn't voice the question. Didn't want the answer because she no doubt worried that Linc's reputation—the reputation hung on him by his last name—would somehow dirty her daughter. "No need. Assure her we are only concerned with giving the orphanage kids a fun party." He hoped Sally believed him.

He certainly didn't. In fact, it was time he analyzed his feelings. He'd like to ask Sally about hers as well, but wondered if the time for that would ever come.

Chapter Ten

Linc spent two hours with Pa and then headed for the farm where Judd and Madge lived. He was familiar with the Cotton farm and knew it was close to the Morgan place. When he reached the driveway, he paused to look toward Sally's house. Would she come over? She hadn't said anything after church. Would she realize they needed to discuss plans for the toys? But he understood why she might stay away. He was a McCoy, and even if he'd been someone else, she made her intentions clear—to marry Abe Finley and enjoy the sort of life he could promise.

Sighing reluctant acceptance, he reined Big Red toward the house.

Judd stepped out as he approached the house. "You like to ride?" He silently admired Linc's horse.

"Prefer it to a motor vehicle." He saw the shiny car by the house. "No criticism meant."

"None taken. I like a good mount, as well. Trouble is it's hard to find decent feed. Hard to pay for gas, too. So mostly we walk, unless we've got a distance to go. Swing down. There's some sprouts of grass over there your horse can nibble at." He waved toward the corner of the yard.

Linc dismounted in the indicated spot and let the reins dangle to the ground. Red would graze contentedly until Linc called.

Judd followed him. "It's really a fine idea to help the orphanage out this way, you know. Anything I can do?"

"You've offered your barn and the needed wood."

"I'd like to do more if it's possible."

Linc grinned. "You want to lead a little pony around?"

Judd grimaced. "A spoiled pony?"

"Yup." His smile widened at the look on Judd's face. "They don't bite…often."

"Thanks for the reassurance. Sure, I'll help."

"Great. I thought of getting at least four ponies, maybe more. The man I know has a dozen, but we won't need that many. However, I need someone to lead each pony so I guess the number I get depends on the amount of help I get."

"Madge would help."

Linc swallowed back a protest. He'd thought of men to do the job.

Judd read his thoughts. "Don't underestimate Madge. She's pretty strong." He chuckled. "And please don't hint that you don't think she could do the job because she isn't a man. I would have to spend the next five years listening to her grouse about it."

"My lips are sealed." Linc raised a hand, as if vowing in a court of law. "You're sure she'd do it?"

"Ask her yourself." They headed toward the house— a sturdy home built to last. The barn was a solid structure, too. He remembered when the former owners, the Cottons, had built it. Although now weathered from the elements, with the paint sanded away by the continual battering of the dusty air, the place was full of promise and possibility.

He turned his gaze from studying the surroundings to the house and almost stumbled. Sally stood beside Madge, her expression a little guarded, a little wary and—he let himself believe—a touch hopeful. He swallowed hard, but it did nothing to push away the lump forming in his throat. The sun peeked around the corner of the house and highlighted her features. She was beautiful. She was lovely.

And she was spoken for.

He tried again to swallow back the thickness, and again failed.

"Sally came for dinner. She thought she should stay and help you pick out pieces of wood for the dolls. She said something about a dollhouse, too." Judd rambled on about the wood he had and suggestions as to what they should use.

Linc heard his voice, but his words were lost in the tangle of his thoughts. He hoped she'd be here but hadn't expected it. Her presence caught him off guard. He fought for control. Sanity. Reason. They were both here for only one reason—build toys for the orphanage. Nothing more. Nothing at all. Though he regretted it with an ache that yawned past the horizon and out of sight.

Slowly his thoughts righted themselves. By the time they were close enough to speak, he hoped he could do so without revealing any of his confusion.

Judd pulled Madge to his side. "Linc needs people to lead the ponies around for the party. You want to help, Madge?"

"I'd love to."

"Thanks," Linc said. His voice sounded calm and steady. "The more help we have, the more ponies I can bring."

"I could take care of a pony, too," Sally offered.

Linc hesitated. "Someone needs to supervise the games and keep the children in order. Like you did at Robbie's party." Mentioning the boy—Abe's son—was a needed reminder to himself of where Sally belonged and where Linc fit into this scheme—the provider of ponies, the builder of toys. His mind said it was okay.

Too bad his heart didn't believe it.

"Let's have a look in the barn." Judd pulled Madge's arm through his and smiled down at her as he led them away.

Linc waited for Sally and fell in at her side, keeping a discreet and safe six inches between them.

The barn smelled of sweet hay, musky mushroom, dank animal droppings—the scent of a barn used often for the purpose intended.

Judd directed them toward the far corner and a neat stack of lumber. "The previous owners left it. Most of it is too small to be of use, but will be suitable for toys." He shoved a square tub toward Linc. "You should find something in here for the dolls and cars." He pushed aside some other pieces. "Give me a hand here."

Linc sprang forward and helped lift out some larger pieces.

"These will be great for the dollhouse."

They leaned the pieces against the opposite wall, and he stepped back to study the wood. Sally edged forward at the same time, and they bumped into each other.

He jerked forward, almost planting a foot in the tub of wood and making a spectacle of himself. He caught his balance, ignored the pain in his shin from his encounter with the metal tub and crossed his arms over his chest, hoping to signify to everyone he was completely in charge of both his body and his emotions.

Sally seemed not to notice and bent to sort through the pieces of wood.

He shuffled back, but the wall crowded him. Judd and Madge blocked the alleyway. The air in the corner was hot, depleted of oxygen, and he began to sweat.

Sally pulled out several pieces of wood, lined them up on the ground and sat back on her heels to study them. "Why don't we make them in different sizes, just like the children? Let's make a mother and father, too."

Madge knelt beside her. "Sally, you always have the best ideas."

Judd joined the girls. Linc stayed apart, arms still across his chest.

Sally glanced up at him. "What do you think, Linc?"

He shifted his gaze to the pieces of wood. He folded his tight knees and crouched beside Sally, the only place there was room. He tried to keep his distance but she reached into the tub, her elbow brushing his arm. His thoughts stalled. He couldn't breathe. It was much too hot and closed in. But when he told himself to get up and leave, his muscles refused to move.

Sally lined up the assorted pieces before him, each

time her arm brushing his. "What do you think? Can we make a family of dolls from this?"

The words zinged through his mind, demanding an answer. He fished around until he could solidify a thought. "No reason why not."

"Feel free to work here," Judd said. "It'll save you hauling stuff back and forth."

They spent several minutes examining wood, choosing some for cars and trucks, some more for the dollhouse. Everyone contributed suggestions. They moved away from the lumber and moseyed toward the door, giving Linc breathing space.

"I'm going to make tea. Come along when you want a break." Madge headed for the house.

"I'll help." Judd jogged after her.

Sally remained, leaning against one side of the door, smiling as she studied the horizon. "This is going to be so much fun."

Linc pressed his shoulder to the opposite side of the doorway, the warm wood scratching through his shirt. He would have a mark on his skin, but he welcomed the pressure and the pain. Did she mean fun to work with him? Or simply fun to make toys for the children? The latter, of course. He knew that was it, but he could not persuade his mind to think along the same lines.

She shifted, favored him with a questioning look that sucked the air from his lungs. "You're certain your grandmother won't mind us using her paint?"

He'd offered to bring half-used cans from Grandmama's basement. "I'm sure." His voice grated. He cleared his throat and tried again. "It's leftover stuff.

Likely most of it will be useless, but we'll find enough to paint the toys."

Her eyes gleamed with what he took for excitement. "Are you looking forward to doing this?"

"Like you said, it's going to be fun." He didn't mean only because they were doing something for the kids. To stall his thoughts before they went any further, he casually mentioned something that had been forming in his mind over the past hour or two. "I think I'll tear down Grandmama's old corrals. She's been after me to do so. With half a dozen ponies to take care of, I need something better. I figure I can salvage enough from the old ones to build something smaller and more solid." He knew he rambled. But talk was his biggest defense. Talk and distance, which right now he didn't seem capable of finding.

"How's your pa?"

"The same. Sometimes I think he's improving. Doc says not to get my hopes up."

"I'm sorry." She touched his forearm with her long, slender fingers. How did she remain so cool when his skin fairly beaded with sweat?

"Is there anything I can do to help?"

Her question, her concern sliced through his defenses, laid his heart open and vulnerable. For one sweet flicker of time he let himself think of taking comfort in her arms, pressing her head against his neck, leaning his chin against her hair.

It could not be, and he fought for reason. Slowly it returned, full of acid regret that Abe could offer her the things she wanted and he, Linc McCoy, could not. "Not much anyone can do, but thanks for offering."

She withdrew her hand, leaving him suddenly cold, his sweat icy on his skin.

"I was surprised you didn't sit with Abe at church."

Her shoulders twitched. When she faced him, her eyes had lost their happy sparkle. He had effectively reminded her of who they were and what the future held, even as she had by asking him about Pa, reminding him of who he was. "Why?"

"Isn't that where you belong?"

She lowered her gaze. "Not yet."

Did he detect regret? He half reached for her, wanting to tip her chin up so he could see her eyes, gauge her emotions.

"Come on, you two. Tea is ready and waiting." Judd's invitation jerked them both toward the house.

Linc was grateful Judd called before he did or said anything foolish. At the same time, he wondered why the man couldn't have waited a few more minutes.

Sally hugged her arms about her and smiled up into the crystal clear sky as she walked across the field the next evening. It was still full daylight out, and she was grateful for a few more hours of sunlight.

She likely should be scowling at the empty sky. The country desperately needed rain. But she couldn't bring herself to worry about drought and hardship at the moment.

The sun poured gold into the colorless grass left over from winter. The strong light gave the budding trees a green shimmer. Spring filled the world with hope and joy. And in no place more so than her heart.

She and Linc had agreed to meet after supper and

work for a few hours on toys, and Sally skipped toward Madge and Judd's place, rejoicing in the beauty of the season and all the good things in her life. Now she was about to share them with the children at the orphanage.

Her steps slowed, and she faced her thoughts honestly.

It wasn't the children filling her mind with such anticipation, but rather, the idea of an hour or two with Linc.

She stopped walking and forced her emotions under control. This was about a party for the orphans. She and Linc only shared the task of preparing for it.

Her thoughts firmly reined in, she resumed her journey, but by the time she reached the boundary of Madge's yard, her joy and her spritely step matched the sun for intensity as she headed directly for the barn.

The interior was dim and still, heat wafting from the corners.

"Hi, there," Linc called from the back. "Glad to see you made it."

"Was it ever in question?"

He didn't answer, and she made her way to the stack of lumber. He sat back on his heels watching her, his expression a combination of welcome and wariness. As if he wondered if she would suddenly realize how dangerous it was for her to agree to work with him, and might change her mind.

She wished she could erase his doubts. He was a good man and he needed to believe it, even if no one else did.

She did. But she dare not tell him. "I said I'd come and here I am." It was all she could offer.

"Great." He jumped to his feet. "Let's take this lot outside." He indicated the pieces of wood she had lined up yesterday. "I'll cut out the shapes."

"I'll sand them. Did you bring paint?"

He pointed toward an odd assortment of cans, and she squatted to examine them. From the drips on the dusty cans she saw there were several colors—green, black, pink and mauve.

"This should do nicely."

"Yep. I thought I would paint the cars and trucks that very girly pink."

His dry tone drew her eyes to his face. Slowly she pushed to her feet and grinned at his mock sorrow. Found she couldn't escape his dark eyes, didn't want to as the look went on and on. With a guilty jolt she realized she had lost all sense of time, space and decency, and lowered her gaze. Had she imagined the moment? She stole another look. No. She had not. His eyes brimmed with a warmth she couldn't deny.

Any more than she could acknowledge.

She cast about for something to otherwise occupy her thoughts, and spied the pieces of wood laid out. "You want them outside?"

He stepped back. "It will be less stifling outside, don't you think?"

"Certainly." Though it was her thoughts crowding her lungs, not the stale hot air of the barn interior. But more space would surely help her keep her wayward mind under control, and she scooped up a handful of pieces and went out to a grassy spot.

Linc followed, carrying more wood and a jigsaw. He studied the selection of wood, chose a piece and started to cut. Within a few minutes, he had fashioned the shape of a little girl. He handed it to Sally along with a sanding block. She settled on the ground and began work as Linc sawed another shape.

He paused to consider his progress. "I feel sorry for those kids in the orphanage. It's bad enough losing one parent when you're young. But to lose both and not have any family to take you in—" He ended on a shrug.

She shuddered. "I know. I can't imagine not having family or a home. Though some do have family, but for one reason or another they can't take in another child or two. One of the girls has an older brother who works on a nearby farm, but he isn't old enough to make a home for them. Another has an old uncle." She chuckled as she thought of the man.

Linc watched her, a bemused expression on his face. "The authorities wouldn't let her live with him?"

She laughed again. "I don't think most of them would care, but he's a recluse. I don't suppose he would welcome a little girl." She held Linc's steady gaze, her thoughts traveling along the road on their own journey while she stayed caught in the warmth and interest in his eyes. "Though now that I think about it, little Janie might be the best thing that could happen to her uncle. She's a spirited young thing. I think she might force him out of his shell."

"Maybe it could be arranged."

"Maybe. But no one seems interested in confronting the recluse. Live and let live."

"Sometimes a person has to be willing to change things."

She tried to blink. Tried to tear her gaze from his.

Tried and failed. It felt like he meant something more than Janie and her uncle.

He continued to speak softly. "Someone needs to tell this uncle that a little girl would benefit by having a real home. If he would welcome her, two people would benefit. Him and Janie."

She continued to stare, seeing a man who wanted things to work out in a kindly fashion. Who cared about others. Perhaps identified with their situation because of the way his life had turned out—judged without cause, shut out unfairly.

"'Course, it takes courage to confront such matters. To admit that accepting things the way they are, without examining other options, is to miss out on something better." He blinked. A shutter seemed to close over the view she'd had of his heart, and he resumed work on the piece of wood.

She couldn't move. Couldn't remember what she'd been about to say. Couldn't even think what she should be doing. She shifted, saw the doll shape in her hands and resumed smoothing the edges. He meant something besides the little girl at the orphanage and all the children there. She suspected he meant something far closer to home, but she couldn't…wouldn't let herself think he meant her…them.

She worked in silence, but between them hung a constraint like a wooden wall. She didn't like it and attacked it with words. "My sisters and I go to the orphanage on occasion. Sometimes we take cookies up to them. Or help with the garden. We play music for them or read to them. But this will be the first party we've done. It should be lots of fun. Not only for them but us, too." She couldn't seem to stem the rush of words. They poured from her mouth like a raging river. "I feel sorry for the children without parents, but they are a pretty happy lot and every time I visit I realize a person chooses how they will face life. Whether they'll wallow in misery or enjoy the good things available to them." The torrent stopped as fast as it started, and she bit her bottom lip. What had possessed her to rattle away like that?

Only one thing. Linc's suggestion that courage was required to change things.

"It takes courage to accept things," she murmured.

"True." But he sounded sad at the thought.

She had nothing more to say on the subject, and they worked in blessed silence for a few minutes.

Linc held out another shape, this one of a boy. "What do you think?"

She studied it. It resembled a figure from a chain of paper cutouts. "With a face and clothes painted on, it will do nicely. Will it stand up?"

"I hope so." He perched it on a slab of wood, and it balanced rather crookedly. He laughed. "Looks like he's about to fall over."

"Or being a boy, maybe he's running after something."

He slanted his attention toward her. "I like your version better." His gaze was open to her.

Again she felt as if he opened his heart and soul and invited her to explore. *My, but aren't I getting fanciful? Wouldn't Madge laugh at my silliness?* She forced her attention back to her task.

And he to his. "I'll check the level more carefully on the rest of these."

The air shimmered between them, full of things she couldn't explain. They caught at bits of her heart, pulling them taut as violin strings attached from some invisible source. All it required to start a melody was someone to caress the strings.

Why did the idea fill her with both dread and excitement?

Linc held out another doll figure and laughed. "I'm trying to think what my cowboy friends back at the ranch would say if they could see me now."

She thought of several things they should say about him. Like he was thoughtful, caring, more concerned with what a child needed than what an acquaintance might say. Her lungs spasmed as she realized he had learned through harsh experience not to let what others said or thought change who he was. He could easily have become rebellious, angry. Instead, he grew patient, kind and perhaps even tolerant. "What would they say?"

He took off his hat and ran a hand through his hair, unaware he set the golden curls into a frenzied dance and left bits of sawdust behind.

"Most of them would jeer, but they'd also grab a saw and help me."

"Sounds like they're a good bunch." She stared at the flecks in his hair.

He concentrated on sawing another shape. "Don't misunderstand me. Some are scoundrels of the worst sort. Others are softies." He favored her with a wide grin. "Though they'd likely threaten to beat me into submission if they heard me say so."

FREE Merchandise is 'in the Cards' for you!

Dear Reader,

We're giving away FREE MERCHANDISE!

Seriously, we'd like to reward you for reading this novel by giving you **FREE MERCHANDISE** worth over $20. And no purchase is necessary!

You see the Jack of Hearts sticker above? Paste that sticker in the box on the Free Merchandise Voucher inside. Return the Voucher promptly...and we'll send you valuable Free Merchandise!

Thanks again for reading one of our novels—and enjoy your Free Merchandise with our compliments!

Pam Powers

Pam Powers

P.S. Look inside to see what Free Merchandise is **"in the cards"** for you!

The Reader Service - Here's how it works:

Accepting your 2 free books and 2 free mystery gifts (gifts valued at approximately $10.00) places you under no obligation to buy anything. You may keep the books and gifts and return the shipping statement marked "cancel." If you do not cancel, about a month later we'll send you 4 additional books and bill you just $4.49 each in the U.S. or $4.99 each in Canada. That's a savings of at least 22% off the cover price. It's quite a bargain! Shipping and handling is just 50¢ per book in the U.S. and 75¢ per book in Canada.* You may cancel at any time, but if you choose to continue, every month we'll send you 4 more books, which you may either purchase at the discount price or return to us and cancel your subscription.
*Terms and prices subject to change without notice. Prices do not include applicable taxes. Sales tax applicable in N.Y. Canadian residents will be charged applicable taxes. Offer not valid in Quebec. All orders subject to credit approval. Books received may not be as shown. Credit or debit balances in a customer's account(s) may be offset by any other outstanding balance owed by or to the customer. Please allow 4 to 6 weeks for delivery. Offer available while quantities last.

▲ If offer card is missing write to: The Reader Service, P.O. Box 1867, Buffalo, NY 14240-1867 or visit www.ReaderService.com ▲

BUSINESS REPLY MAIL
FIRST-CLASS MAIL   PERMIT NO. 717   BUFFALO, NY

POSTAGE WILL BE PAID BY ADDRESSEE

THE READER SERVICE
PO BOX 1867
BUFFALO NY 14240-9952

NO POSTAGE
NECESSARY
IF MAILED
IN THE
UNITED STATES

Their gazes connected and clinched. She felt the sun on her shoulder, saw the way it slanted through his eyes, making it impossible for her to escape.

"You have a smudge on your cheek." He brushed it away with a fingertip, sending little sparks through her veins to pool into a sunlit puddle in the bottom of her heart.

She swallowed hard, tried to control her heartbeat, which threatened to hit runaway speed. "You have sawdust in your hair." Not giving herself time to consider her actions, she leaned closer and picked the flecks from his curls, surprised at the coarse texture of his hair. She was even more surprised by the way her heart thundered against her rib cage.

He caught her wrist and lowered her hand, resting it against his arm.

"Sally."

Her name sounded so sweet and inviting on his lips that she was caught in a web of wanting, yearning, wishing, hoping—foolish impossible thoughts all tangled into one long ache.

"Sally." His voice deepened, and he searched her gaze.

Linc held her hand against his arm. It was so small. The touch of her fingers on his head had started a stampede of emotions he feared would get out of control if she continued. He still couldn't suck in air enough to relieve the pounding of his pulse.

Yes, he knew she had plans to marry Abe. Yes, he knew her mother didn't approve of him. Why, if she knew how he felt about her precious, sweet daughter at this moment, she'd likely run him out of town on a rail.

He did not want Sally to marry Abe.

He fought for the return of reason. He could not offer her the things she wanted. Not here. Not with the judgment of local residents hanging over his head like a conviction. Maybe some other place....

He allowed himself to stroke the back of her hand. To explore the tender flesh of each fingertip before he released her and took up the saw again. "Sally." Her name tripped over his tongue like honey fresh from the comb. "Have you ever considered living anywhere but here?"

She jerked as if shocked at his words. "Never. My family is here. My home is here."

He nodded, slowly released her hand and returned to the task of sawing human shapes from scraps of wood. Her security was here. Her memories, too. Leaving and forging a life to the west obviously wasn't an option.

He paused and considered slapping himself across the side of the head. As if she would consider going anywhere with him. He had nothing to offer her.

But his heart.

Not enough.

He forced his thoughts back to creating toys for the children. Soon he had a row of little wooden boys and girls and two larger figures to represent a mother and father. He bolted to his feet. "I think I better start on the dollhouse."

He dragged out large pieces of wood, and a little later had a shell constructed. While he worked, Sally watched and continued to sand the little figures.

He stood back to study the house. "Now what?"

Sally stood beside him. "Rooms, I suppose. Maybe a window or two. Right here."

She reached for the spot at the same time as Linc, and their arms brushed.

Such a jolt ran up his nerves, she might as well have plugged him into a light socket. But he didn't jerk back. It was like their skin had been melded together by the heat. She turned her face to him, her eyes wide with shocked awareness.

He held his breath, wondering if she would acknowledge the emotions sparking in the air between them.

It seemed she had forgotten to breathe.

"Sally," he whispered.

Pink stained her cheeks. She blinked. Moved away. Turned her attention back to the dollhouse. "We need a kitchen, a front room, some bedrooms." She rattled on and on about what the dollhouse needed.

He jammed his hands into his pockets. Too bad she wouldn't admit what she needed.

Trouble was, she had, but he didn't like it because she didn't need him.

For half a minute he considered abandoning this project in order to avoid her. But he knew he wouldn't. Knew he would allow himself to savor every moment they shared.

Above all, he wanted to avoid thinking of the inevitability of it coming to an end. But it would, unless he did something. He jerked his hands from his pockets and turned to face Sally, grasping her shoulders in his palms, feeling her slenderness and wanting to pull her into his arms and protect her from every unhappiness.

"Sally, I like being your friend. It means a lot to me."
He wasn't saying what he felt and tried again. "But is it
possible for us to be more?"

Her eyes flashed sunshine, and her lips parted.

He'd surprised her—that was plain. He wanted to say
how much he cared, but he was afraid to lose what they
had. If she refused even friendship…he couldn't begin
to think how he'd deal with it.

She ducked her head, hiding her expression. When
she lifted her face again, he dropped his hands and
stepped back. Even before she spoke, he knew her
answer. "I like being your friend, too." Her words were
soft, pleading.

He nodded, understanding what she didn't say. It was
all she could offer.

Because he did not have the stability, the reputation,
the security Abe had to offer, and she couldn't accept
anything else.

"Friends it is." At the uncertainty in her eyes, he
forced a gentle smile to his lips. "Friends who trust God
to care for them." Would she hear his words as a challenge to trust her future to the Good Lord rather than
Abe? *Please God, help her see this truth.*

Until she did, Linc would never have the place in her
heart he ached for.

Chapter Eleven

Sally pretended she didn't know what Linc had suggested—something more than friendship—and succeeded in ignoring it until bedtime as she opened her Bible and prepared to read a chapter.

Overwhelming emotions tore at her heart, making it impossible to think.

Oh, Father. I miss you still. I suppose I always will.

She looked at the passage she was about to read, but the words blurred before her and she simply stared at the page, trying to sort out what she felt. Sorrow and sadness at her father's absence. Confusion over her feelings for Linc.

Yes, she had feelings for him. As a friend?

Her conscience begged her to be honest. Did she care for him more than she should? As more than a friend?

She groaned. How could she? She wasn't fickle, working for one man's approval while enjoying offers from another man. Nor was she one to run after romance and adventure. It was too risky. And that's what Linc signified. Not stability and security. Caring about him beyond friendship made her quiver with fear, made her want to run to the little corner in the loft and build walls of hay about her.

Oh, God, help me know the right way.

Blinking away the sting of tears, she focused on the Bible in her lap. The pages fluttered in a breeze coming through the window and stopped at a place where she hadn't planned to read. The Psalms. She chose chapter sixty-eight, and at verse six read, "God setteth the solitary in families." She need not read further. God had directed an answer to her confusion. Families for the solitary. This was a sign for her. She wasn't totally alone, though she sometimes felt it. She belonged in a family, and Abe could offer her that.

Closing the Bible, she stared through the window. In the darkness a light flickered at Madge and Judd's, bringing back a rush of memories of Linc and their time together. He was a good man, even though so few were prepared to believe it.

What he offered was frightening. Like flying. People weren't made for flight. Flying was for the birds.

With determination she stuffed back every remnant of confusion. She would not falter in doing what was right for her.

The next morning she watched for Linc, wondering if he would be different after asking for more than friendship. He crossed the yard toward the barn, glanced at the house and saw her. A smile wreathed his face, and he waved.

She waved back, a weight of worry dropping from her heart. He seemed happy enough to continue being friends. She returned to her work. A few hours later, she realized she sang under her breath…one of the songs Linc so often belted out, as if his heart couldn't contain his joy.

It wasn't until Carol came home from school and they gathered for coffee that Sally and Linc had a chance to talk, though with the children present they could not speak of anything personal. She couldn't say if she was more relieved or disappointed that it was so as she handed him coffee and offered cookies from a lard pail. Her heart twisted with apprehension. Would he somehow punish her for her decision?

He accepted the coffee, chose three cookies then looked up at her and smiled. "Thanks. I've been looking forward to this all afternoon."

Dare she think he meant more than cookies and coffee? Her smile curved her lips and filled her heart as she sat beside Carol and enjoyed a cookie.

But by evening, when it was time to go to Madge and Judd's to work on toys, her doubts returned. Would he still be happy to see her?

He saw her crossing the field. "Hi, Sally." He waved and jogged out to meet her.

Her heart took flight at the way his smile welcomed her. She should have known he wouldn't let her decision affect their friendship.

"Grandmama found some bits of wallpaper she said we might like to use for the dollhouse. What do you think?" He held out a bundle of rolled paper.

She unrolled it to see several different patterns. "This is perfect. Look, I can put this in the living room." She indicated a swatch with big red cabbage roses. "This will be lovely in a bedroom." The piece had tiny pink medallions on a pale green background. "Maybe there's something for a boys' room." She flipped the pieces until she discovered a green foiled pattern. "What do you think of this?" She looked at Linc for his opinion.

His eyes were warm as fresh coffee. "I like it." His gaze did not drop to the piece of wallpaper she meant, but held hers in an endless look that seemed to hold her close.

She could not tear her gaze away. Perhaps because she did not try, though it entered her mind she should do so.

Linc let out a deep sigh and turned away, leaving her dizzy. With relief, she explained to herself. Though it felt a lot more like disappointment.

"I got here early and cut out trucks and cars." Together they walked to the hillside by the barn, where Linc had laid out the toys under construction.

They settled down to work. Sally, content to be here, sharing this project, thought Linc seemed equally at ease.

"Look." He drew her attention to Madge's cat, stalking a magpie. "He doesn't stand a chance at catching that bird."

"Macat is pretty determined. The bird harasses her constantly. She can't cross the yard without the bird diving at her."

"So it's revenge she wants?" Linc parked himself beside Sally to watch the cat.

With a great deal of effort, Sally kept her emotions under control. No reason she should be so aware of how close he sat or how his arm brushed hers.

Macat inched forward. The magpie danced away, pulling a bit of meat with her.

"The bird has stolen her dinner. Poor Macat." Why did her tongue feel so thick? Was it something she ate? She knew it wasn't.

Macat pressed to the ground and didn't move, but her gaze never left the bird who squawked as it pulled at the meat. Sally was about to give up waiting to see what would happen when Macat sprang. She leaped into the air even before the bird took flight and managed to catch the bird in her claws. But the magpie wasn't about to be caught, and flapped his wings in Macat's face. With a yowl of protest, Macat released the bird. The magpie flew to a nearby branch and scolded loudly as Macat stalked off.

Linc roared with laughter. "Poor bird," he managed to say.

"Poor Macat. She almost had him. Now the bird will make her life even more miserable."

He patted her shoulder. "The bird has the advantage. He can fly."

Fly. The word reminded her of her thoughts of last night. "Being able to fly is good." One foot seemed poised to leave the ground.

He patted her shoulder again. "For the most part, I prefer to have my feet solidly on the ground."

"Me, too." She pulled her thoughts back from the edge.

Four more delightful evenings Sally worked at Linc's side. The dollhouse was coming together well, with the dolls and trucks progressing nicely.

Her conscience was at ease about spending time with

him. She was doing good work, and they had plenty of supervision, though Judd and Madge only wandered out to offer a few words then disappeared to tend to their own concerns. Most of all, she had made it clear she wanted only friendship from him, and he seemed content with her decision.

But more and more, the word friendship sounded and felt empty.

Not that she could contemplate the idea of losing his friendship. Seeing him, working with him and talking to him strengthened her for each day's work. The idea didn't seem quite right, but she didn't bother to examine it more closely. Doing so made her uneasy. Her plan to marry Abe was sound. He offered what she needed. Unbidden, not really welcome, Linc's words flashed through her mind. *Friends who trust God to take care of them.*

What did he mean? Did he refer to his own situation?

She reached the door to her home. Tonight, as every night, Mother waited for Sally as she returned from Madge's, but this time her displeasure could not be ignored. "If you weren't with Madge and Judd I would forbid this." When Sally started to protest she was doing the work for the children, Mother raised a hand to stop her. "I know you think it's only a good deed, but Sally, you need to bear in mind the dangers of spending so much time with Lincoln McCoy."

"Dangers? Do you think he would harm me?"

Mother grew very serious and insisted Sally sit down. "He could very well harm your reputation. Abe is a church leader. He is an upright man. A good man, but don't presume to take advantage of his good nature. I doubt he would overlook indiscretion on the part of the woman he is considering for his wife and the mother of his children."

Sally drew up tall and straight. "I assure you I am not being indiscreet, nor do I intend to be." She'd made it clear to Linc they could only be friends. What more could she do?

Mother sighed deeply. "I'm sure you are sincere, but sometimes, my dear, your emotions cloud your judgment."

Guilt stung her cheeks. Yes, her thoughts were not as innocent as they should be. But what could she do? She couldn't back out of this commitment to the orphans. But the truth was, she couldn't imagine walking away from what she and Linc were doing. Silently she informed her brain that what they were doing was planning a party for the children.

She would guard her thoughts and actions. She had tried her best to do so.

From now on she would strive even harder.

Every day Sally continued to work at Abe's house, caring for his children and his home and doing her best to live up to his expectations. And her own.

The afternoon after Mother had spoken to her, while she finished cleaning the kitchen she watched out the window as Robbie played in the yard. He spent less time at his fort since the birthday party, when he'd become the owner of a horse made from a wooden sawhorse with a blanket pad for a saddle and the make-believe cow he tried constantly to rope. Linc had given the boy a few lessons on roping, and Robbie could almost get a loop over the wooden cow head.

She laughed as he gave up swinging the lariat and sauntered over to drop the loop over the cow, and then backed away holding the rope and acting as proud as if he'd successfully lassoed it.

The children at the orphanage would enjoy the games and pony rides as much as Robbie. When the party was over, the children would be the proud owners of the same games Robbie now enjoyed, plus a fairly large dollhouse, various-size wooden dolls and enough cars and trucks for each boy to own one. She and Linc managed to spend an hour or two most evenings working on the project. The matron suggested they have the party the last weekend in May, lending a sense of urgency to get everything ready.

At the same time, Sally often found herself taking far longer to paint on a face, or smooth out the edges of a piece of wood than it required. The hours spent working with Linc held a special sweetness.

Perhaps Mother was right. She walked a dangerously thin line between right and wrong. However, she was determined to stay on the right side of that line. Even while allowing herself to enjoy preparations for the party.

As Sally watched Robbie play, she told herself she was doing nothing wrong. It wasn't as if Abe had asked her to marry him, even though the understanding had been clear when she started working for him. He had told Mother what he had in mind. Sally knew and had agreed in principle. In fact, she promised herself she'd prove she could pass inspection, be a good mother, run the home efficiently. She and Linc were working together on a project, one Abe approved of, one that was good for the community and one that displayed Christian virtues. After all, didn't the scriptures command them to visit the fatherless and widows in their affliction? That's exactly what they were doing. No one could fault her on that issue.

Carol would be home from school soon, and they had begun taking the after-school snack outside. From the first, Abe had instructed her to give Linc coffee, so she did.

Not that it was a hardship. It was, if she were honest, another highlight of the day. She liked the way Linc talked with the children and told them stories about ranching in the west country.

She put the cups of sweet iced tea on a tray along with a plate of cookies as Carol clattered into the house and raced upstairs to change her clothes.

Sally waited for the girl to join her, then they went outside. Linc had built a crude bench on the north side of the house, out of the blazing sun and somewhat sheltered from the wind.

Robbie saw them and dropped his lariat to run over.

"Go call Linc," Sally said.

"I'm on my way." Linc strode from the barn, his head bare, his hair frosted with dust and wood shavings. "The barn will soon be a garage."

Then he'd be done. Abe had no more jobs for him. What would he do? Would he stay? Leave? Doubtlessly it depended on his father. Was he improving as Linc hoped and prayed he might, or fulfilling the doctor's dire prediction?

She waited to ask until they lounged against the wall of the house, indolent in the heat. "How's your father?"

Linc dangled his hands between his knees, the glass of tea empty in his grasp. "He's noticeably weaker."

"Is he going to die?" Carol asked.

Linc turned the glass round and round. "I don't know. Maybe."

"You'll be an orphan if he does."

"Hadn't thought about it, but I guess so."

"Did your mama die a long time ago?" Both children seemed keenly interested in Linc's situation.

He put his glass on the bench beside him and grasped each child by a shoulder. "My mama is in Heaven. I miss her, but I know I will see her again. If I knew the same about my pa, it wouldn't be so hard."

Robbie pressed to Linc's knee. "Mama made me promise to never forget about Heaven. She said Daddy would tell me how I could go there when I was big enough. Do you think I'm big enough now?"

Linc shared a happy smile with Sally. "Indeed I do. You talk to your father tonight."

"Do you want my father to talk to your pa, too? Tell him how to be ready to go to Heaven?"

Linc looked across the yard toward the place where his father lay. "I wish that would do it."

Carol leaned her head against Linc's shoulder. "I miss my mama. Sometimes I wish I could forget her so I wouldn't miss her so much."

Linc bent his head to rest it on Carol's forehead. "You don't ever want to forget her, even though remembering sometimes makes you ache inside. After all, she gave you life. She'd want you to be okay. To enjoy your life."

Carol nodded. "I guess so." She sprang to her feet. "I'll try my best. Come on, Robbie. I'll play cowboy with you." Robbie always wanted his sister to join him, but normally she chose to play by herself.

The pair scampered away.

Sally pressed her lips together to hold back the rush of emotion. She missed her father but would never forget him. "You're so good with them."

"I suppose it's because I know how they feel. But then, so do you." He pushed to his feet. "I better get back to my task. Will you come to work on the toys tonight?"

"I'll be there." And if she intended to be an efficient homemaker, she needed to finish supper preparations.

She spared no effort in creating a particularly nice supper. She'd purchased a roast on Abe's credit. Rich aroma wafted from the oven where it cooked. Because of the heat she'd even forced herself to use the gas stove. Abe would no doubt be impressed. She mashed potatoes to creamy perfection. The succulent gravy was without a single lump. She'd resorted to tinned vegetables, but made a white sauce for the peas and added a few tiny white onions from another can. For dessert she'd made a raisin pie. Pie baking wasn't one of her best skills, but this one turned out rather well. A white cloth covered the kitchen table and the better dishes sparkled in the late summer light.

Abe stepped into the house. "It smells great in here." He looked at the table. "Is this a special occasion?"

"No." Suddenly her efforts felt like a child trying too hard to get attention. "I just wanted to do this." Did he appreciate it? Had she done a good job, or would his wife have done better?

Why did she feel like she was on trial? Probably because she knew she was. He'd said to Mother, "If Sally proves to be adequate…" Sally had listened shamelessly beyond the door as the two of them talked. Mother had said, "She will be more than adequate." Yet she was never certain she measured up to Abe's invisible mark. A contrast to the way she felt as she painted dolls and trucks in Judd's barn. She didn't have to measure up for Linc.

Perhaps it was guilt over such thinking that compelled her to make this meal better than ordinary.

"It looks very nice. I'm impressed."

"Thank you." The children had washed until they shone, and at their father's signal sat at the table, Abe at one end, Sally at the other. She watched for him to bow his head. This time she wouldn't be caught off guard.

Without so much as a glance at the others, Abe lowered his head and said grace.

The meal was well received, the pie tasty and the children well behaved. Sally silently congratulated herself on a job well done.

Abe pushed his dessert plate away and leaned back. "Very nice, Sally. Children, you may be excused."

They pushed their chairs back and glanced longingly out the window. Sally understood they wanted to go out and play in the warm evening, but their father preferred they play indoors after supper so they went to the front room to find inside toys.

Sally rose, gathered up dishes and carried them to the sink.

Abe, for some reason, did not immediately leave the table. "Sally, sit down please. I'd like to talk to you."

Her fingers gripped the stack of plates so firmly she couldn't release them. Was he about to fire her? Or— her fingers tightened even more—ask her to marry him? She forced her hands to relax, set the dishes on the counter and returned to her chair, schooling her face to reveal nothing. "Yes?"

His smile seemed stiff. "You've worked hard. I want to show my appreciation by taking you out for dinner."

A myriad of emotions rushed to her mind—embarrassment at his praise, pleasure that he cared to show appreciation, hope his approval meant something more, fear it did. The thoughts tangled and twisted like autumn leaves caught in a tiny whirlwind. "That...that would be nice," she managed to stammer.

"Can we make it tomorrow—Friday? I've asked Mrs. Anthony to watch the children."

It would be just the two of them? Her heart banged against her ribs. She'd never been alone with him. What would they talk about? She realized he waited for her to speak. Had he asked a question? Oh, yes, tomorrow. "That would be fine."

"I'll pick you up at your place about seven. That should give you enough time to clean up before we go out."

She looked down at what she wore. If she removed her apron would it not be good enough? Or was he referring to her hair? Only by squeezing her fingers together did she stop herself from running her hands over her mop. No doubt it was as untidy and unruly as ever. Somehow she must find a way to control it before they went out. "That will be fine." She squeezed her words from a tight throat.

"Good." He rose and left the room.

She stared at the table. Her insides felt empty, swept clean by a harsh wind. She couldn't think. Couldn't push to her feet. Suddenly a flood of urgency swept through her, sending nervous energy to her limbs. She must hurry home and find suitable clothes. Experiment with combs to tame her hair. She sprang into action, cleaned up the kitchen in record time, called a breathless goodbye to the Finleys in the other room and rushed out the back door.

By the time she drew abreast of the turnoff to Madge and Judd's place, her heart raced from her haste and she stopped to stare. She'd promised to help Linc tonight. Her gaze shifted to her home in the distance. She needed to prepare. Her eyes returned to the nearby barn. The party was planned for Saturday, and the toys needed to be finished. Linc needed her assistance.

The moments ticked past as she studied the situation, feeling as if her heart was being torn in two directions. In the end, wisdom won over emotion and she decided to hurry home. But first she needed to explain her absence to Linc. She turned her feet toward Madge's house, determined she would not change her mind.

Linc didn't go to Judd's place Friday evening. The toys were finished—the last coat of paint drying. The party was to be on Saturday. Sure, there was last-minute stuff to do, but last night Sally had said she wouldn't be there.

"Something else to do," she'd murmured, avoiding

his gaze. She offered no explanation but left shortly afterward. Usually they worked at least two hours. Sometimes they joined Madge and Judd for tea and cookies. Often they set aside the work to sit in the shelter of the barn, watching the sunset. He meant to make the most of their "friendship." Every night he prayed Sally would allow more. Last night she had rushed away before he could enjoy any of those pleasures.

"Are you done reading?" Pa asked, his voice weak.

"No, Pa." He brought his thoughts back to the present and read more of the story.

After a few moments, Pa touched Linc's knee. Linc lowered the book to see what he wanted. "Why aren't you making toys tonight?"

"We're finished." Every day he'd given Pa a description of what they'd done. "The games and toys are ready to take over. We just have to wrap the smaller things and load them for transport."

"Is Sally wrapping the presents alone?"

"No. Sally had other plans tonight. Madge will look after doing it."

"Oh. That explains it."

It explained nothing. He could have gone out to Judd's if he wanted. He returned to reading so Pa couldn't ask any more questions or voice any more assumptions.

After a bit Pa grew tired and Linc closed the book. "I'm going to check on the ponies." He had brought them in that morning.

Pa nodded. "I'd like to meet Sally. Do you think she'd be willing to visit me?"

"I'll ask her." Linc could no longer deny that his

father grew steadily weaker. His face had a pasty color. He ate nothing and drank very little. He'd be pleased if Pa met Sally while he was well enough to appreciate her fine qualities. Oh, but how he hated to admit his father was dying. Needing to find release in physical work, he hurried outside. He had completed one pen to hold the ponies, but an old section near the corner of the barn still needed to be rebuilt.

As he lifted heavy posts and nailed salvaged planks, he prayed for his pa. *Lord, please don't let him die before he chooses to prepare for Heaven. Give him enough days. Please.*

He'd taken down most of the old corrals, allowing a clear view from Grandmama's kitchen window into the Finley backyard. Soon that was all he'd have—a view. He'd about finished converting the barn for Abe. He was grateful for the work the man had provided. But what next?

He didn't know. He felt as if his life had stopped. Except for the time he spent in Sally's company, when he felt more alive than he could remember. He stopped hammering nails and stared at the Finley yard. He'd tried to tell her how he felt, but she'd stopped him. Did Sally consider herself duty-bound to proceed with the agreement with Abe? Was it really what she wanted? Would she consider something else? Maybe something not as solid as what Abe offered, not as secure, but safe in that his love would never be conditional.

The way his smile stretched his mouth, he was glad no one could see him standing there grinning up into the sky. He loved her and freely admitted it. Seemed until she and Abe made formal promises to each other, it was fair to let her know. But every time he came close to saying something, she shied away as if knowing the words on his tongue and not wanting to hear them. Yet he couldn't miss the way her eyes sought his, her expression tentative until he gave her a smile as full of assurance as he could manage. He let himself believe she needed his approval, his acceptance…his love…although she wasn't ready to admit it.

Given time, she'd realize love was more important than anything else she had her heart set on. He saw no reason to hurry. One of these days she would be willing to trade security for love.

He went back to building the fences, hope exploding through him until he wanted to shout. Instead, he settled for singing loudly, not caring who heard or what they might think.

Mother had helped Sally alter a dress. They'd removed the soiled collar and given it a plain neckline. It wasn't the latest fashion, but Sally thought the dark blue satin suited her. Four combs half subdued her curls. She would have to slip out to the ladies' room partway through the evening and do it over.

"Here he is." Mother tried to sound nonchalant as Abe drove up in his big car, but she missed doing so. "He's coming to the door."

Nervousness set in with the grip of a winter storm. "Mother, do I look okay?"

"You look fine. Really fine." She hadn't said so, but Sally knew she hoped this evening would produce a firm offer of marriage from Abe. Mother would not be happy until she made sure all three of the girls found good men to marry. She was satisfied with Judd and Emmet as mates for the older girls. And only Abe would do for Sally. Linc's face flickered across her thoughts. Mother didn't approve of him. She'd even gone so far as to list her reasons. No home. A shady family history. A bit too brash for her comfort.

Abe knocked.

"Goodbye, Mother," she murmured as she went to the door.

Abe stepped in at her invitation. "I'll have her home in good time, Mrs. Morgan."

His assurances might have pleased Mother, but they made Sally feel about as old and responsible as Carol.

However, he held the door for Sally and complimented her on her dress, so she pushed aside any resentment.

"I thought the hotel dining room would be nice."

She hadn't thought to ask where they would eat. The dining room at the hotel was the fanciest place in town, where visiting dignitaries ate, where travelers on the railroad ate. Or at least they had before the Depression hit. Not many people visited anymore.

But the dining room still operated, still gleamed with a polished wooden floor, tables covered in white linen set with sparkling china, silverware and glasses.

Young Alice, wearing a black dress and a little white apron, hurried forward as Sally and Abe stepped into the quiet room.

"Hi, Alice," Sally greeted the girl.

"Welcome. Please let me show you to a table."

She'd known Alice since the Morgans moved to Golden Prairie. The girl had been three years behind her in school. If even Alice felt it necessary to be formal in this place, it must be reserved for serious business only. Sally's nerves returned.

She sat when Abe held the chair. She took the black clad menu when Alice practically placed it in her hands. The menu offered a four-course meal with little in the way of options, and she gladly let Abe order for them both.

They received steaming bowls of beef noodle soup, and she gratefully turned her attention to it.

The soup bowl was empty far too soon. The air around them drowned in quiet. Only two other parties dined. A pair of businessmen poring over documents and a very stern man with a younger woman across from him. They had little to say to each other.

Sally stole another peek at them. They might have been herself and Abe.

Abe leaned back as they waited for the next course. "When is this party you are doing for the orphans?"

"Tomorrow."

"So soon?"

"Yes." She couldn't remember the last time she'd been so tongue-tied and unable to add anything to a conversation.

"Are you ready?"

"Apart from a few last-minute details."

"Good. It's a very nice thing to do." He cleared his throat and continued. "I'm pleased you are concerned with the less fortunate in the community."

"Thank you." She barely met his gaze, but even so, her eyes stung with embarrassment.

Thankfully Alice served a salad. They scarcely finished before she put the roast beef meal before them.

The pair of men shuffled their papers and sat back as if done with their business. The man and woman lingered over tea, neither of them speaking. Sally wondered if Abe was aware they were equally silent.

The plates were whisked away, and Alice brought chocolate mousse served in very pretty glass bowls. Sally tasted it, sweet and rich. It clogged her throat and she set aside her spoon.

"Is there a problem?" Abe asked. "We could send it back. Get something else."

"No, it's fine. I'm full." She wondered if she could swallow anything…more from tension than eating too much, however.

Abe ate his dessert and sat back. When Alice appeared at his side, he asked to have the table cleared and tea brought.

The tension in Sally's nerves increased with every passing moment. Alice set a pot before her and asked if she wanted to pour.

Sally shook her head. "You do it." She wondered if she could lift a cup to her mouth, let alone pour from a full pot.

Then they were alone. The businessmen departed. At some point the other couple had silently stolen away.

"Sally." Abe's voice startled her. "I brought you here for a special reason."

She nodded.

"I'm very pleased with how you manage my home and how the children have settled down."

Her gaze crept to him.

"I think it is time to make our arrangement formal. Sally, would you become my wife, a mother to my children?"

She stared at him unblinkingly. Was that all there was? No word of love or affection or promise of forever? Of course, the latter was understood.

"You will be free to run the home as you see fit, so long as you maintain the standard you have shown yourself capable of. I will see you have a reasonable allowance for household expenses and your own needs. You will be well taken care of."

He offered security, safety. Her tension eased. It was what she wanted. What she'd prayed for. If a tiny rebellious part of her wondered if there could be more, she pointedly ignored it. Abe meant all the things that had disappeared when Father died. Words from Linc's mouth reverberated through her head. *Friends who trust God to take care of them.* Surely this was God's way of taking care of Sally. She tried to fill her lungs, but they seemed to be made of wood.

"I accept."

Abe's smile was genuine. "Very good. I'm pleased. Come." He got to his feet and eased her chair back. "We're done here."

She waited as he took care of the bill and then let him lead her back to the car. He settled her inside and closed the door firmly. The click of the latch echoed in her head.

He turned the car back toward home, but stopped at the bottom of the driveway and turned to her. "I didn't buy you a ring. We can wait until we get married. But I'd like to seal our agreement in the time-honored way."

She had no idea what he meant.

"With a kiss. If I may?"

"Oh. Of course."

He leaned toward her. She leaned toward him. Her hands remained demurely in her lap. One of his hands rested on the steering wheel, the other on the back on the seat, bare inches from her shoulder. They met halfway. His lips were firm and cool as they touched hers for one second. Another. She didn't know if she was expected to pull back first or if he should be the one.

He sat up.

She straightened.

"I need to get back to the children."

"Of course."

"Do you want me to inform your mother?"

"No. I'll tell her if that meets with your approval."

"That's fine. I could make an announcement at church on Sunday."

"Do you mind waiting a few days so I can tell my sisters before they hear it from some other source?" She'd have to write Louisa.

"Of course. I should have considered that."

They reached the house. Abe jumped from the car, and she waited for him to open the door for her. He held out his hand and helped her alight. Apart from the kiss, it was the first time he'd touched her.

But it wouldn't be the last.

She better get used to the idea. "Thank you for the nice evening."

"My pleasure." He walked her to the door, bowed formally and stepped back.

She hurried inside and pressed her back to the closed

door, listening for him to drive away. As the sound of the car faded in the distance, she turned to the kitchen where Mother awaited.

As she crossed the floor, her legs began to vibrate so hard she barely made it to the nearest chair.

Mother looked up, her expression one of anticipation. As soon as Sally sat down, Mother reached across the table and took her hands. "Oh, my, your hands are like ice."

Sally nodded. The coldness went clear through to the marrow of her bones and the deepest depths of her heart.

"Did you have a nice evening?" Mother leaned forward, anxious to hear all the details.

Sally could recall nothing of the evening save for one thing, which she blurted out. "Abe asked me to marry him and I accepted."

"Thanks be to God. I've prayed daily for each of my girls to find a good, solid man."

Abe was that all right, but shouldn't she feel something besides admiration? "Mother, am I doing the right thing?"

Mother gave their clasped hands a shake. "Of course you are. Why do you ask?"

"I'm not sure."

Mother tsked. "I saw this coming. You've spent too much time with that McCoy man. You've let his charm sidetrack you. Sally, charm is deceptive and for the most part, self serving."

Linc wasn't self serving. But Sally knew if she tried to defend him she would never hear the end of it. "Shouldn't I feel something…well, special?"

"For Abe? Certainly you should. But love isn't simply an emotion. It's a decision, as well. Choose your love wisely, and it will grow to maturity."

"Did you choose Father wisely, or did you feel something in your heart that couldn't be explained or dismissed?"

Mother smiled. "Your Father was a good man. I loved him deeply. But—" Her expression hardened. "It was the fact he was a good man that allowed our love to grow."

Sally wanted the kind of love her parents had. Was it built on choosing wisely or loving deeply? Must she choose between the two? Could they not be found in the same person? She vibrated with a chill.

"Sally, you are young and impressionable. But there are certain things you simply can't ignore and hope to be happy in the future. You thrive best in an organized, safe and secure world. Abe can offer you what you need. You thought so when you went to work for him. What has changed since then?"

Safe, organized? These concepts were supposed to make her feel secure. Yet they also seemed constricting. As if her wings had been clipped, and she'd meekly allowed herself to be placed in a gilded cage. "Nothing's changed." Tears clogged her throat, but she would not weep and let Mother guess at how confused she was. In Mother's mind, there was nothing to be uncertain about. Abe was simply the best choice for Sally. No questions allowed.

"Then I believe you have chosen the right path in accepting Abe's offer of marriage."

Sally nodded, mute with emotions she couldn't name.

"Sally, your father would be very proud and happy at this moment. Don't you recall how he often said, 'A good name is rather to be chosen than great riches'? He would approve of Abe as a husband for you."

"He would, wouldn't he?" She sucked in air until her insides had room for nothing more. No more doubts. No more confusion. No more comparison between Abe and Linc. She had chosen the man most suitable to her needs. One her mother approved of. She'd soon enough get comfortable with the idea.

Chapter Twelve

Linc arrived at Judd and Madge's place at noon, as he and Sally had agreed. Judd and Madge were climbing into their car as he swung off Red. "We have to leave right away," Judd explained. "We promised to help organize the children. We'll see you at the orphanage in a few minutes." They drove away, leaving him alone.

He hadn't realized how dusty and dry the yard was until they departed. The wind had a lonely sound to it as it whined around the corner of the barn.

Shaking his head to clear away such thoughts, he turned his mind to anticipation of the afternoon and chuckled for no good reason other than he and Sally would be working together. His grin widened as he went to the barn to wait for her.

The party was going to be barrels of fun. He'd already secured the ponies a quarter of a mile from the orphanage to produce an hour into the party. He let himself picture the children jumping with excitement when he led the ponies to the orphanage. Doing something for these parentless children filled him with joy.

Sally drove in and parked the old rattletrap of a car at

the barn door. The wind's whine turned to a hum. The yard no longer seemed dry and empty. He leaned against the door jamb as she climbed from the car. She wore a flowery cotton dress in shades of blue that brought to mind endless summer. Her brown curls danced in the wind. The sun flashed across her face, turning her eyes pine tree green. Her skin glowed like the pretty china Grandmama kept in her cupboard. Taking the party to the orphanage with Sally at his side was going to be better than any Christmas he could remember.

She closed the door and turned, suddenly noticing him. Her hand remained poised midair. Her smile of greeting turned to a look of surprise. "Linc?"

He knew he didn't imagine the tentative eagerness in her voice. He didn't care that she'd read his thoughts and was uncertain what to do. There was no uncertainty in his mind. He wanted to pull her into his arms and speak the words of love crowding his brain. He half reached for her, then changed his mind and crossed his arms over his chest. If he kissed her at this moment, admitted his love and received hers, they might well forget the task ahead of them. Now was not the time or place.

Except perhaps it was. They were alone, and how likely was that to happen again today? Somehow he would make certain it happened. He'd manage to find a time when they were by themselves and free from outside obligations so they could enjoy sweet confessions of their feelings. "My pa would like to meet you."

"He asked?"

"Why is that so surprising?" His words were slow and lazy. He wondered she didn't read his love simply from his tone of voice.

"He doesn't know me."

Linc chuckled. "Which is why he wants to meet you. He likes to hear about my day. You're part of that."

She studied the flat dry landscape. The seconds ticked by. He thought he heard a clock marking time then realized it was his heart. Was she reluctant because of his father's reputation? "My father did not steal those jewels."

Her head came round. "I didn't suggest he did."

"You haven't agreed to see him."

Her eyes didn't quite meet his. "Of course I'll meet him. Why wouldn't I?"

Because people might consider it foolish. But he wouldn't say the words aloud. She'd agreed. That was enough. Once she met Pa, once she'd heard Linc's confession of love, she would change her mind about Abe and grow comfortable visiting in Grandmama's house. "This afternoon after we're done with the party?"

"If it works out." She shifted her attention to the stack of toys. "We better get this stuff loaded. The children will be waiting."

"Let's get to it." He'd wait for a time and place when she wasn't distracted by other things to tell her how he felt.

Madge had wrapped the smaller gifts and labeled them for each child. They stowed the games in the back. Sally draped a sheet over the dollhouse, and they managed to cram it in, as well. Then Linc crawled into the passenger side, edging himself in between the saw horse that would become the body of a cow and the piece of wood shaped like a cow's head for the kids to rope.

They drove up the hill. Madge and Judd, plus two

young ladies who accompanied the children to church each Sunday, had the children lined up on the step awaiting Sally and Linc's arrival. The children knew there was to be a surprise, and they looked ready to explode in twelve different directions as they waited.

Sally grinned at Linc. "Have you ever had such an eager welcoming party? I know I haven't."

"Must confess I haven't, either." Though he had allowed himself to dream of being welcomed by a hazel-eyed, curly-headed woman. And perhaps, in time, a few children. He pushed those thoughts to a corner of his mind to wait. For now he must think of these children and give them a fun party they'd never forget. He knew what it was like to lose his mother. Soon he'd know what it was like to lose his father. He also knew what it felt like to be on the fringes of society—tolerated more than accepted. Today he would focus on proving to the children that people cared about them and wanted them to have fun. His private concerns would have to wait.

The children strained forward. Linc and Sally remained in the car. He turned to her and grinned in anticipation of the next few hours. He grabbed the wooden cow head and the saw horse. "Are you ready?"

She lifted the beanbag board and nodded. In unison they stepped out. Together they set up the two games. All the adults yelled "Surprise!" Then the helpers released the children, who swarmed Linc and Sally.

"It's a party," Sally shouted over the melee. "Games and cake."

The kids were soon enjoying the games. Linc shot Sally a look of pure pleasure, underscored with admiration and love.

She grinned back, then, seeing what his eyes said, her mouth sobered. She turned to little Johnny at her side.

But he'd seen something in her eyes, too. A guarded awareness. A promise of more. He clamped his teeth together to stop a shout of joy from escaping.

Soon it was time to bring the ponies up the hill. Linc slipped away, welcoming the chance to think. Having admitted to himself he loved Sally, he discovered his heart was capable of so much more than he had known. Even though his attention was on the children, he heard her voice, felt it surround his heart like a hug. Even without looking, he was aware of every move she made, almost as if something invisible—but tough as the strongest lariat—stretched between them. As he led the ponies he rehearsed what he would say to her.

Billy, the rowdiest of the kids, spotted Linc. "He brung us horses!" With a whoop echoing for miles, Billy headed directly for the ponies. Only the fact that the animals spent most of their lives in a circus, carrying rambunctious children on their backs day in and day out, kept them from reacting.

"Slow down, Billy," Linc called. "You'll scare them."

The boy took one more step, then seemed to consider the consequences if he continued his headlong rush. "Can I help lead them?"

"Sure. Here. Take this rope." He let Billy lead the second pony, knowing nothing short of a tornado would persuade it to leave the others.

The rest of the children waited noisily.

Sally organized the children, and Linc handed a pony off to each of his helpers. Little eight-year-old Sharon's older brother, Andy, took one. Judd and Madge each took a pony, leaving Linc with the last.

"We'll start with the oldest children." Besides getting noisy Billy on one, Linc figured it would give the more nervous younger kids a chance to see how safe riding the ponies really was.

A little later, he looked at the kids lining up for a second ride. But by his count, only ten had ridden the ponies. He glanced around to find the missing two. A tiny girl sat under the lone tree in the yard, two fingers in her mouth. Her big blue eyes studied him across the space separating them.

Linc turned to Sally, who tried to persuade some of the children to return to the games. "Is that Emmy?"

Sally nodded. "She's a fearful child. I don't think she'll get within shouting distance of these animals."

The fear in the child practically scorched him from across the dusty grass. She pressed back, as shy as a fawn. "Here." He handed the rope of his pony to Sally. "I'm going to talk to her." He strode over and sat beside Emmy, his legs sticking out several feet in front of them. Sort of made him feel awkward and protective at the same time.

"Hi, Emmy."

"Hi," she mumbled around her fingers.

He put the child at about four or five. Awfully young to be without either mother or father. It took two hard swallows to get rid of the lump choking him. "You ever had a pet?"

The fingers came out of her mouth and she studied him, her eyes wide and hungry, making his throat tighten until he could barely breathe.

"Once I had a kitty. Miss Dolly. Before Mama and Papa and baby May died." Tears pooled in her eyes and threatened to overflow.

If she cried, he would be sorely tempted to join her. Instead, he forced his voice to work. "Kitties are nice. Soft and cuddly." He tore his gaze from the child's and looked toward the ponies. Sally watched, her smile a little uncertain, and in that moment he knew they felt the same regret, the same sadness over the plight of little Emmy. Again it seemed something reached from his heart to hers, binding them together. He knew it was love. Two hearts beating as one. Two souls feeling as one.

"I miss Miss Dolly," Emmy whispered on a shudder.

He guessed Miss Dolly was not the only thing she missed, and his heart twisted so tight he wondered it could still beat. "One of those ponies over there is hoping a little girl named Emmy will choose to be his friend."

She shifted her attention. "They're awfully big."

"Nah. They're not that much bigger than a full-grown kitty."

Emmy laughed, a sweet tinkling sound. "Kitty that big would sure scare away the mice."

Linc let out a roar of laughter. The little one had a sense of humor hidden behind her fear. Who'd have guessed it?

Sally's eyebrows came up, as if asking to share the joke.

Linc bounced to his feet and held out his hand to Emmy. "Come on. I'll show you what nice pets they are."

Emmy considered the ponies, considered his hand then stared into his eyes.

He let her see that he meant her no harm…that he liked her and wanted to help her, wanted to be friends.

Holding his gaze in trust, she took his hand and walked to the ponies. Allowing Sally to continue holding the lead rope, he picked up Emmy, amazed at how little she weighed. "Now this here is Pat the pony. He likes being petted."

Pat hung his head and never so much as twitched a muscle as Linc rubbed his hide and scratched behind his ears.

"See. Just like a big cat."

Emmy giggled and reached out one tiny hand, but quickly drew it back and buried her head against Linc's neck.

He had never known anything half so sweet as the feel of the little girl in his arms. He met Sally's gaze and knew from the look in her eyes that she guessed his reaction, and he wondered if it would make it easier for her to accept his confession of love. Perhaps in the future he would hold a tiny girl like this with a mop of curly hair and big hazel eyes like Sally's.

He pushed back a rush of emotions and turned his attention back to sweet little Emmy, who gave him blue-eyed consideration. They studied each other for several seconds, then she smiled. He smiled back. Mighty good thing she couldn't read his mind, because if she could, she'd know she could have asked him for the moon at that moment, and he would have tried to rope it and give it to her.

"Why don't you sit on old Pat's back for a moment? He'll think you don't like him if you refuse."

Emmy considered Pat's sad appearance which, in Pat's case, was a permanent state. "Okay. But you have to keep hold of me."

"I will. I promise." He perched her on Pat's wide back, his hands around her waist.

She clutched his arms.

He lifted his gaze to Sally's across the horse. Let her see how much he enjoyed holding Emmy and protecting her. Let her see all that his heart held…hope for a future full of love and little children. Shared with her.

Her eyes widened and turned pine green. Her cheeks blossomed pink roses. She opened her mouth. Closed it again and jerked away to stare across the yard.

Emmy squeezed his arm hard. "'Nough."

He turned his attention back to the child and lifted her from the horse. She clung to him, her feathery hair tickling his nose.

But one more child had still not ridden a pony. "There's someone missing," he told Sally.

She glanced about. "Claude Knowles. He was here earlier playing beanbag toss. I wonder where he's gone."

Billy overheard them. "Claude's a big crybaby. He's probably hiding inside 'cause someone laughed when he missed every single hole in the game." He made a sound of derision. "He should have been a little girl."

Linc handed Emmy to Sally and squatted down to Billy's eye level. "Son, it pains me something awful to hear you made a younger child unhappy." Billy's expression grew hard. If Linc didn't miss his guess, the boy meant to make someone pay for Linc's reprimand.

He didn't want to be responsible for that happening. "I had a big brother. Harris was his name. He spent hours teaching me how to bat a ball. He taught me how to skate and showed me how to pretend sword fight."

Billy's eyes lit up at the mention of sword fights.

Linc knew he had to do more damage control. "We only used little bits of wood and never ever hurt anyone. My point is, my brother helped me learn to do stuff I didn't know how. Probably would have never learnt if not for him."

Billy considered him curiously. "So where is your brother now?"

"Billy, I buried him a few weeks ago. He was killed in a mining accident." He wiped his hand across his face. "He was a good big brother. I will always miss him."

Nodding sympathy, Billy turned away.

Linc could only hope and pray Billy would choose to help the younger ones in the home rather than mocking them.

"I'm going to see if I can find Claude." He let himself enjoy Sally's wide approving smile, then turned away to search for the boy.

Matron assured him Claude was not in the house, so he circled the yard and found the boy nearly invisible as he pressed to a wooden box in a corner near the road, where he could observe the activities from a very safe distance.

He sat beside the boy. "Claude. You gonna join the others?"

"No."

"Miss Sally and I sure would like it if you did. And there's a pony waiting to give you a ride."

"I prefer not to ride a pony, thank you."

"Okay. But maybe you can tell me why not."

"Don't care to."

Linc considered the statement, but discovered he didn't believe it. "Fine, but everyone gets a turn."

"I don't want a turn. Thank you, anyway."

Linc got to his feet, walked up the little hill, took the pony from Sally and led him to Claude. He sat beside Claude again with the pony's lead rope in his fist. "Everyone gets a turn. It's up to you how you use it. You can ride or not."

Claude didn't answer, though Linc felt his careful, guarded study of himself and then the pony.

In a few minutes, Linc got to his feet. "Time for everyone to get a second turn." He hoped Claude would realize Linc included him.

Sally waited until he had one of the children on Pat's back to whisper, "What was that all about?"

"He's ready for adventure but needs a little encouraging."

He gave all the children another ride, let Emmy sit on Pat's back with Linc's hands holding her, then took the pony down to Claude again. Still Claude didn't move.

Another round of rides. This time Emmy allowed Sally to lead the pony a few steps, so long as Linc remained at her side.

As soon as Emmy was done, Linc took the lead rope and went to Claude. Before he got there Claude bolted to his feet. "I'll ride."

"Up you go then." He lifted the boy, pleased at the

look of triumph on the child's face. His gaze connected with Sally's, and a bolt of joy shot up his spine at her blatant approval. Then she glanced away, as if aware of how much she'd silently communicated.

He hoped she wasn't wishing she could take it back, and pressed tight to his heart the sweet knowledge of how she felt.

They spent the next two hours giving the children rides. Several times he caught Sally watching him. As soon as she saw that he saw, she looked away, pretending to be terribly busy with something else. But not so fast that he didn't see a flash in her gaze that made him wonder what she was thinking and when she would tell him. He almost laughed aloud at the sweet assurance that she seemed more aware of him than she might be willing to admit.

Later, she'd meet his pa. He hadn't realized how much he wanted it until now. He didn't want to be an outsider anymore. He wanted to be accepted by the community as an equal. A person to be respected. He wanted to be accepted by Sally, her friends and family.

Sadly, he guessed, unless he achieved such acceptance, Sally would continue to have doubts about him. Security was so important to her and meant more than a permanent address. It included things such as safety, a solid job and a secure position in society.

And yet, what more could he do than what he was doing? Live an honorable life. Attend church. Help others. *Lord God, help people to see that I am a good man.* God accepted him. So did his grandmother. But it was no longer enough.

The ponies were tiring. "Time to let them rest."

"Aw. One more ride," Billy begged. The others anxiously but silently added their request.

"'Fraid not. But why don't you see what Sally has in the car for you?"

As they turned her direction, she laughed and raced them to the car, arriving seconds ahead of the older children. She stood, her back to the car, and waited for the younger ones to catch up and for the adults to join them. Her face glowed with joy and her curls bounced around her head.

Linc handed the ponies off to the others, who were to take them back to the shelter and feed and water them. Then he jogged over to help Sally. He edged past the children and stood shoulder to shoulder with her at the side of the car. For a moment, he let himself swim in the pleasure of her nearness, her warm skin against his, her wildflower and cinnamon scent filling his senses.

The children pressed closer, reminding him of where his thoughts belonged. "Okay, you lot. Back up two steps and sit in a semi-circle."

They tripped over each other as they obeyed.

Linc took Sally's hand, telling himself it was necessary in order to pull her to one side. He didn't believe it, but perhaps the others did. He opened the door and handed her the wrapped dolls to distribute to the girls. He took the wrapped trucks and passed them to the boys. Then he and Sally leaned against the warm side of the car, their shoulders again touching, and watched the children unwrap presents.

He loved the expressions of joy on each face. "They really like the gifts."

"Not often they get something for no reason."

"Then I'm glad they learned there doesn't have to be a reason to do things for people we care about." He wasn't sure what he was talking about, except it wasn't only about the children. Did she hear the way his voice caught in his throat as he mentally put her on top of the list of people he cared about? Could she tell he meant to do everything in his power to make her happy?

The children were about to move away to play with their toys. "Hang on a minute."

Sally grinned at him—sending his heart into full gallop—as they pulled the dollhouse from the car, hidden under a draped sheet. "Katie, do you want to take off the cover?"

The tiny girl with a tangle of blond hair shyly came forward. She pulled off the sheet and stared at the dollhouse. It was the oldest girl, Maddie, who said, "It's a dollhouse."

The girls oohed and aahed as they gathered round to examine it. Soon they were putting their dolls in various rooms.

The boys looked disappointed. "Who wants an old dollhouse?" Johnny muttered.

Linc chuckled. "It's a new dollhouse. But you boys get to keep the wooden horse and cow and the bean bag game. You can practice riding and roping and tossing beanbags." Whooping their joy, they raced back to play.

Linc sighed. It felt so good to bring joy to these children.

Sally moved to his side. "It's great to see them enjoy themselves."

"It is indeed." He readily admitted he got as much

pleasure out of sharing the day with her as in seeing the children have such fun.

Judd had slipped away a few minutes ago and now returned, Mrs. Morgan beside him in his car.

"Here's Mother with the cake." Sally hurried to help her.

Linc's heart dropped to the soles of his feet. Mrs. Morgan made no secret of her disapproval of him. She nodded a sober-faced greeting to him and favored the others with a wide smile. The children called, "Hello, Mrs. Morgan."

"I wonder if they'll be able to tear themselves away from the toys to eat cake," Madge said.

The matron laughed. "I doubt we'll have to call them twice."

A table had been carried outdoors. Sally placed the cake on it and called, "Who wants cake?"

Linc laughed when the children left their toys immediately.

Sally laughed, too, and he allowed himself to glance at her. Their gazes caught, full of shared warmth and something more. Something he hoped went far deeper than pleasure over the children. Something that would meet the deepest needs of his heart and allow her to admit her love for him because, more and more, he was convinced she loved him even if she didn't yet acknowledge it.

Mrs. Morgan nudged Sally and she jerked away, suddenly very interested in adjusting the cake so it was precisely in the middle of the table.

Linc shifted his gaze to meet Mrs. Morgan's warning stare. He held steady for a heartbeat, silently informing her he would not be intimidated, and then he turned to watch the children who each ate two pieces of cake then dashed back to their play. The adults lingered over their thinner slices, served with tea.

"This was a great party," the matron said. "Thanks to Sally and Linc for their hard work."

The assembled adults clapped.

Linc grinned at Sally, not caring if his look was tender, telling. Let Mrs. Morgan think what she wanted. Let the others speculate. "We're now old hands at this, so if anyone wants to reserve our services for a future party…" Sally's eyes darkened, warning him not to go too far. "Well, I'm sorry to say we won't be available."

Judd clapped him on the back. "How long are you hanging around?"

The question, innocent enough, reminded Linc they all saw him as transient. Perhaps hoped for it. "I've no plans."

Mrs. Morgan didn't sniff. Yet her expression said as much as if she had. *A man with no future.*

He didn't mean it that way. "I can't make plans until I see how my father does."

Judd murmured sympathy. "Sally says he isn't doing well."

"I hope and pray he will get better, but the doctor doesn't offer any encouragement."

Sally turned to him, her eyes awash in understanding. "I can't imagine how difficult it is for you. I remember when my father died. It was hard to watch him go downhill, but at least he didn't linger for ages in pain. I guess, in hindsight, I should be grateful."

Her concern touched him in a spot deep inside that

he had not been aware of until this very moment—a tender spot that welcomed the balm of her sympathy.

The others remained quiet, as if lost in their own sorrow.

Madge broke the silence with a long sigh. "I miss him a lot."

They drew together to hug each other, Mrs. Morgan in their midst.

Linc stood outside the circle. He was tired of being on the outside looking in. He wanted more—to be accepted, to belong, to matter. To be part of a family.

Mrs. Morgan straightened. "We all miss him, but he would want us to get on with our lives. I want you to come to dinner tomorrow after church."

Linc understood she meant her family. Sally knew, too, but at least she managed to look a little regretful.

The sisters gathered up the remnants of the tea and carried them to the house. Judd watched one of the boys trying to throw the lariat and hurried over to help him. The littlest child fussed, and Matron picked him up and headed for the house.

Linc's nerves twitched as he realized he was alone with Mrs. Morgan. He glanced about for something to take him elsewhere, but before he chose a direction, she began to speak.

"My oldest daughter married a young rancher. They're doing well for themselves and their two daughters."

Linc nodded without comment.

"Judd bought the Cotton farm, and they have a good solid home. He will no doubt do well once this drought ends."

"Which will be soon," he murmured. "God willing."

"Amen to that."

He could think of nothing more to say. He didn't need an advanced university degree to understand why Mrs. Morgan had told him these things. She meant for him to understand her daughters married men she approved of. Not men like Linc, with a tainted past and an uncertain future.

He wasn't good enough for her daughter.

But he wasn't about to let her make his choices. He felt something special for Sally. Had seen the depths of emotion in Sally's gaze often enough to think she might have similar thoughts. He'd let Sally decide what she wanted. A man of substance and reputation like Abe— or a man with a heart that belonged to her.

Sally stepped from the orphanage, and her footsteps faltered. Mother and Linc talked together. Her heart did a funny little flip-flop. Were they talking about her? Then she remembered the one thing she'd tried to avoid thinking of all day long. She'd agreed to marry Abe. Her heart lurched to her throat. Surely Mother wouldn't tell him. They'd agreed to make a formal announcement at Sunday dinner with the family there, along with Abe and his children.

She hurried closer.

"I need to get back to Pa," Linc said.

Sally's air whooshed from overanxious lungs. They'd been talking of his father. "I'll give you a ride."

Mother gave her a look that normally would have Sally apologizing and changing her behavior. But this time, she only smiled sweetly.

"It will get him home sooner. In case his pa needs him."

Mother's expression did not lose its disapproval, but neither did Sally change her mind.

"You take him home," Judd said, blissfully unaware of Mother's concern. "I'll see Mother Morgan home."

The others joined them. Amidst a flurry of thank-yous and goodbyes, Sally and Linc climbed into the car.

She finally persuaded herself to relax when they were almost back to Golden Prairie. But for the life of her, she couldn't think of anything to say to Linc. Her thoughts seemed stuck in a knot.

He sighed expansively. "Another party done. What do you think? Should we do this for a living?"

His teasing eased her mind. "Yeah. Sure. Let's take it on the road."

His laughter danced across her mind and she grinned, pleased at making him laugh.

"I can imagine how much you'd enjoy living in temporary quarters. Say a circus tent. Moving from place to place like some kind of kid-size Wild West show."

She wrinkled her nose. "I don't think I'd like it much."

They reached town and she eased the car toward the barn, where the ponies would by now be happily munching their feed.

"Come with me to check the ponies?"

His eyes said so much more than his words, begging for her company. She wasn't ready to go home and face her mother's disapproval and demanding questions, so she murmured agreement.

He took her hand as she stepped from the car and retained it as he led her into the barn. They checked each animal and came to Big Red's pen. The horse nickered a greeting. Only then did Linc drop her hand to toss some hay at his horse. He leaned against the pen and considered Sally, his gaze steady.

She didn't move away. Didn't shift her gaze. Something about the way he studied her gave her a feeling of being blessed. The look went on and on until she felt as if he'd read every secret longing, every hidden wish. Not only read them, but promised to fulfill them.

He grinned. "It was a good party, wasn't it?"

Was that all they had to talk about? "I thought so." She could hardly find her voice.

He reached out and plucked a bit of straw from her hair, his knuckles brushing her cheek, sending a wave of warmth up her skin. "Do you want to meet Pa now?"

Sally's thoughts went crazy. *Did you think he meant to kiss you? And if he had, were you going to stand there and let him? No, of course not.* She had promised to marry Abe. She would never do something so dishonorable. She'd been raised better than that. "Now is as good a time as any."

"Good." Again he took her hand as he guided her from the barn. As if she needed guidance. The alleyway was wide and clear. She had only to head for the door. But she didn't pull away.

He dropped her hand as they stepped into the sunlight. "Sometimes Pa is too groggy to talk."

"That's fine." She clasped her hands together at her waist. She did not miss his touch, she told herself several times as they crossed the yard and stepped into a big kitchen warm with evening heat and welcoming smells of cooking and home.

Mrs. Shaw sat in a small wooden rocker, eyeglasses perched on her nose as she bent over needlework. She glanced up at Linc's entrance and blinked twice when she saw Sally at his side.

"Pa wants to meet Sally," Linc said.

"Hello, Mrs. Shaw." Sally knew the woman from church and community events. "I hope I'm not intruding."

"Oh my, no. You are most welcome. Come in. Linc, check on your father first."

He signaled for Sally to wait while he hurried from the room.

"How did the party go?" Mrs. Shaw asked.

"Very well."

"Linc was so pleased to be able to…you know, do something for the community."

Sally nodded. Mrs. Shaw sounded like Linc didn't expect anyone would let him be involved. "The children love him. What are you making?" She bent over the handiwork. "Why, it's beautiful." Deep red roses with a touch of pink on an emerald green background.

"It will be a cushion pad for my little wing chair in the front room."

Sally stared, drawn by the colors and the carefully executed flowers. "I've never done counted stitch work."

"It's time-consuming but very rewarding. Take a peek in the other room." Sally moved to the doorway. "See the picture over the desk?" It was a big scene of an English countryside.

"It's wonderful."

"It took me three winters to complete."

"But what a masterpiece."

"Why thank you, dear. If you want to learn how to do it, I can teach you."

"I might take you up on your offer. Winters are long."

Linc stepped from a doorway across the living room and saw her looking at the picture. A smile flashed across his face, as if pleased to see her there. "I see Grandmama is showing off her skills."

His grandmother snorted. "I am not showing off. Sally admired my roses so I thought she might like to see that picture. She called it a masterpiece."

Linc jostled Sally with his elbow. "You've earned yourself a special spot in her heart with that comment." He kept his voice low, but his grandmother still heard.

"If you keep it up you might find yourself cooking your own meals."

Linc pressed his hand to his heart. "Oh, please. Not that. I'll be good. I promise."

His grandmother laughed. "Go away with you."

Sally chuckled. It was good to see the affection between them. She liked a man who got along equally well with his elders and children. The thought stung her brain with accusation, which she ignored. But then she instantly excused herself. Of course it was okay to like Linc. Wasn't she supposed to show kindness to everyone?

Linc squeezed his grandmother's hands, then turned back to Sally. "Pa's awake. He's anxious to meet you."

She knew the man was bedridden. Had been since his accident. But suddenly she realized she'd agreed to step into a man's bedroom.

Linc watched her closely and read her hesitation. "It's okay." Linc held out his hand and she took it, finding strength and reassurance in his touch. He pulled her to his side. "He's weak but likes to hear what's going on around him. I said we'd tell him about the party."

They stepped into the room. A shrunken man lay against a pillow, his skin almost as white as the cotton cover. Yet his brown eyes—so much like Linc's—regarded her with unblinking curiosity. Linc pulled her forward. "Sally, this is my father, Jonah McCoy."

"I'm pleased to meet you." Sally held out her hand, then realized he didn't have the strength to lift his arm. Instead she reached down and squeezed his hand where it lay on the bedcovers. His skin was cool.

"So you're the young lady who has been keeping Linc occupied."

She shot a glance at Linc. What had he said? But Linc regarded his father, a look of sadness on his face. Sally swallowed back the tightness closing off her throat. She couldn't imagine watching her father suffer his way to death. "He helped put on a very successful party for the orphans."

"Tell me about it."

Linc pushed a chair toward her, and she sat at Mr. McCoy's bedside. "He taught a little boy how to throw a lariat. You should have seen the look on young Johnny's face when the loop actually landed over the wooden cow head. Johnny always pretends to be tough, but I thought he was going to hug Linc when he succeeded." She told of the games. How Maddie, the oldest girl, organized the others for the beanbag throw. How she managed to get Linc to take part in the game and how Maddie had blushed and giggled when Linc lost to her and congratulated her on her strong right arm.

Linc leaned against the head of his father's bed and seemed as keen on the stories as his father, so she continued, dredging up each and every detail. How young Claude Knowles—

"Wait. I used to know a man named Claude Knowles. A widower who lived over to the west."

"That would be young Claude's grandfather. He and Claude's parents died a year ago."

"And the boy has no other relatives?"

"Not that I'm aware of. Or perhaps they couldn't afford to take him."

"Sad. Everyone should have family and a home. Son," he spoke to Linc, "I'm sorry I didn't give you that." He drew in a breath that caught partway. He coughed and grimaced with pain.

Linc grabbed a bottle. "Pa, here's more medicine."

But Mr. McCoy waved away the offer. "Not just yet." His voice was thin with his pain. "I want to hear the rest of Sally's story."

So Sally continued. How Linc had picked up little Emmy and the girl had clung to him. Her heart squeezed tight as she recalled his gentleness with Emmy and how the girl adored him. This fearful, shy child trusted Linc instinctively. That said a lot about a man, as far as she was concerned.

She told Mr. McCoy how Linc had gone to Claude's side and given him the time and space he needed to choose to take a pony ride. Linc seemed to understand that sometimes a person needed time to get his head around an idea. She related how Claude sat in the grass and ate his cake so neatly that not a crumb fell, while the older boys, Johnny and Billy, had wolfed down two pieces each with no regard for what ended up on their face and clothing. How the little ones chased after each other and rolled in the dusty grass simply for the joy of playing. "Of course, the ponies were a big hit. I guess the children will remember it for a long time." She went on to describe the children receiving the toys. "Linc is responsible for all of them. He cut them out. He made the dollhouse."

"It wasn't just me," he protested. "You finished everything."

She couldn't tear her gaze from Linc's, feeling a deep connection as she shared this time with his father.

Mr. McCoy coughed again. "I believe I'll take some medicine now."

Linc measured it out. "We'll let you rest now, Pa."

"Thank you, Sally, for visiting a weak old man." He could barely manage a whisper.

"It was my pleasure." She squeezed his hand again.

Linc led her from the room, gripping her hand as if he feared to let go. She held on tight, understanding how difficult it must be to see this every day. She wanted to assure him his father would get better, but one look at the man and she knew it wasn't going to happen.

Linc led her through the kitchen, still holding her hand. "We're going to check on the ponies," he told his grandmother.

At his expression of sorrow, the older woman pressed her lips together and her eyes glistened with tears. The look she gave Sally seemed to beg her to help Linc as best she could.

Linc strode from the house, Sally in his wake. He didn't slow his steps until he reached the spot beside Big Red's pen where they had stood previously. He let out a long, shuddering breath.

With her free hand, she touched his shoulder. "I'm sorry. This must be very difficult for you."

He pulled her into his arms and held her tight. She let him, wrapping her arms around him, offering comfort the best way she could. He shuddered, clung to her. After a bit, his breathing eased and he pressed his cheek to her hair. "Sally."

The thickness of his voice, ringing with emotion, strummed something inside her. The way he said her name filled her with longing she couldn't explain.

He eased back, caught her chin with his finger and tipped her head so he could look in her eyes. "Sally."

His gaze dipped deep into hers.

A tiny nudge in the back of her brain tried to get her attention, tried to tell her something. She ignored it.

He studied her lips so longingly, she forgot to breathe. He shifted his gaze, ran it slowly across her cheeks until he meet her eyes. "Sally," he said a third time, his voice so deep it rumbled in her heart.

She was mesmerized by the look in his eyes, the ache in his voice. Her heart seemed to stretch, widen, maybe even open.

He lowered his head, paused and sent her a questioning glance.

She couldn't move. Couldn't think.

He touched his lips to hers. Warm, gentle, tentative.

Her arms wound around Linc's waist, her palms pressed to his back. Her heart pounded against her chest. This was how a kiss should make her feel. Not cool and distant like Abe's had.

Abe. The man she'd promised to marry. She jerked away, pressed her arms to her side and stepped back, forcing herself from his embrace.

"No," she groaned. "I can't." Her words came in hard bullets. "Abe asked me to marry him last night, and I said yes."

She panted as if she'd run a mile.

Chapter Thirteen

Linc clamped his lips together and let her words blast through his brain before he spoke. "You what?"

"Abe and I are getting married."

"Why?" It didn't make sense. She'd kissed him as much as he'd kissed her, and not unwillingly. In fact, she had sighed softly and leaned into his embrace as if she'd found home. He reached for his hat to shove it forward, then remembered it hung on a hook in the house and settled for rubbing his hair. "Why?" he asked again.

She rocked her head back and forth. "It wasn't unexpected. Both of us know that's why I'm there. He's happy with how I run his home and the way I care for his children."

"It sounds like a business agreement. You do the housework and he'll provide you with a house."

She lifted her chin but couldn't quite meet his eyes. "He's a good man."

"Granted." He could tell her Grandmama wanted Linc to take over the farm, and he had about decided to do so, but he didn't want her to choose him in order to get a roof over her head.

"I'm not marrying to get a house."

"Do you love him?" It hurt to even say the words.

She sighed as if dealing with a rebellious child. "You don't understand."

His knees almost buckled. She hadn't said she loved Abe—the one argument that would make Linc walk away. Her omission gave him hope. "I do understand. But you can't marry a man to replace your father. You can't marry him for security alone. Sally." He took a step toward her, but she held up protesting hands and he drew back, not wanting to scare her off. "Sally, you talk about faith. Said your faith required security, safety. No person on this earth can promise you that completely. Nor should you expect it. Only God holds the future. There will come a time when you will have to trust Him because there is nothing else left. Why not do it now? Don't marry Abe for security. Trust God for it. Marry me for love. Choose me. I can't promise circumstances won't change or bad things won't come into our lives. But I can promise to love you and cherish you every day of my life." His words struggled past the tightness in his throat. "Sally, choose me."

She continued to rock her head back and forth, her eyes clouded with uncertainty.

Again he tried to close the distance between them, but she held up her hands once more.

"I can't. Mother would never understand. She'd not forgive me. The dinner tomorrow is to announce to the family my engagement." She pressed her fingers to her mouth, and with a little cry, dashed away.

He didn't follow. She'd made her choice clear. She would not, could not, go against family expectations.

She would never give up the security of someone like Abe for a man like Linc, with a history of wandering, a hint of scandal attached to his name and nothing to offer but his love.

The sound of a motor mocked him as Sally drove away. All he could do was pray. And he poured out his heart and longing to God in a way he had never before done. *Oh, God. You know I love her. I could live with this mind-shattering ache if she loved Abe. If I thought Abe loved her—but I think he only wants someone who will do his bidding and run his house well. She wants something she can only find in trusting You fully. I have lots to learn about faith, too. We could learn and grow together if she would let it happen. God, please make her see love is what matters in the long run.*

Darkness had fallen by the time he left the barn. He tiptoed into the house, turned off the light Grandmama had left on in the kitchen, paused to make sure Pa was comfortable. When he saw his father slept, he trudged upstairs to his bedroom and fell, fully clothed, on the bed.

The next morning, Linc woke with a pounding headache and headed down the stairs for a cup of coffee. Grandmama was up and the coffee perked on the stove.

Grandmama looked at him and her eyes widened. "My word, what happened to you?"

"Fell asleep in my clothes," he murmured as he filled a cup and took several swallows, not caring that the hot liquid burned his tongue.

"Why?"

"Don't ask." He didn't mean to be curt, but he had

no desire to discuss how he'd made a fool of himself kissing Sally and then begging her to choose him. Yet he'd make a fool of himself again if he thought it would convince her to change her mind.

Grandmama shook her head. She opened her mouth as if to say something, but at Linc's warning glare, thought better of it.

The coffee did little to ease his bad mood. He didn't expect it would. "I'll check on Pa." He strode away, ignoring Grandmama's questioning look. He couldn't explain his mood to her.

Pa twisted restlessly, moaning. Linc thought he was asleep, but his eyelids rose halfway at Linc's entrance. Linc sprang forward. "You need your pain medication. You should have called. I would have given it to you earlier."

"Thought I could hold off."

"Well, don't try it again." His words were soft with concern. He administered the medicine then sat beside Pa, singing softly until the medicine did its work. He knew from the lines gouging Pa's thin face that the relief was minimal. He hated to disturb him, but Pa needed cleaning up so he got a basin of water and washed him all over, as gently as he'd wash a newborn baby. He carefully rolled his father from side to side as he replaced the soiled sheets with clean ones. He took the sheets to the back porch and put them to soak.

Grandmama waited in her Sunday best when Linc returned to the kitchen.

He'd forgotten about church. "You go ahead without me. I'll stay with Pa. He's having a bad day."

"I can stay if you need me."

"We'll be fine."

Grandmama touched Linc's cheek in a loving gesture. "He's fortunate to have such a loyal and caring son. I will be praying for you both. He doesn't have much time left to make a decision."

Linc hurried back to Pa's room, afraid to speak. If Pa had to die, all Linc wanted was for him to choose Heaven before he did. He picked up *Pilgrim's Progress* and started to read.

Pa interrupted him. "I like Sally."

"Good."

"Seems you do, too."

"Pa, she's agreed to marry Abe Finley."

"I'm sorry to hear it."

Not near as sorry as Linc. He was grateful for an excuse to miss church, to miss seeing her sit at Abe's side or seeing Abe sit up front, knowing Sally would soon join him. Not that he was glad for Pa to be suffering.

"Son, you're a good man. Never got into trouble like Harris."

Linc didn't bother pointing out how Pa and Harris got into trouble as a pair. Neither of them would be doing so again. The future looked lonely to Linc.

"There's something I need to tell you." Pa took a deep breath that brought on a bout of coughing. "It's not something I'm proud of." More coughing cut off his words.

"Pa, rest."

Pa nodded. "You're a good man. You deserve someone like your ma to share your life."

Linc wondered what else his pa meant to say. But he

didn't seem inclined to try again, and Linc didn't want to tire him. "Do you want me to read?"

Pa nodded, and Linc read for an hour. Pa's discomfort increased. "Let's see if you're more comfortable on your side." He rolled his father and placed two pillows at his back. "Does that help?"

"Some."

Linc rubbed the exposed shoulder gently. Pa sighed, finding comfort in the motion so Linc continued until his father relaxed. Then he slipped from the room, praying Pa would rest for an hour or two.

He wandered the house, but it felt crowded and he strode out to the barn. He needed to do something. Something physical. He didn't care to dishonor God by working on Sunday, but he had to do something to relieve the aching of his bones. He grabbed a shovel. A big old post at the corner of the barn had broken off and needed to be dug out. He drove the shovel in the ground and stomped on it. Over and over he lifted dirt from a growing hole. The post must be buried halfway to China. Whoever put it in the ground had meant for it to stay.

Two feet down, his shovel hit something hard with a clang. He tried several different spots, but each time hit the obstruction. Likely a rock. He welcomed the challenge of digging it out. Soon he could tell the object had a flat top. Then he saw the corners were square. He dropped to his knees and leaned over to scrape away the dirt by hand.

What he found was a metal box. He pulled it from the hole and stared at it. What was a container doing here? Had it been buried by accident? Something someone had lost? Or hidden? The lid was bent, and it stuck so he couldn't open it. He went into the barn, found a screwdriver and pried the lid up.

"No. It can't be." He sank to the floor and stared at the contents of the box.

Sally glanced about the table. Abe sat at her left, in the place where Father would have sat, Carol on her right. Robbie sat on the other side of his father, Madge and Judd next to him. Mother sat at the far end of the table facing Abe. Everyone was there except Louisa and Emmet and their girls. Yet it wasn't their absence she felt. Only one person's absence blared across her senses, even though he'd never been in the Morgan home and likely never would be. Still, he seemed to hover like an invisible guest.

Linc hadn't been in church, either. Mrs. Shaw had stopped to speak to her and explained Linc's father wasn't up to being left alone. Sally wished she could tell Linc how much she cared about his father's sufferings. But last night when she'd tried to comfort him, it had ended up in a kiss.

Her cheeks stung, and she suddenly found it necessary to adjust the napkin in her lap.

Mother stood at her place at the other end of the table. "Dinner is ready, but before we eat, Abe and Sally have an announcement. Abe?"

Abe stood and cleared his throat. "Sally and I are going to get married."

Sally held her head high and faced her sister and brother-in-law. They would never have reason to suspect she had stolen a forbidden kiss in the secrecy of the Shaw barn.

Madge's look lingered on Sally, full of unspoken questions.

Sally smiled.

"About time," Judd said. "You've got a prize in Sally."

Moisture pooled in Sally's eyes, but she widened them. She would not cry.

"I'm aware of that." Abe squeezed her shoulder. "She's proven herself very capable."

He appreciated her. Valued her. She wanted nothing more. Not promises of love to last a lifetime. Love was cold comfort without a roof over one's head. Not that she was marrying Abe solely for that reason. He was a good man. A solid citizen. And what, a demanding voice asked, is Linc? Is he not a good man? A solid citizen? Of course. But he had no roots. As far as she knew, he planned to return to cowboying, and she'd listened to enough of his stories to know what kind of life that was. Following a herd of cows. Living on the range for much of the year. Where did that leave a wife?

Abe sat down, and Mother asked him to say the blessing.

Sally knew enough to bow her head immediately. At Abe's amen, she realized she was only being foolish when her heart should be overflowing with gratitude. This was what she wanted. Had wanted for a long time—a man with stability. A man who would—

Abe handed her the bowl of potatoes, and she took them with wooden hands.

She'd been about to say, a man who would make her feel as her father had. But what did that mean? Her father had cherished her, protected her, guided her. Is that what she expected from Abe? Would she get it? Would he love her like Linc did? Oh, how her wicked thoughts tortured her. She pushed them aside and turned to assist Carol.

Carol ignored the offer of potatoes and studied Sally's face. "Does this mean you are going to be my new mother?"

Sally nodded. "But I don't expect to take your mother's place. No one ever should. Is that okay?" She would have preferred to discuss this with the children in private, but Abe insisted they hear the announcement along with everyone else.

"I guess so." She took potatoes and passed them to Mother.

Sally turned to find Robbie glaring at her.

"I don't want a new mother. I don't need one. You can be the housekeeper. That's all."

Abe's expression grew stern. "Robbie, you will apologize. Sally is to be your mother and you will behave."

Robbie glared from Abe to Sally and said not a word.

"Robert Abraham Finley." Abe's warning tone was unmistakable.

Sally knew how explosive Robbie could be. "Let it go for now," Sally whispered, and received a look from Abe to match the one he gave Robbie. She instantly wished she could pull her words back.

"He is my son and he will obey me." Although he kept his voice low, everyone at the table heard him.

Sally longed to melt into the floorboards. "Please, Robbie," she whispered.

Robbie must have felt sympathy for her discomfort. "I'm sorry."

"Sorry, who?" Abe prompted.

"I'm sorry, Sally." No mistaking the slight emphasis on Sally's name, stubbornly informing one and all she would never be anything else.

For a moment, Sally feared Abe would correct the boy further, but he let it go.

"That's fine." He faced the others. "Sorry for the disruption."

There was a sudden rush of passing food and comments about the meal. Slowly the tension drained from the room, and Sally thought it might be possible to swallow a mouthful of potatoes and gravy.

"Abe, you should have come to the party at the orphanage. Sally and Linc did an excellent job." Judd didn't seem to think it odd to link Sally's name with Linc's, but Sally's potatoes stuck partway down her throat and would go no farther.

"I saw their work at Robbie's party and was impressed." Abe smiled at Sally. "As I told her, I'm pleased she is involved in community efforts."

"Sally has always been the one to help others," Madge said. "Remember how she took soup and covered dishes to the Anderson family for three months when the parents were so sick?"

"I just like to help others."

"It's your way of keeping things safe."

Madge's words stung. As if she meant Sally helped others for selfish reasons. As if Sally had a need to control life. She didn't. No matter what Madge or any of them thought. No matter what Linc said.

"Maybe I help just because it needs to be done. Because God says true religion is to help widows and orphans. To share with others."

Mother cleared her throat, subtly letting them know they were not to argue.

Thankfully the subject was dropped, but Judd and Madge returned to talking about the party at the orphanage, which did nothing to help Sally forget Linc. Heat stung her cheeks at the memory of that kiss. She hoped if anyone noticed, they would put it down to excitement over her engagement.

The meal seemed to go on and on. Would it never end? Would they ever leave her in peace?

Finally Abe pushed away from the table. "An excellent meal, Mrs. Morgan. Thank you."

Mother nodded. "I hope it's the first of many, now that you are to be my son-in-law."

Sally wondered if maybe the roast had been a little off, though no one else seemed to be bothered in the slightest.

"Children, thank your hostess."

Carol and Robbie dutifully thanked Sally's mother.

"It's time I took this pair home."

Even Carol looked unimpressed with the idea of leaving. Sally understood they would have to play quietly in the front room for the rest of the day. Would Abe allow her to change any of his rules when they married? She guessed he would resist the idea. She, too, could look forward to Sunday afternoons confined to the house, reading or perhaps writing letters. Maybe she'd find a distant pen pal and write long, chatty letters once a week. Someplace exotic, like Africa or South America.

Abe and the children said goodbye to everyone. Robbie made certain to give Sally a most fearsome scowl when he thought no one else was looking. Then they were gone.

She grabbed the dishes still on the table, carried them to the worktable and poured hot water in the basin. Madge came to her side. "I suppose I should offer congratulations."

Mother joined them. "Indeed. This is a wonderful opportunity for Sally. Father would be well pleased."

Madge sighed as if she didn't agree, but she kept her thoughts to herself, for which Sally was grateful. She wasn't sure she could deal with any more doubts or questions at the moment, and kept her attention on washing dishes.

Finally the kitchen was clean. Judd and Madge departed for home.

Mother patted back a yawn. "I think I'll have my Sunday afternoon nap."

A few minutes later, Sally was thankfully, peacefully alone. She glanced around the room where the family spent so many enjoyable hours, and realized she'd never felt more alone or lonely in her life. Of course she would miss the home she'd known with her parents and sisters. A certain amount of sadness was to be expected.

The walls felt too close…the heat oppressive. She fled outdoors, her racing feet carrying her to the barn. Panting far harder than the short run should cause her to, she scrambled up the ladder. Her foot slipped on a rung, and she cried out. But she was safe and scrambled to the wooden floor, then made her way to the far corner. Every bit of hay had been fed to the cow, so she couldn't build walls about her. All she could do was pull her knees to her chest and press her face to her arms, still out of breath and overheated from her run. She waited for her heartbeat to return to normal, then lifted her head.

The loft door was closed, leaving the interior in gloom. A musty smell permeated the air. Pigeons cooed on the roof overhead. Sally tried to concentrate on every detail in a vain attempt to still the raging emotions inside her chest. Emotions she couldn't understand or even name, but they roiled and twisted until she thought she couldn't bear it.

"Oh, God," she moaned. "Help me."

But her turmoil did not ease. Was it guilt? "Forgive me for kissing Linc. That was wrong."

No relief came with her confession. Had she omitted doing something God expected?

But what did God expect?

To trust Him to take care of her.

But she did so, to the best of her ability. She sucked in dusty air and coughed. She must work this out, straighten out her confusion. But the more she flung about trying to sort her troubling thoughts into order, the more tangled they grew.

A rustling below drew her attention, then she heard someone on the ladder. She drew back into the corner, hoping she would be invisible.

Madge's head popped through the opening. She scanned the loft. "There you are. I thought I might find you here." Not waiting for, nor likely expecting, an invitation, Madge climbed up and slid across the floor toward Sally. "We used to have a lot of fun playing up here." She sank down to sit beside Sally. "Seems a long time ago."

Sally made a noncommittal sound, not wanting to relive the earlier, happier times.

"Things have to change as we grow older." Madge grew quiet and still. Neither of them spoke. But Sally knew it wouldn't last. She could sit and keep her thoughts to herself all day long, but Madge never could. It was only a matter of minutes before she'd say what was on her mind, what had brought her here on a Sunday afternoon when she could be with Judd.

"Sally."

Yes, here it came. Not that it mattered. Nothing Madge could say would erase Sally's confusion. Maybe there was no solution for it.

"Sally, why did you agree to marry Abe?"

"What?" The question startled a response from Sally. "It was the reason I went to work for him. You knew that from the beginning."

"But I've seen you with Linc." Madge wiggled her eyebrows, as if to suggest she'd seen more than the two of them working on toys.

Sally hoped the dim lighting hid the way her cheeks burned. "So what?"

"Come on, Sal. You can't be so dense you don't feel the sparks between the two of you."

"Guess maybe I am." The sparks meant nothing. They couldn't. "What kind of a girl would I be if I agreed to marry one man while I harbored feelings for another? Father would certainly have had something to say about that."

Madge gave Sally a long hard study. "Do you think Father would approve of your engagement to Abe?"

Sally nodded. "He's a good man."

Madge shook Sally's arm. "You can't marry a man simply because he's well respected. Nor because you think Father would approve. Sally, this is your life. Until death do you part. You have to listen to your heart in matters like this."

Easy for Madge to say. She always knew what she wanted and went after it. Likely she'd never entertain contrary feelings. But Sally felt as if her heart was in a tug-of-war. She simply couldn't sort out the confusion. The only way was to choose the wisest thing and forget everything else. "I have to do what I think is best, and that's marrying Abe."

Madge crossed her arms over her chest and sighed heavily. "I will, of course, support whatever decision you make."

Sally smiled for the first time all afternoon. "Even if it kills you to do so. Right?"

Madge chuckled, then suddenly sobered. "It's not me who will have to live with the decision. It's you. So please—" She flung about to face Sally. "Please, dear little sister, make sure it's the right one."

"I'm trying to."

Madge looked about ready to say more, then pressed her lips together and wrapped her arms about Sally.

Sally leaned her head against Madge's firm shoulder. Not everyone could be as strong and sure of things as Madge. People like Sally simply had to push ahead, trusting God to guide them even when they couldn't see where their path led.

She must listen to her head more than her heart, and like Linc said, trust God to take care of her.

Next morning, Sally's resolve had deepened. She knew Abe was the man God had put in her life to provide for her needy faith. As she made her way to the Finley home, she wondered how she would endure Linc's presence as he finished the barn. Seeing him, knowing how he felt would make it difficult to stick to her decision. She hated to hurt anyone. But breakfast was over and the kitchen cleaned, and still he had not appeared. She stared toward the Shaw backyard, the new corral fences allowing her a good view.

Was it just two days ago that she and Linc had shared such a wonderful day? The party at the orphanage. The visit to his father. The forbidden kiss in the barn. Her insides flooded with guilty heat. She must never think of it again.

But like rebellious children, her thoughts returned to reliving events of that afternoon. They'd fed and petted the ponies.

The ponies. Of course. He'd taken them back today.

It was as if the sun broke through the clouds in her mind. She glanced at the sky. Strange, no clouds interrupted the blue. She sang one of Linc's silly songs as she carried the dishwater to the garden.

Robbie crouched in his fort. "Where's Linc?"

"Taking the ponies back."

"Oh." The answer seemed to satisfy him, and he returned to his play.

Sally hurried to work once more on Tuesday. Life was good. And it had absolutely nothing to do with the possibility of seeing Linc today. So what if the thought cheered her unreasonably? What was wrong with being friends with the man? After all, Abe didn't seem to object. But then, he didn't know about the kiss.

No reason he should.

But the morning passed without Linc showing up. She didn't get so much as a glimpse of him, even though she spent a great deal of time staring at the yard across the alley.

Robbie stomped to the doorway and glowered at her. "Where is he?"

"Maybe his father is too sick to leave."

"It's your fault. You're going to marry my father, so Linc won't come anymore."

Sally had not let herself consider the idea, but it hovered at the edges of her brain. Had he left town? Was he avoiding her?

She gave herself a mental shaking. Best she get used to the idea. Being Abe's wife would make it impossible to continue as she was with Linc.

No more kisses. But couldn't they be friends?

Only if Linc welcomed it.

And if she kept her thoughts in proper submission.

Chapter Fourteen

Linc had prayed for something to change, but this was not what he had in mind. Not by a long shot.

He had dusted the metal box off and carried it inside. "Pa, what's this?"

Pa grunted awake.

Linc put the box on the chair and opened the lid to reveal several necklaces and brooches and two rings with enormous stones. "These are Mrs. Ogilvy's missing jewels, aren't they?"

"I hoped you wouldn't find it."

"You stole it? And all this time I have defended you. Held my head high, telling myself and everyone who would listen that the McCoys were innocent."

"I tried to tell you but then decided no one need ever know. How did you find it?"

"I dug out an old post."

"At the corner of the barn."

"That's right."

"It was the worst decision I ever made. What can a man do with jewels? Once the Mountie sent a description of them across the country, I could never cash them in. So I buried them and moved on."

"Now what?"

Pa coughed weakly. "I guess it's up to you."

"Thanks, Pa. Thanks a lot."

"I'll go to my grave with this over my head."

Linc's anger and resentment melted. "Pa, you can go to your grave forgiven and ready for Heaven if you choose."

"God ain't likely to forgive a man like me."

"God says in His word, 'If we confess our sins, He is faithful and just to forgive us our sins, and to cleanse us from all unrighteousness.'"

"I guess that applies to ordinary sins."

"When the Roman soldiers crucified Jesus, he prayed they might be forgiven. Doesn't seem to me there is anything much worse than killing God's son."

"I suppose it is worse than stealing and lying."

"I'd say so. Pa, you can have your sins forgiven and be ready to enter Heaven. Please, won't you choose it?" Silently he prayed God would crack open his father's stubborn heart.

"I'll think about it. Now what are you going to do with that stuff?"

"The jewels? I'll have to think about that, too."

He had to return the ponies to their owner on Monday and welcomed the opportunity the trip provided for him to think about what he should do. If he turned the jewels over to the Mountie, his pa would be arrested. If he held them until after Pa's passing, he would be as guilty as Pa of hiding the truth. But oh, how he wished he didn't have to face the fact that the McCoys were guilty.

The faint hope he had that Sally might reconsider her plans to marry Abe and choose Linc instead died a painful death. He would never be worthy of such a woman. She would never consider linking her name with that of a McCoy. Everything people said about the McCoys was true.

He prayed as he took the ponies back. He prayed as he returned to Golden Prairie. He sought something besides the only answer he could find. But nothing more came. He must do what was right, even though it was hard. Harder than anyone would ever know.

His pa was dying, and Linc was about to turn him over to the law.

Tuesday morning, he spared a brief glance at the Finleys' backyard and caught a glimpse of Sally watering the garden.

Setting his mind to do what he must, he walked away from the view, stuck the metal box, now covered with a blanket, under his arm and marched down the street toward the Mountie's office.

He set the box in front of the lawman and began his explanation. "My pa and brother stole the jewels and buried them in this box behind the barn. I discovered it while fixing the corrals. Only thing I ask is you let my pa die in peace."

"Sorry, son. I must question your father and get the truth. I will be mindful of his condition, however."

Linc had to console himself with that assurance. "I want to return them to Mrs. Oglivy and apologize as best I can."

"By rights this should be kept as evidence, but I suppose we can take pictures of the contents. First, I need you to give me a written statement." He pushed paper, pen and ink to Linc.

Linc wrote the facts out as precisely as possible, then he and the Mountie marched down the street. There wasn't much call for a photographer, so the business was combined with undertaker. Linc stalled on the doorstep. He'd soon enough be visiting this man for the latter.

The photographer asked no questions, but Linc could practically hear the cogs in his head working at high speed. No doubt he had figured out what he took pictures of. Although the Mountie had reminded him this was official business and was to be kept under wraps, Linc wondered how long it would be before the whole town knew the McCoys had Mrs. Ogilvy's jewels in their possession all this time. Over six years. Six years of living a lie, believing a lie.

Mrs. Ogilvy looked surprised when she saw the Mountie and Linc on her doorstep. She noticed the metal box but said nothing.

"Can we come in?" the Mountie asked.

"By all means." She stepped aside. "Forgive my lack of manners. Come and sit." They trooped into a big living room with a large number of red items—red cushions, red drapes, red pictures. The walls were practically covered with pictures. What didn't have a picture held a china cupboard or shelf loaded with knickknacks. He guessed many of the contents of the room were valuable. He sat stiffly on the red couch.

The Mountie sat beside him. "Linc has something to say."

So he repeated the story as the Mountie handed her the box of jewels.

She waited until he finished then slowly, tenderly lifted each item from the box. "Everything is here. The necklace and rings my grandmother brought from Russia. The pearls Grandfather gave to her on their wedding day. This necklace, my own dear Harold gave me on our wedding day. These are like children to me. Each one reminds me of a loved one and their life." She reached for Linc's hand and squeezed it. "Thank you for returning them to me."

It was all Linc could do not to bolt to his feet. He had done nothing worthy of thanks. Shame stung his thoughts. Shame that his family was as bad as people said.

"Now, young man, tell me again where you found this."

He told her about fixing the corrals and digging out the broken post.

"You say you weren't involved?"

"For the past six years I've believed the McCoys were falsely accused." No doubt his bitterness and disappointment dripped from every syllable, but he didn't care.

"Where were you that day six years ago?"

"I was helping my grandfather cut some hay in a slough. You know, the one west of town. He owns that land." He'd been blissfully content for the first time since his mother died. He liked working the farm. Grandfather had suggested Linc buy a few head of cows and start his own herd. His grandfather had already paid him wages in the way of a sorrel gelding that he rode every chance he got.

Mrs. Ogilvy nodded. "He used to get a good stock of

hay off that slough." She directed her attention back to Linc's story. "Where have you been and what have you been doing since you left here?"

He told her everything.

"You like working on the ranch, it seems."

"I do."

"Will you go back there when you're done here?"

He wondered at her line of questioning, but considering what the McCoys had done to her, he willingly answered. "I don't know what I'll do. Grandmama needs help but—" He shrugged. "Might be best for her if I leave."

"I understand your father is not well."

"He's dying."

She gasped. "Oh, how dreadful. I understand he was in an accident. Tell me about it."

Linc did not want to think about the accident, the death of his brother, the impending death of his father and now the guilt of the McCoys. He wished he could run away from all this, but he knew no matter how far he went, his past would accompany him. In short, precise words, he told of the mining accident, burying Harris and then transporting Pa home. "I hoped he'd recover, but I accept now that he won't."

Mrs. Ogilvy patted the back of his hand. "You've been through a lot, young man." She turned to the Mountie. "What happens now?"

"I must investigate," the Mountie said.

Mrs. Ogilvy shook her head and turned to Linc. "I'm sorry this has to happen while your father is dying."

They left a few minutes later. "If your story proves

correct, I won't be arresting your father, though I will lay charges."

"If it proves correct? Do you think I'd turn in my father falsely?"

The Mountie gave him a hard look. "It's mighty convenient to have your brother dead, your father soon to be joining him from what I hear, and you as innocent as a baby, if one believes your story."

"Then get busy and find your proof." He stormed away. How had things gotten so complicated?

"I'll be over in an hour to question your father. Don't go anywhere."

Linc spun around. "I think if I planned to leave town, I would have buried the jewels again and not said a thing." He told Grandmama to expect the Mountie then retreated to the barn. But he found no peace there, only the sense of dread hanging over his head. Even memories of Sally and the one kiss they'd shared failed to ease his mind.

He forced himself to remain in the barn, telling Big Red how mixed up life had become until it was time for the Mountie to come, then he returned to the house. Grandmama hovered at the stove and jerked about when Linc banged the door.

"My, you startled me. I'm as nervous as a young bride. Last time I had the police in my house…well, they were accusing your father of stealing from Mrs. Ogilvy. I never believed it possible. Still don't."

"Pa regrets it, if that's any consolation."

"Can't say it is, with a Mountie about to march into my house. I expect all the neighbors will have their noses pressed to their windows."

Linc tried to sound caring but failed. "There is no such thing as a secret in a small town." He went to Pa's room to prepare him for the visit.

Pa twitched. "Is he going to arrest me?"

"No. He's just coming to discover the truth."

"I'll tell him. You can count on it."

"Yeah, Pa."

Linc sat with Pa as the Mountie questioned him. After Pa finished, the Mountie asked, "You're saying Linc had nothing to do with this? No knowledge of it?"

"That's correct. He was just a boy."

"He was sixteen. About the same age as when Billy the Kid started his life of crime."

The hair on the back of Linc's neck stood up at being compared to such a notorious criminal. "My father says I'm innocent and I am."

"I guess if I was about to die, I'd do what I could to clear my son's name, too."

Linc bolted to his feet. "Sounds like you're calling both me and my pa liars."

The officer's expression remained impassive. "I'm saying you'll need more proof than your father's word." He didn't wait for Linc to show him out.

Linc ignored his pa's call. He ignored Grandmama's plea to cool down. Instead, he raced to the barn, threw a saddle on Red and rode away from town as fast as he could.

How did he prove his innocence? Grandfather was the only one who could vouch for where he was, and he was gone.

His mad ride took him by Judd and Madge's farm. He would not think of all the good times he'd enjoyed there with Sally. Then he passed the Morgan place. He'd never be welcome there now. Not with guilt hanging over his head.

He rode farther then, finally, out of consideration for his horse, slowed. Still he rode on. If only he could ride until he reached a place where no one knew him. He'd change his name and never have to face the shame of being a McCoy. But eventually his anger cooled. His pa was dying. And Linc would not abandon him to die alone, or leave Grandmama to care for him. So he turned Red about and headed back to town, his heart feeling cold and heavy in his chest.

Sally had seen the Mountie stride into Mrs. Shaw's house and wondered what was wrong. He left half an hour later without a backward look. And then Linc raced to the barn, and a few minutes afterward rode Red away at a furious pace. Sally longed to know the cause of all this commotion. She considered going to the house and asking Mrs. Shaw.

But she cleaned the kitchen and prepared a dessert as she considered it. Would Mrs. Shaw find her concern unwelcome? Finally, she could stand it no longer. She must find out what was wrong, but before she could put action to her thought, a knock came on the front door and she went to answer it.

"Madge, what are you doing here?"

Madge stepped in and hurriedly closed the door behind her. "Have you heard?"

"What?" It wasn't like Madge to be so mysterious.

Madge pulled her to the kitchen and insisted she sit. "What is this all about?"

Madge sat beside her and took her hands. "The McCoys have suddenly found Mrs. Ogilvy's jewels and turned them in. The Mountie questioned both Linc and his father. Everyone is talking. Apparently Mr. McCoy claims to be solely responsible and says Linc is completely innocent."

"How do you know all this?"

"People have seen the Mountie and Linc going to Mrs. Ogilvy's with a metal box. No doubt the missing jewels, and someone overheard the Mountie talking about the McCoys' explanation."

"Lots of someones involved."

Madge never even took note of Sally's sarcasm. "Of course, everyone speculates they've figured it all out so Linc would get off the hook, and his father will not live to go to trial. Mighty convenient, people are saying. You were right. It was wise to choose Abe."

Sally jerked her hands away. She hadn't chosen Abe because she suspected Linc of being involved in anything shady. "Is that what you think? That Linc is guilty and seeking to escape judgment this way?"

Madge didn't answer, but her eyes revealed her doubt.

"You saw him at the party. How he loves kids." Sally felt a storm of words building and did nothing to stop it. "He came back so his pa could die at home. Why would he do that? Why not stay away rather than face what people are saying? And why would he turn in the jewels at all? Why not keep them hidden? Didn't I hear you saying what a nice man he was just two days ago?" She jerked to her feet. "Nice men don't steal and lie. Furthermore…" She lowered her head to within a few inches of Madge's face and favored her with a glower. "Nice people don't make such accusations."

Madge sank back, her expression stubborn. "Perhaps you're right. But we'll never know the truth."

Sally let out an explosive sound. "I know the truth. He would not steal. Nor would he take advantage of his father's illness to clear his own name. None of this makes sense. Where did he find the jewels?"

Madge shrugged. "Guess he knew where they were. How else would he find them?"

"You are wrong. Everyone is wrong."

"Right. Everyone is wrong but you. I suggest you consider why you need to believe he is innocent." She pushed to her feet and stuck her face close to Sally's. "Perhaps you better consider what Abe will think of such rabid defense of another man." She stalked from the room, heading for the door, then stopped and returned. "Sally, I know you feel you have to defend the underdog, but in this case there is more to consider." She again left the room, and the outer door clicked shut behind her.

Sally sank to the closest chair. How could Madge have done such an about-face, going from defending Linc, even so far as to tell Sally to follow her heart, to believing his guilt? Linc was innocent, even if no one believed it. She knew it with all her heart.

She pushed her way through the rest of her chores and made an adequate supper for Abe and the children, though she had no appetite.

Abe waited until they'd finished and the children left the room to speak to her. Of course he'd heard the rumors and must address the situation. "Did you hear that Linc found the Ogilvy jewels?"

"Madge came by and mentioned it."

"Seems he isn't the upright citizen I believed he was. I don't want you or the children to associate with him any further. I'll tell the children right away." He left the room, taking for granted Sally's agreement.

She studied the fourth finger on her left hand. Abe would one day, and probably soon, put a ring on that finger. He had the right to expect her to agree with his decisions. She rubbed a fingertip around the spot where the ring would be. Wasn't this what she wanted? To be safe and secure in a house with a man who would always take care of her, always believe he knew what was best for his family? It held a certain protective quality. She wouldn't have to deal with hard things. Abe would see to that.

Just as her father had done his best to protect her. When he died she'd felt so vulnerable. All sorts of bad things had happened. The drought and Depression had hit. Men were swept away to relief camps. People went broke and moved away, as broken as their bank accounts. The Morgans had lost most of their land and almost lost their house. She did not have the strength to face such adversity anymore. Abe would take care of her.

In the other room, Robbie yelled at his father. He obviously did not like Abe's instruction to stay away from Linc.

A little later Sally left and walked home. The road seemed longer than usual, the heat more oppressive, the dust harsher.

Mother waited at the kitchen table. "You're late."

"The heat slowed my feet."

Mother studied her long and hard before she spoke. "Madge told me about the McCoys. I trust you have had nothing further to do with that man."

That man. "I suppose you mean Linc?"

"You know I do. I was right to tell you to avoid him."

Sally tried to control the words rushing to her tongue. She succeeded only in controlling the anger accompanying them. "Mother, I can't believe you judge Linc without evidence. In fact, against evidence. He found the jewels and turned them over to the police. I understand they were returned to Mrs. Ogilvy. What would you have him do? Why not continue to hide them to protect himself and his father? I think he did the only noble thing he could do, and it must have taken a great deal of courage. Though I expect he thought he would be heard without prejudice and judgment. I suppose that was his mistake. To trust people to treat him fairly."

Mother stared at Sally like she'd announced she intended to shave her head. "Are you planning to defend him against all others?"

"What would be the point? People will believe whatever they want." A weariness like nothing she'd ever known tugged at her bones. She wanted to go to her room and sink into her bed.

"Sally, you are engaged to Abe. I hope you will conduct yourself in a manner that honors that."

Her mother needn't have bothered with her warning. Linc had made no effort to see her or speak to her in two days. She didn't expect he would do so in the future. After all, he knew she was planning to marry Abe. He would respect that.

The next few days proved the accuracy of her thoughts. She glimpsed Linc once or twice, but he didn't even glance in her direction. The Mountie returned once that she saw. He might well have been there other times.

Sally wanted to go over and ask how Linc's father was. She wanted to tell Linc she didn't believe what everyone was saying, but Linc needed nothing from her and Abe had been clear about not speaking to him.

She looked around for Robbie. Twenty seconds ago he was playing in his fort, but now he was missing. Again. Since Linc no longer spent time with the boy, Robbie had returned to his practice of disappearing, disobeying and generally letting one and all know how unhappy he was.

Stepping outside, she called his name. No response, of course. She trudged to the barn and again called his name. A faint rustle alerted her to his location, and she went to where he huddled in the far corner. She sank down beside him.

"He's not a bad man," Robbie mumbled.

She knew he meant Linc. "I know that."

"Then why can't I see him?"

"You have to obey your father."

"But he's wrong."

Sally didn't reply. She agreed with Robbie, but it would be wrong to speak against his father.

"Do you think he'll leave?"

The question scraped her heart hollow. Who would blame him if he rode away and never returned? "I expect he will stay with his father." It was likely the only reason he remained. Sally had not given him any other reason. Nor could she. She had promised to marry Abe.

She waited for a sense of peace and security to ease through her.

But she waited in vain.

Chapter Fifteen

Linc sat at his pa's bedside, watching the covers over his chest to make sure they continued to rise and fall. Pa barely roused from his uneasy rest anymore.

Doc stepped into the room and shook his head. "It won't be long now. Call me if you need anything, though there is little I can do at this point. I'm sorry."

Linc nodded without taking his gaze off Pa. Seemed there was little anyone could do to solve any of Linc's problems. He simply had to accept life would not be what he had allowed himself to dream.

The Mountie had returned a day ago and said Linc's name was cleared. The statement left by the only eye-witness was vague, but the Mountie had been able to locate the man and he was certain there were only two men, and Linc wasn't one of them.

He'd said charges wouldn't be laid against Pa because of his weak condition.

Not that it made any difference. People would believe what they chose to believe. There was no point in expecting them to change and suddenly decide Linc

McCoy would be welcome in their midst—accepted as a noble, honest man.

He'd return west, join up on a ranch and hope he could forget this time in his life. But his heart refused to find peace with his plan. He wanted to stay. He wanted to live here in Grandmama's house, raise a family with Sally. Be part of the community.

But the community would never accept him.

Sally would not be part of his dream. Moreover, she didn't deserve to have her name associated with his. Far better to be Mrs. Abe Finley, an accepted and respected member of the community.

Grandmama hugged him when he told her he would not be staying permanently. "I'm sorry, Linc. I hoped and prayed things would turn out differently. I will continue to pray for things to change. I need you." She drew back to look into his face, studying him so hard he had to force himself not to break eye contact. Her eyes clouded with tears. "I think you need things you can only find here."

His only reply was to hug her back. What he needed and wanted were not choices he had. He returned to Pa's bedside, afraid to leave him alone.

Pa stirred and opened his eyes, clouded with pain and confusion. He tried to pull in a deep breath and coughed, pain spasming through him.

Linc knelt at the side of his bed. "Pa, just rest."

Pa shook his head. "Call your grandmother."

Linc hesitated. Was this the last? He sniffed back a rush of tears and went to the doorway. "Grandmama?" His voice was low, but he couldn't have made it louder if he tried. His throat seemed to have closed off.

Grandmama hurried from the kitchen. "Is it...?"

"Pa asked for you." He waited for her to join him and led her to the chair close to Pa's head.

She took his hand. "Oh, Jonah. I hate to see you like this."

"Mother Shaw, you have been a true Christian woman."

Both Linc and Grandmama leaned close to hear what Pa said. Linc took Pa's other hand. He couldn't speak past his pain, but no matter how much it hurt to watch, he would stay with Pa until the end.

Pa turned his gaze to Linc. "You have been a good son. Always. I'm glad your name is cleared." He fell silent. His eyes drifted shut. His breathing was so shallow Linc feared it had stopped. "Oh, Pa. Don't die without making things right with God."

Pa's eyes flew open.

Linc couldn't believe the flare of life in them. Maybe the doctor was wrong. Maybe Pa would fight back and live.

"I wanted you both here so I could tell you. I made my peace with God. He took away my sins. My burden and guilt are gone." His smile was the sweetest thing Linc had ever seen. "I only wish I hadn't been stubborn so long."

Tears streamed from Grandmama's eyes as she leaned over and kissed Pa's cheek. "Jonah, my prayers have been answered." Her voice broke, and she couldn't go on for a moment. "Be sure and say hello to Mary for me."

Linc pressed a kiss to Pa's cheek then. He thought Pa was crying, then realized the moisture on his cheek came from his own tears. He hadn't even realized he cried.

"Go to sleep now, Pa. I'll see you in Heaven." His heart cracked. He wanted to share life with Pa as a Christian, but it would never happen.

He and Grandmama continued to hold Pa's hands. Linc stroked Pa's forehead and tried to sing the words to the old song, "In the sweet by and by, we shall meet on that beautiful shore." His throat grew tight but he forced the words out, not caring that the melody was lost in the cracking of his voice. Any more than he cared about the tears flowing freely down his face and dripping to the bedcovers.

"He's gone," Grandmama whispered. "Gone to Heaven." She choked back a sob.

But neither of them moved. Finally Linc closed Pa's eyes, crossed his hands over his chest and stood at the side of the bed. He pulled his grandmother to her feet to stand beside him. "I will miss him more than anyone will ever know."

Grandmama turned into Linc's arms and sobbed.

He led her into the kitchen and eased her to a chair, then made them tea.

Grandmama sniffed and dried her tears. "Mary is gone. Harris is gone. Now your pa. And you'll soon be gone, too." She let out a shuddering breath. "I will be alone again."

Linc squeezed her hands. "I will be here long enough to make arrangements for Pa's burial. I wish I could stay longer."

Grandmama gave him a fierce look. "There's no reason you can't stay. You're a good man. You know it and I know it. Why not give the people around here a chance to discover it?"

"I thought I had. Seems they are only waiting for a chance to see me as anything but good."

"If you want something badly enough, you will fight for it."

Did she mean his reputation or Sally? He didn't care enough about the first to remain. He cared too much about Sally to stay and watch her marry Abe.

Grandmama patted his hand. "I guess you say how much you care by what you do."

This time he knew she meant Sally. He pushed to his feet. "I need to call the doctor and the undertaker."

Sally saw the doctor and undertaker both go into Mrs. Shaw's house as she crossed the yard after taking the lunchtime dishwater to the garden. She dropped the pail and pressed her hands to her mouth. Linc's father had died. And she hadn't been there to comfort him.

It was not her right. In fact, she was forbidden to speak to him.

Choking back a cry, she grabbed the pail and dashed for the house. She sank to the nearest chair and buried her head in her hands. Weeping for his loss. Weeping for her loss.

Her loss? She jerked her head upright. She had chosen what she wanted. A secure life. A solid home. A man who had a steady job.

But the words echoed in her empty heart.

What would her father say? Mother was certain he'd approve of Abe. Her father was a solid, steady man who provided a secure home. Even when they moved from

Edmonton she had not worried, although they'd lived in a tiny sod shanty while the big house was built. Even there she'd felt safe and secure.

Because her father was taking care of her.

Because she trusted his love.

A fleeting truth fluttered through her head. Something important that she couldn't quite capture and identify.

She retraced her thoughts. Her father took care of her. She trusted his love. Trusted his love. She heard his voice helping her memorize Psalm chapter ninety-one. "Sally, my dear little daughter, whatever happens, remember God loves you and will always be with you. He will cover you with His wings. You need not fear the terror of the night or anything that comes against you. God is your refuge. He will guard you in all your ways."

She missed her father. His steady presence. His care and love. But she didn't want someone to replace him. He would be disappointed if he thought she needed someone to provide the protection he'd taught her to find in God.

God was her Heavenly Father. He would care for her.

Not seeing anything before her, she stared long and hard. What did it mean? What was she to do?

By suppertime she was a bundle of confusion. "I can't stay. Just leave the dishes and I'll do them in the morning."

Abe's look demanded an explanation.

She couldn't provide him one and gave a vague shrug, as if to insinuate it was something she couldn't discuss. He nodded as if he understood. Probably thought it was a woman thing. Her cheeks burned with embarrassment, but let him think what he wanted. She had to get home.

Mother was in the garden when Sally approached the house, but she managed to slip by unnoticed. She hurried to her room, picked up her Bible and found Psalm ninety-one. She read it over and over, feeling as if the answer was in front of her face. Yet she couldn't put her finger on it.

Oh, God. I feel like something is missing. Show me what I need.

Trust in the Lord. Trust His love and care.

Linc's words came to her as clearly as if he stood before her. *Friends who trust God to take care of them.* Was her confusion because she had put her trust in what marrying a man like Abe could give her…security and a nice home?

She looked closely at the idea. How could she expect a man to do that for her? Shouldn't her trust be in God?

Thoughts swirled through her head as she assessed the choices before her. Trust God, or trust Abe to give her what she needed?

The words of a hymn flooded her mind. "Be not dismayed whate'er betide. God will take care of you." Softly, she sang all four verses. It was the answer she sought. God was her refuge and shelter. Her anchor. Not a house. Not a man. Not trusting in things of this earth that proved so fleeting and insecure. It was God who would take care of her. It wasn't even fair to expect Abe to take on such an onerous role.

She fell to her knees beside the bed. "Thank you, Father God."

She rose from the floor and laughed. She'd been looking for security in the wrong places.

Her heart flying free, her feet light, she descended the stairs.

And came face to face with Mother.

Her mood dipped, and then she stiffened her shoulders.

"Mother, we need to talk."

"When did you get home?"

"A few minutes ago. I slipped by you because I needed time to think and pray." She led her mother to the kitchen and indicated she should sit down.

She sat across from her and considered how to break the news. Gently as possible. "Mother, I have been seeking a replacement for Father. I wanted a man who could guarantee to make me feel as safe and secure as he did."

Mother smiled. "He was a good father."

"Yes, he was. And if he knew how I've been thinking, I feel he would be disappointed with me."

Mother looked startled. "Why?"

"Didn't he teach me to put my trust in God, not man, not possessions, not circumstances or belongings?"

Mother hesitated. "Yes. But I don't see—"

"Both you and I thought Abe could do for me what Father did. You know, provide security, safety." She didn't say love because that had not entered the agreement. "Father's job was to guide me from childhood to adulthood by teaching me not to seek all those things in a person, but in God, and he did his job well."

"I'm sure Abe can provide as well as your father did."

"But Mother, I can't marry a man and expect him to do what only God can. Only God can promise to take care of me. To guard and guide me. It's what Father taught us all."

"Yes, but—"

"Mother, I can't marry a man I don't love. Do you think Father would want me to?" It was a loaded question and not entirely fair, but Mother had used the same argument to persuade Sally and now needed to understand she couldn't do it.

"I suppose you think love will keep you warm. Give you a roof over your head?"

"That's the whole point. I need to trust God to take care of me. He is my Heavenly Father. Doesn't the scripture say, 'If God so clothe the grass, which is today in the field, and tomorrow is cast into the oven, how much more will he clothe you, O ye of little faith'?"

Mother shook her head. "Maybe I'm of little faith. I want to see you married to a man who can take care of you."

"I thought I wanted that, too. But it isn't enough. And it's putting my faith in the wrong place."

"Are you—?" Mother swallowed hard. "Are you thinking of marrying Linc?"

The question burned through her like a fire-tipped arrow. "I'm not sure that's a possibility." She'd abandoned him. She'd dismissed him. Why would he give her another chance? "His father died today. I saw the doctor and undertaker go into the house."

"I am sorry."

Sally heard a "but" in her voice and got to her feet before Mother could put it in words. "I'll tell Abe tomorrow I can't marry him, and I'll offer to continue as his housekeeper until he finds a replacement."

"I'm sure he won't have any problem finding someone else."

"Exactly." And if she could so easily be replaced, then he should do it. She wanted a relationship where a man thought she was irreplaceable.

The next morning she took a cake and a covered dish with her when she went to the Finleys'. She would take them across the alley as soon as she got a chance.

Abe stepped into the kitchen, looking as fine and polished as ever.

She faced him bravely. "Don't call the children yet. There is something I must tell you."

His look was impatient. But he didn't ask what was so important that it couldn't wait until a more convenient time. More convenient for him. He crossed his arms over his chest and waited.

"Abe, I've changed my mind. I'm afraid I can't marry you." She rushed on, ignoring the disbelief in his eyes. "It wouldn't be fair. I love your children." It was the one thing that gave her pause. "I admire you. But I would be marrying you for all the wrong reasons."

"I can offer you a good home."

"I know. And there was a time when that and your position in the church and community were enough. Or at least I thought they were. I will continue to look after the children until you find a replacement. If that suits you."

"Fine." He plunked down, then remembered he hadn't called the children and got up again to go to the bottom of the stairs and call them. He returned and stood behind his chair. "A cousin of my late wife's has

offered to come. I'll let her know I accept her offer."
He sat.

It was over as easy as that. No regrets.

Except for the children. She waited until Abe left to
tell them.

"You going to marry Linc?" Carol demanded.

"I don't know. I think he will be leaving."

"You could go with him. I would."

Robbie was far more practical. "Who's going to look
after us?"

"Your father said he had someone in mind."

"Good." But she caught a glimpse of hurt in his face
before he scowled at her.

"Robbie, I hope we can still be friends. Maybe you
can come out to visit, and I'll take you to the loft where
I used to build a fort. Remember me telling you that?"

He managed a nod but his expression remained as
defiant as he could make it, as if afraid he would cry if
he didn't make himself angry.

She understood his hurt. The boy longed for safety
and security as much as she did. Knowing they needed
to learn the same lesson she'd been so slow to learn, she
sorted through the Bible story cards until she found the
one about Abraham and read it. "Abraham trusted God,
and God took care of him. Your mama trusted God. She
wanted you to, as well." She looked from one child to
the other. "I'm learning that same thing."

Carol nodded. "I'll try to remember what Mama
taught. And you."

Robbie looked thoughtful, though he tried to hide it.

Carol hugged her before she left for school. "I wanted

you for a mother, but you love Linc and should be with him."

Sally laughed. "How is it everyone but me saw what I needed?"

Carol gave a shy smile. "Linc loves you, too. I saw that."

"You are a very astute little girl." She hugged Carol one more time, loath to let her go. She'd miss these children more than anyone would guess possible.

Later, she took the food over to the house across the alley. Mrs. Shaw opened the door. "Why thank you, my dear."

Sally glanced past her.

"I'm afraid Linc is not here. He had to see to the grave digging. We're burying Jonah tomorrow."

"I'm sorry. Please relay my condolences to Linc."

"Of course."

Sally left. Restless, she took Robbie to the store to pick up supplies for supper. A gaggle of women watched her as she entered the store.

Mrs. Brennan poked her head forward like a curious turkey. "I understand you were friends with that McCoy man."

Sally smiled and nodded. She was not going to give these gossips anything to titter about.

Miss Carter nudged Mrs. Brennan. "Don't expect there will be many folks at the funeral. Good riddance to bad rubbish, I say."

"How charitable of you," Sally murmured.

"I hope that young McCoy plans to leave. Our town doesn't need the likes of him around. The Mountie says he is satisfied the boy had nothing to do with stealing from Mrs. Ogilvy, but it's not easy to pull the wool over my eyes."

Sally felt like she'd had a sheet over her eyes for years, and now it was gone and she could see clearly for the first time. "I'll be at the funeral."

At least three of the ladies gasped, as if the idea was beyond comprehension.

"You have claimed to be Mrs. Shaw's friend for years. Shouldn't you be there to show her support, if nothing else?"

The women gaped at her. Quiet, compliant Sally, they seemed to say, speaking out like this?

"I'll be there, too."

Sally spun about to face Mrs. Ogilvy, who smiled at Sally then steamed by to confront the other women. "I'm convinced Linc McCoy is innocent of any wrongdoing. He's done his utmost to make things right. He's endured the scorn of this town to stay at his father's side until he died. In my view, that makes Linc McCoy an honorable man. I'm proud to know him."

The women looked uncomfortable. A couple of them would have sidled away, but Mrs. Ogilvy stopped them in their tracks.

"I'm not done. I will remind you of something our Lord said. 'He who is without sin among you, let him cast the first stone.'" Then she regally sailed past and ordered her supplies.

The women were suddenly in a great hurry to leave.

Sally went to the counter to conduct her business. Mrs. Ogilvy turned to her. "You're the young woman who is planning to marry Abe Finley, aren't you?"

"I was. I've since reconsidered it. Our engagement is off."

"I see."

The way she continued to study Sally made Sally wonder what she saw. Something more than the announcement that she wasn't marrying Abe.

"Is there a particular reason? Or perhaps another man you find you care for more?"

"I realized my reasons for such a marriage were all wrong. Seeking security. Afraid of love."

Mrs. Ogilvy chuckled as she patted Sally's hand. "My dear, never be afraid of love. Any more than you would any great adventure."

Sally recalled Linc's words about Claude. How he was ready for adventure but a little fearful, or something to that effect. It perfectly described Sally. But no more. If love was an adventure, she was ready for it.

She only hoped she hadn't waited too long.

That evening, after supper—which was strained with vibrant disapproval from Abe—she broached the subject of the funeral. "I'm going. I wondered if you would allow the children to attend. It might be nice for them to let Linc know they care about his loss."

Abe looked ready to refuse permission.

Carol had tiptoed into the doorway and overheard Sally's request. "I'd really like to go. I remember how good it felt to see how others cared when Mommy died."

Abe studied his young daughter. "Robbie, are you there?"

Robbie popped around the corner, and Sally knew he'd listened to the whole conversation.

"What do you want to do?" Abe asked his son.

Robbie hung his head and mumbled, "I might like to go and say goodbye."

"Very well then. You may take them. But don't linger about afterward."

Sally thanked Abe, but her gaze returned to Robbie. Who did he want to say goodbye to? He'd never met Linc's father. He must want to say goodbye to Linc.

And she wanted to say hello.

She prayed she would get a chance.

The next day she dressed the children in their Sunday best, changed into a black dress she seldom wore because it reminded her of her father's death, and they went to the church.

The gossips in the store were right. Very few people attended the funeral. Linc and his grandmother were in the front row. Farther back sat several older ladies, friends of Mrs. Shaw's. Mrs. Ogilvy marched in and went to the pew directly behind Mrs. Shaw.

Linc's grandmother turned, saw the other woman and nodded her appreciation.

Linc turned, too. Sally saw his start of surprise and his mouthed, "Thank you." Then his gaze continued on to Sally and the children. He let his gaze slide past her.

The pain slicing her heart had less to do with Linc's loss than her own disappointment at the way he ignored her. But then, what did she expect? He didn't know she'd broken it off with Abe and, honorable man that he was, he would never allow himself to seek comfort from a woman engaged to another, even in this dark hour of his loss.

The service was short. Then they followed the casket

to the cemetery. Only Linc and his grandmother stood close to the grave. Out of respect, the others remained a few feet away.

The casket was lowered into the ground, then the few who weren't family members marched by and squeezed Linc's hand and his grandmother's.

Suddenly Sally was face to face with Linc. "I'm so sorry," she murmured.

His expression was hard as granite. "Thank you."

She had planned to ask if they could talk later, but his sternness robbed her of all thought.

He turned to the children, effectively dismissing her, and hugged each of them. "Thank you for coming."

Carol clung to him, sobbing. "Are you going to leave now?"

"Soon." He straightened and avoided looking at Sally.

She hugged Mrs. Shaw, offered her condolences and hurried home. The children seemed relieved to have seen Linc and spoken to him.

Only Sally struggled to hold back tears.

He was leaving soon. Would he give her a chance to tell him she no longer planned to marry Abe?

Would it matter to him any longer?

Chapter Sixteen

Numb from head to toe, Linc led his grandmother home. It was over. He tried to find relief in knowing his father's suffering had ended. He tried to console himself with the knowledge Pa had gone to Heaven.

But he simply felt empty.

Grandmama sank to a chair and sighed, a sound so heavy it seemed to scrape the floor. "I could use some tea."

Linc, welcoming a reason to do something, filled the kettle and put it on to boil. Then he sat down and stared at the tabletop.

"What now?" Grandmama asked.

"I don't know."

"I realize you haven't had time to deal with your father's death, but are you planning to leave soon?"

"I figure I can join up with some ranch."

"Pardon me if I say you don't sound enthusiastic."

"I don't feel anything." The kettle boiled. He made the tea, waited for it to steep and poured a cup.

"Aren't you having any?"

Linc shook his head. "I think I'll go for a ride and clear my head."

"Linc, there is something I want to say. Now is probably not the best time, but I want you to think about it. I've already made it clear I want you to stay and take over this place. But it's more than that. Linc, I'm getting old. I don't want to be alone. I need you here."

She'd said it before, but never so clearly expressing both her want and her need for him to stay. "Grandmama, I don't know if I can stay." The idea of seeing Sally married to the man across the alley was more than he could deal with right now. Perhaps he'd never be able to deal with it.

"Linc, I wish you'd reconsider. If not for me, then for that Morgan girl."

"She's going to marry Abe."

"Does she love him?"

Linc shrugged. What did it matter? She was willing to sacrifice love for her idea of security. Maybe he couldn't blame her. There were times he longed for the things she wanted. The difference was, he didn't see any chance of getting them here. He looked about the room, realizing how much he loved this place. Too bad it was tainted with the misdeeds of the McCoys.

"Like I said before and will say again in the hopes of persuading you to reconsider leaving, you could stay and prove the McCoys are good people."

"I'm not sure anyone would ever believe it."

"Eventually they would. Just promise me you'll think about it."

"Okay." He left then and rode Red long and hard.

He passed Judd and Madge's place without sparing

it a glance. He approached the Morgan farm. Steeled himself to keep his face forward and look neither to the left nor the right.

Soon the orphanage was ahead of him. He heard the laughter of one of the children, but rode on. Every place he passed was full of memories of Sally and the times they'd enjoyed together

Six years ago he'd said goodbye to this place, even though he'd wanted Pa to stay and prove their innocence. Small wonder he didn't agree to. Hard to prove a lie.

Now Linc was leaving again.

Running away again.

Now where did that come from? He wasn't running from anything.

Except people's judgment. And Sally. Acknowledging he would be running from Sally made him lean over the saddlehorn and groan.

He pulled Red to a halt and led him up a small hill, where he sat and stared at the drought-ravaged countryside.

The drought would eventually end. Those who managed to hang on would be glad they had stayed through the tough times. They would have their land and homes still.

The thought tangled with something Grandmama had said about staying. Stay and prove the McCoys were good people. Stay and fight for Sally.

Like those who stayed and fought for their land through the present trials.

Of course, they had no assurance when the drought would end. Could they even know for certain it would?

Could he have any hope his circumstances would change? Did it matter? Or was faith enough?

He'd taken to reading his Bible every night, feeling a connection to Sally as he did so, but also something deeper, more secure, more necessary—a connection to God. Out of curiosity about what those books at the end of the Old Testament with the funny names were about, he'd read several. Some of the verses were like songs of faith.

They listed a number of disasters—drought and failed crops—then concluded by saying, "Yet I will rejoice in the Lord, I will joy in the God of my salvation. The Lord God is my strength, and He will make my feet like hinds' feet, and He will make me to walk upon mine high places."

The verses filled him with fresh hope and strength.

Should he stay and fight for his name? For Sally? What if he stayed and nothing changed? What if people still accused him of stealing? And Sally married Abe?

If it didn't turn out the way he wanted, it wouldn't change God's love for him. Nor God's promise to give him the strength to go forward.

And at least he would have tried.

He bowed his head and prayed, asking God for wisdom and strength to do what he should, asking for God to intervene so things would turn out the way Linc wanted, but if they didn't, he asked for faith and trust to go on without bitterness.

Peace colored his thoughts, and he remained on the hillside for a long time, simply breathing in contentment.

Dusk had spread its skirts across the sky when he

made his way back to town. Grandmama burst out crying as he strode into the house, and he rushed to her side. "What's wrong?"

"I thought you might have gone without saying good-bye."

"I'm not going."

She stopped crying immediately and wiped her eyes. "Did I hear you correctly?"

He told her what he'd decided and why. Before he finished, she squeezed his hands and smiled widely.

"Good for you."

The next morning Linc wakened and bolted to his feet. Then he remembered he didn't have to check on Pa and sank to the edge of the bed. It would take time to accept that his father was gone. Not that he wished him back. But he missed Pa and Harris. He missed his mother.

However, the future beckoned and he again sprang from his bed.

Today he would find a job to tide him over until the farm could be brought back into production.

Finding a job turned out to be a challenge, just as it had before Abe offered him a chance. But after two days he saw a small sign in the window of the hotel. Handyman wanted. He strode inside and said he'd like the job.

The manager looked him up and down. "What do you have to recommend yourself?"

"I'm a hard worker, and I'm hungry."

The man laughed. "I need someone to make repairs on the building, do some painting, wash the windows, keep the floors clean. Can you do that?"

"I can do it so good you'll never have a complaint."

"Pay isn't much."

"Don't expect much. Just enough to keep me and my grandmother fed." And maybe save a little to restock the farm. But he wasn't going to worry about that. He would trust God for the future. Right now he wanted a job for more than the money it would bring. He wanted… needed…to make himself visible. Prove to the good townspeople of Golden Prairie that the McCoys could be trusted.

"You got a name?"

Linc didn't hesitate. "Lincoln McCoy." He held out his hand. "Didn't catch your name."

"Orville Jones. Say, aren't you the young man who found Mrs. Ogilvy's jewels?"

"I am." Linc would not hide from all that meant. "I was also accused of having a part in stealing them. But I didn't do it. Is that going to be a problem?"

Orville studied Linc long and hard. "Why would you return them if you weren't innocent? Besides, didn't the Mountie investigate and decide there was no evidence against you?"

Linc nodded.

"That's good enough for me."

"Thank you. Now point me to the work."

He left later in the afternoon, knowing Orville was satisfied with his work. Now he was ready to speak to Sally.

A trickle of worry trailed through his thoughts. As soon as he recognized it, he reminded himself he had made a choice to trust God.

He hurried home. This was about the time of day

Sally left the Finley place to head home. He paused long enough to tell Grandmama about the job and explain he was going for a ride.

"I trust you are going to find Sally."

He chuckled. "Seems a man can't have any secrets around here."

She tweaked his ear. "I'll be praying."

His heart full of gratitude, he hugged her and trotted out to saddle Red.

The dusty road ahead was empty. There was no sign of Sally. Was he too late? Or too early? He looked over his shoulder and saw only the dust raised by Red's hooves.

Drawing near Judd's turnoff, he slowed. Perhaps Sally had stopped to visit her sister. But he didn't turn in. Only one person he wanted to see, and he wanted to see her alone.

He signaled Red to go forward at a walk, all the time scanning the road, the driveways, the landscape for Sally. Nothing. Not so much as a flicker of movement.

He swallowed hard and sank low in the saddle. He'd practiced what he'd say. Tried to guess how she'd respond. It hadn't crossed his mind he wouldn't see her.

Where is she, God? Sometimes it was hard to trust.

He rode on two more miles, loath to return disappointed. But there seemed no point in going farther, and he finally reined around. "Let's go home, horse." His chin almost rested on his chest as he headed back to town.

Big Red neighed, causing Linc to jerk his head upward.

There she was. At the end of the laneway staring at

him. He dropped to the ground and strode toward her. "Where were you?" As if she had to inform him of her whereabouts!

"I went to visit Madge."

"I didn't see you." Did she hear the ache in his voice, or only the demanding note of his question?

"I saw you. I thought—" Her voice cracked. "I wondered if you were leaving the country. Are you?"

He heard in her voice more than her words said. A longing. A wish that he wasn't leaving. And it gave him hope. "Guess you haven't heard."

"What?"

"I got a job at the hotel. Orville seems to think I'm worth taking a chance on."

"You aren't leaving?"

"Nope. I'm taking over Grandmama's farm. She needs me. I need a home." He needed more, but only Sally could give him what he truly needed. He feared to ask her to give him a chance. "How are Abe and the children?"

"Good. I no longer work there."

He couldn't think what she meant. He would not allow himself to hope and dream without reason. "Really?" When had his voice ever before sounded so strained? "Why is that?"

"His wife's cousin is taking my place."

He tried not to look confused, but guessed he failed miserably when she giggled.

"Why? You— She—" He gave up and lifted his hands to beseech her to explain.

"I told Abe I couldn't marry him."

"You did?" Had he swallowed a whistle to make his voice so squeaky? "Why?"

"I realize my security is not based on a house or marriage to a man who can take care of me."

He nodded, silently asking for more.

Her smile was as sweet as the kiss of morning sunshine. "I've chosen to trust God to take care of me and my future."

He grabbed his hat and slapped it against his thigh, whooping so loudly that Red snorted and sidestepped away. "Me, too."

"You, too, what?"

"I decided to trust God even when life doesn't look like a bed of roses. When people are saying my name with twisted expressions on their faces, when the girl I love is saying she plans to marry someone else."

She looked serious, though it appeared to be a strain. "You love someone?"

He tossed his hat to the saddle and faced her, close enough to see the green in her eyes shift through a variety of shades. "I love you, Sally Morgan. With my whole heart. What do you think about that?"

She ducked her head. "It sounds very nice."

He caught her chin with his fingertip and lifted her face upward so he could study her. Her eyes were warm and welcoming, her lips curled softly with pleasure. "Will you marry me?"

His confidence dipped. What if she didn't say yes? He rushed on before she could answer. "I can't promise you we won't have struggles. I can't say life won't be hard. I don't know what the future holds. I only know God holds our future, and He is the only One strong enough for the job. But I can promise you I will love you as long as I live. I will do my best to make you happy and keep you safe and secure." He ran out of words and waited for her reply.

"God will take care of us."

"Us?"

"I can't think of anyone I would sooner share the challenges of life with than a cowboy by the name of Linc McCoy."

"You'll marry me?"

"Yes, I'll marry you. I love you. I choose you."

The words poured through him like molten honey. His heart filled with joy until he thought it would burst. He caught her mouth with his and kissed her soundly and thoroughly, in a way that didn't begin to express the depths of his love for her. He leaned back and smiled at her. "I've come home."

She wrapped her arms around his waist. "You need to come to my home." She tilted her head toward the house up the lane.

Reality hit with a thud. "Your mother won't be pleased."

"Let's give her a chance." She withdrew her arms enough to take his hand. "Come on."

Sally clung to his side as they strode toward the house. The closer they got, the more tension she felt in his body. A tension that burned along her nerve endings. She'd made it clear to Mother she would only marry for love. No doubt Mother suspected it was Linc she loved, but she still trembled at facing her parent's disapproval.

All her life she had tried so hard to be good, to do

what her parents wanted, to be compliant. But she was no longer a child, and she could not live a lie. "It will be okay," she said, as much for herself as Linc. "Mother will understand." *Oh, Lord, make her see I must follow my heart. And that Linc is a good man.*

They hesitated at the door. She turned to look into Linc's face, and love for him flooded her thoughts. Nothing else mattered. "Come on."

They stepped inside. Mother must have seen them coming, for she stood in the kitchen doorway waiting for them. A myriad of emotions crossed her expression—resistance and disapproval—but then she studied each of their faces and acceptance appeared.

"Come in. I'll make tea and you can tell me all about it." She turned back into the kitchen.

Sally grinned up at Linc. "She's giving her approval."

Linc's eyes blazed with joy, and he pulled her into the hallway and kissed her quickly, then tucked her arm through his. "That's to remind you what's in here." He patted his chest to indicate his heart.

She imitated his gesture. "And what's in here."

Epilogue

May 24, 1935

Sally stood in the midst of the crowd, Linc at her side. It was the official opening of the Ogilvy Central Park. Mrs. Ogilvy had donated funds for a park in the heart of town. The town fathers had discussed what they wanted. But no one took action.

Then Linc had stepped forward with a design.

She leaned over to whisper in his ear. "I think it should have been called the McCoy Park. You did most of the work." He'd drawn up plans and presented them to a town meeting. There were those who wanted to dismiss his ideas because he was a McCoy, but Mrs. Ogilvy had silenced all criticism by announcing to one and all she bore no ill will toward the McCoys, and certainly none toward Linc. "He's an honorable man I consider myself privileged to know." Sally had heard her say those words before, as had a handful of women, but now the whole town heard them and knew Linc had Mrs. Ogilvy's approval.

After that, the majority were happy enough to let Linc volunteer to do the work.

He'd spent so many hours this spring leveling the ground, planting flower beds, putting in trees that Sally had started taking meals to him. Together they had sat in the half-developed park and talked about the future.

"You don't mind Grandmama living with us?" His words brought her back to the present.

"Of course not. Where else would she go?" She and Linc had discussed it extensively before their marriage, but as Sally said, it was her home. They were the intruders. "Besides, she's teaching me to do counted stitch pictures." One was a secret between Sally and Linc's grandmother. They'd used a photograph of Linc's parents taken shortly after their wedding, and Sally was turning it into a picture to give to Linc on their first anniversary.

Linc pulled her to his side, and from the look in his eyes she knew he would have kissed her if they weren't in such a public place. They'd married in late October and had enjoyed a blissful winter of learning more and more about each other.

"This couldn't have happened without the efforts of Linc McCoy," Mr. Reimer, spokesman for the town council, said, drawing both Linc and Sally's attention back to the ceremony. "Thank you, Linc. We consider you an asset to our community." A roar of agreement went up from the crowd.

Sally wrapped an arm about Linc and held tight. She dare not look at him, knowing this acceptance and approval meant more to him than anyone but herself would ever know. "You deserve it," she whispered, then stood at his side as people filed by, shaking his hand and thanking him.

When the line of well wishers had passed, Linc draped an arm about her shoulders and smiled at her. "Are you happy, my sweet?"

"I'm happy and so proud I could almost burst."

Sally's mother stopped by. "You did us proud, Linc."

He dropped a kiss to her cheek. "Thank you, Mother Morgan. Your approval means a lot."

She lifted her face, a regretful expression pulling at her lips. "I'm sorry I ever misjudged you. I hope you won't hold it against me."

Linc grinned. "I've long since forgotten it. You should, too."

"Thank you." She patted his cheek. "Don't forget we're all getting together at my house for supper."

"We'll be there."

Sally's mother went to speak to Linc's grandmother.

Linc leaned close to whisper in Sally's ear. "We wouldn't miss it."

Their secret warm between them, Sally adored him with her eyes, knowing she could inform him with words and kisses how much she loved him when they were alone.

Later that day they gathered around the table at the Morgan home—Louisa, Emmet and the girls, who had come for a visit, Emmet's aunt, Madge and Judd and Mother and Linc's grandmother—now as much a part of the family as anyone.

Mother looked around at her family. "I am so blessed. I have prayed for my girls to each find a good man, and God has honored me beyond my expectations."

Emmet cleared his throat. "We would like to make an announcement." He and Louisa looked at each other with such devotion, Sally's eyes stung with unshed tears to watch them. "We are going to adopt a baby. A young woman came to us and asked if we would take her child. The baby is due in September." The two little girls beamed so bright, Sally knew they were thrilled about the news.

Sally and Linc grinned at each other, then joined in congratulating the pair and asking questions.

A minute later, Judd signaled for quiet. "Madge and I have an announcement, too. We are having a baby in October. There'll be two cousins close in age."

Linc laughed. "Make it three. We're having a baby in October, too."

Mother lifted her hands in the air in a gesture of worship. "Three grandbabies at the same time. I am so blessed."

The three sisters echoed her sentiments, and the three cowboys-turned-husbands nodded agreement.

Later, after the dishes were done, the three sisters wandered outside.

"Babies together." Sally laughed, her heart full. Louisa and Madge laughed, too.

Sally studied her eldest sister. "If only you lived closer so the babies could grow up together. Like we did."

"Do you ever miss this place, Louisa?" Madge asked.

Louisa's expression was so serene that Sally knew her answer before she spoke. "I miss Mother and you two, but I wouldn't sacrifice a minute with Emmet. Besides, we'll come often to visit, and you must bring your babies to visit me."

Sally and Madge nodded agreement.

Madge turned to stare at the barn. "Do you think Father would be pleased if he could see us?"

Sally reached out and drew her sisters into a three-cornered hug. "He taught us well. Now it's up to us to live what he taught us and teach it to our children."

Louisa kissed Sally's cheek and grinned across at Madge. "When did our little sister become so wise?"

Madge chuckled. "When she learned to listen to her heart and welcome a cowboy home."

Sally nodded agreement, and then, arms entwined, the girls returned to the house and their loved ones. Sally's heart felt ready to burst with joy, and she guessed from the expressions on her sisters' faces that they shared her happiness.

She could ask for nothing better.

* * * * *

Dear Reader,

I love writing happy, healthy families, and the Morgan family is one of those. Not that they don't have their problems. After all, no family is perfect. In fact, I wish I could tell everyone that people simply do the best they can with the information they have…at least in healthy families. Furthermore, healthy adults have healthy relationships with their family. Of course, in a dysfunctional family, being healthy might mean something entirely different. I'm fully aware of that, as well.

I hope this story shows how to function in a family—each member with faults and failings. My prayer is we might all be encouraged to be responsible for doing what we can to make family life better. In the words of a prayer by St. Francis of Assisi,

Lord, make me an instrument of your peace.
Where there is hatred, let me sow love.
Where there is injury, pardon.
Where there is doubt, faith.
Where there is despair, hope.
Where there is darkness, light.
Where there is sadness, joy.
O Divine Master,
Grant that I may not so much seek to be consoled,
as to console;
To be understood, as to understand;
To be loved, as to love.
For it is in giving that we receive.

It is in pardoning that we are pardoned.
And it is in dying that we are born to eternal life.
Amen.

I love to hear from readers. Contact me through email, linda@lindaford.org. Feel free to check on updates and bits about my research at my website, www.lindaford.org.

God bless,

Linda Ford

Questions for Discussion

1. Sally is the youngest daughter in the family. Has that position influenced how she views life? How?

2. What other events have influenced her view?

3. Can you see how your position in your family and events in your life have influenced you?

4. How is Sally seeking to deal with uncertainties in her life? How do you?

5. Linc believes he and his family are innocent and should prove it to the community. What changed his mind? Or did he change his mind?

6. What things did Linc do that made you think he was a good, honorable man?

7. Life can throw some unhappy surprises at us. Have you had such? How did you deal with them? Can you learn anything from the way Sally and Linc handled life's unpleasant things?

8. What important lesson about trusting God did they learn?

9. Sally perhaps came across as the weakest sister of the three. Do you think she was weak? Why or why not?

10. We know the Depression ended. The rains came, ending the drought. Do you think Sally and Linc prospered when this happened? Do you think the improved circumstances would make them forget the lessons they learned? Do improved conditions tend to make us forget our lessons?

11. Are you concerned about Abe's children? Do you think Sally and Linc will continue to be involved with them?

12. Is there one specific thing in this story or series that you can apply to your life to make it better or more satisfying?

INSPIRATIONAL

Love Inspired *celebrating* 15 YEARS

HISTORICAL

COMING NEXT MONTH
AVAILABLE APRIL 10, 2012

THE WEDDING JOURNEY
Irish Brides
Cheryl St.John

BRIDES OF THE WEST
Victoria Bylin, Janet Dean & Pamela Nissen

SANCTUARY FOR A LADY
Naomi Rawlings

LOVE ON THE RANGE
Jessica Nelson

REQUEST YOUR FREE BOOKS!

2 FREE INSPIRATIONAL NOVELS
PLUS 2
FREE
MYSTERY GIFTS

Love Inspired
HISTORICAL
INSPIRATIONAL HISTORICAL ROMANCE

YES! Please send me 2 FREE Love Inspired® Historical novels and my 2 FREE mystery gifts (gifts are worth about $10). After receiving them, if I don't wish to receive any more books, I can return the shipping statement marked "cancel". If I don't cancel, I will receive 4 brand-new novels every month and be billed just $4.49 per book in the U.S. or $4.99 per book in Canada. That's a saving of at least 22% off the cover price. It's quite a bargain! Shipping and handling is just 50¢ per book in the U.S. and 75¢ per book in Canada.* I understand that accepting the 2 free books and gifts places me under no obligation to buy anything. I can always return a shipment and cancel at any time. Even if I never buy another book, the two free books and gifts are mine to keep forever.

102/302 IDN FEHF

Name _____ (PLEASE PRINT) _____

Address _____ Apt. # _____

City _____ State/Prov. _____ Zip/Postal Code _____

Signature (if under 18, a parent or guardian must sign) _____

Mail to the Reader Service:
IN U.S.A.: P.O. Box 1867, Buffalo, NY 14240-1867
IN CANADA: P.O. Box 609, Fort Erie, Ontario L2A 5X3

Not valid for current subscribers to Love Inspired Historical books.

Want to try two free books from another series?
Call 1-800-873-8635 or visit www.ReaderService.com.

* Terms and prices subject to change without notice. Prices do not include applicable taxes. Sales tax applicable in N.Y. Canadian residents will be charged applicable taxes. Offer not valid in Quebec. This offer is limited to one order per household. All orders subject to credit approval. Credit or debit balances in a customer's account(s) may be offset by any other outstanding balance owed by or to the customer. Please allow 4 to 6 weeks for delivery. Offer available while quantities last.

Your Privacy—The Reader Service is committed to protecting your privacy. Our Privacy Policy is available online at www.ReaderService.com or upon request from the Reader Service.

We make a portion of our mailing list available to reputable third parties that offer products we believe may interest you. If you prefer that we not exchange your name with third parties, or if you wish to clarify or modify your communication preferences, please visit us at www.ReaderService.com/consumerschoice or write to us at Reader Service Preference Service, P.O. Box 9062, Buffalo, NY 14269. Include your complete name and address.

LIH11B